THIS MIGHT HURT A BIT

THIS MIGHT HURT A BIT

BY DOOGIE HORNER

Simon Pulse

NEW YORK   LONDON
TORONTO   SYDNEY   NEW DELHI

SIMON PULSE

An imprint of Simon & Schuster Children's Publishing Division
1230 Avenue of the Americas, New York, New York 10020
First Simon Pulse hardcover edition June 2019
Text copyright © 2019 by Doogie Horner
Jacket illustration copyright © 2019 by Adams Carvalho
All rights reserved, including the right of reproduction in whole or in part in any form.
SIMON PULSE and colophon are registered trademarks of Simon & Schuster, Inc.
For information about special discounts for bulk purchases, please contact
Simon & Schuster Special Sales at 1-866-506-1949 or business@simonandschuster.com.
The Simon & Schuster Speakers Bureau can bring authors to your live
event. For more information or to book an event contact the Simon & Schuster
Speakers Bureau at 1-866-248-3049 or visit our website at www.simonspeakers.com.
Jacket designed by Sarah Creech
Interior designed by Tom Daly
The text of this book was set in Adobe Caslon Pro.
Manufactured in the United States of America
2 4 6 8 10 9 7 5 3 1
Library of Congress Cataloging-in-Publication Data
Names: Horner, Doogie, author.
Title: This might hurt a bit / by Doogie Horner.
Description: New York : Simon Pulse, [2019] | Summary: Relates a
seriously bad day in the life of Pennsylvania teenager Kirby Burns, in which he
faces dangerous classmates, discovers that a friend is hiding a terrible secret,
and grapples with the one-year anniversary of his sister's death.
Identifiers: LCCN 2018027694 (print) | LCCN 2018033577 (eBook) |
ISBN 9781534427198 (eBook) | ISBN 9781534427174 (hc)
Subjects: | CYAC: Grief—Fiction. | Friendship—Fiction. |
Bullying—Fiction. | Pennsylvania—Fiction.
Classification: LCC PZ7.1.H6643 (eBook) | LCC PZ7.1.H6643 Th 2019 (print) |
DDC [Fic]—dc23
LC record available at https://lccn.loc.gov/2018027694

Dedicated to Mom, Dad, and Melanie.
Scott and Anya, I'll get you next book.

CHAPTER 1

THE THING THAT BOTHERS ME MOST ABOUT UPPER Shuckburgh—and it's hard to pick only one—is that there's no Lower Shuckburgh. Why didn't the founders simply name this rustic rolling valley *Shuckburgh*? Of course, a better question is why didn't they give it a name that wasn't so close to *Sucksburgh* or *Upchuck* or so many other delightful variations, but maybe curse words were different in the 1700s.

Dad said our town is named after a city in England. I looked it up on a map, to see if there's a Lower Shuckburgh in England, and there is indeed—*north* of Upper Shuckburgh.

Madness.

The laws of logic hold no sway here in Upshuck County. Our mountain is blue, our dogs are the size of horses, and right now it's colder inside Dad's hangar than outside. We haven't spent a winter here yet, but I'm sure that when we do, hot snow will rise from the ground and fall up into the sky.

My phone says it's forty-eight degrees outside, but the big thermometer on the wall—a glass tube in a rusted frame that says VIN FIZ over an engraved biplane—says it's forty-three degrees in here, and even though that's impossible, I believe it, because all things are possible in Sucksburgh.

I pull my arms inside my sweatshirt like a turtle and nudge the useless propane heater a little closer with my shoe. The hangar smells like gasoline and oil, a rich aroma that reminds me of all the times Dad and I used to go flying together.

Dad's white sneakers and clean blue jeans stick out from under the Phantom like the Wicked Witch of Walmart, the ultralight's sleek black cockpit and aluminum landing gear jacked up so he can work on the wheels. The left wing waggles over my head as Dad struggles with a stubborn bolt.

"Can you hand me a wrench?" Dad extends a greasy hand from under the plane and flaps it expectantly, a surgeon waiting for his scalpel. "Three-sixteen—no, uh . . . I guess three-sixteenth."

My knees crack like icicles as I stand up off the stack of spare tires and examine the twenty identical wrenches lined up in Dad's toolbox.

"How am I supposed to know which one is the—"

"Or a half inch," Dad corrects.

"Okay, well, which one is the—"

"I guess gimme both." The soft *clink* of a bolt falling onto the gravel under the plane. "Ah shoot," Dad says, and I hear him searching through the gravel for the lost bolt. "And gimme a bolt, too." Another *clink*. "Make that two."

I realize the sizes are engraved on the wrench handles, hand him the right ones, and retake my chilly seat beside the space heater, giver of life.

Dad built the hangar himself when we moved in over the summer, pronouncing it complete after falling off the roof twice but before putting in any insulation. The inside looks like an aviation-themed Applebee's, every inch of wall covered in tools, spare parts, old tin signs, propellers, and tacked-up photos of Dad's ultralights over the years. Blurry snapshots of small, bright planes swooping low over farmers' fields, of Dad standing proud with his arm up on the exposed engine, smiling behind aviator glasses.

Ultralights are small planes that seat one or two people, and they're very light because they're made of hollow aluminum tubing with fabric stretched over them. You don't need a pilot's license to fly them, and you can even fly them out of your own backyard, assuming you've got enough backyard to do it, which—now that we live in Sucksburgh—we do. Our "backyard" is nine acres of grassy field that stretches back to a horse farm. The horses hate the ultralight and run back into their stable every time Dad takes off or lands, the Phantom buzzing low over our house like a giant dragonfly.

It's a beautiful little plane, and flying in it is a real kick.

Takeoffs are especially thrilling. Dad pushes the throttle wide open and the prop becomes a blur, the engine so loud we have to wear earmuffs under our helmets. My teeth clack together as the Phantom bumps over the field until suddenly the ride gets totally smooth, like we've hit a patch of ice—but really the wheels are floating just an inch above the ground. Then the plane floats up and backward a little bit, weightless as a leaf, and we're flying.

Everything looks small from up there. We climb past cotton-ball clouds, soar over patchwork farm fields and model-railroad towns. Every now and then an eagle or a goose will fly along with us for a little while, and Dad wags the wings at them before they peel off. He gets a big kick out of it. "Did you see that, bud?" he asks over the intercom built into the earmuffs. "Roger," I reply, trying to sound all business, like pilots do in the movies.

Dad's bummed that I haven't gone flying with him since we moved. I told him it's because it's been so cold, but he must know that's not true. I mean, we were here all summer, too, and I didn't fly with him then, either. I told him it was too hot. I'm like an antisocial Goldilocks.

Dad's still always trying to drag me out to this dirty freezer. I swear he asks every night after dinner, "Hey, bud, wanna come out to the hangar with me? I could sure use an extra set of hands." I said yes tonight only because Mom whispered to me as I was putting my plate in the sink, "Do you hate your father?"

The question shocked me. "What? No."

"Well, he thinks you do."

I don't care what Dad *or* Mom thinks, but I didn't feel like getting in a fight in the kitchen with my arms in the suds and Mom glaring at me with those lion eyes she gets when she's determined, so I just said, "No, of course I don't hate Dad," to which she replied, "Great. Have fun helping him in the hangar." I know she's upset because tomorrow is Melanie's anniversary— she found a way to bring it up *twice* during dinner—and from the look on her face, it seemed like she might be going for the hat trick, so I was more than happy to retreat out here.

Is this heater even on? The coils are glowing red, but my hands are turning blue.

Dad is so happy I'm hanging out with him that it's getting on my nerves. He's humming "Poor Boy Blues" as he wrenches and screws and clangs. He hasn't said much to me since I came out here, but I realize now that Mom wanted me to visit the hangar so Dad could talk to me about Melanie. He begins his attack while he's still under the plane, a boxer throwing soft jabs to test his opponent's defenses.

"So, bud," he says, the small gear of his ratchet wrench methodically turning, "how's it going?"

I take a deep breath. "Good. It's going good."

"Good," he says. "Good, good." He says nothing else, waiting for me to say more, the steady small *wrench, wrench, wrench* of his ratchet tightening the silence until I'm ready to scream.

"Do you have to keep making that noise?" I ask.

The wrenching suddenly stops. Dad pauses. "Well, only if I

don't want the wheels to fall off when I'm flying." A flurry of frantic wrenching and then Dad stops. "Okay!" he announces cheerfully. "All done!"

He slides out awkwardly from under the Phantom and wipes his hands on his high-waisted dad jeans. I love the way he dresses, a businessman's idea of what a mechanic would wear: dark red chambray shirt tucked into ironed blue jeans. It's so dorky I love it, and I can't help but smile.

"What?" Dad asks, grabbing his leather flight jacket from the Phantom's prop and putting it on. He's tall and has to duck under the wing as he walks over to me, combing his fingers through his neat salt-and-pepper hair. "What's so funny?"

"Nothing."

Dad smiles, and for a second I'm terrified he might hug me, but he settles for a manly clap on the shoulder. "I'm glad you're smiling. I was worried that tonight might be tough for you. That tomorrow might be tough for you."

Oh, fuck you. I never should have given him that smile. I look down. "It wouldn't be tough if you didn't keep bringing it up."

"What do you mean 'keep bringing it up'?" he asks, honestly confused. "When's the last time I brought it up?"

I try to remember, and I'm discouraged to realize I can't think of a single time in recent memory. I've been so antisocial with my parents that they've pretty much given up talking to me about *anything*, Melanie-related or not. I want to tell Dad, *You don't have to bring it up; I see it every time I look in your eyes,* but that seems true enough to be dangerous, so instead I say,

"All the time, that's when," which sounds lame even to me.

I hop off the tires, my ass frozen solid. "Get some fucking chairs in here," I mumble as I walk toward the door. I hope that cursing will divert Dad from the subject, but it doesn't. The old man's as sharp as the crease in his jeans.

"Bud, c'mon, look, if you're upset . . ."

I turn around and give him an angry glare. I dare him to keep talking.

Dad spreads his hands, gently trying to defuse this bomb. "If you're upset . . . that makes sense. Mom and I just want you to know . . . you don't have to be upset alone."

"I'm not upset," I say, and I honestly don't know if I'm lying or not. I would prefer not to know, thank you very much.

As I open the hangar door and step halfway over the threshold, Dad calls, "Last chance," and without looking back, I say into the dark outside, "Good."

I slam the steel door behind me, and the hangar's frame shakes with a satisfying *clang* that makes me feel a little better. There's nothing worse than when you angrily slam a door and it just kind of silently whooshes shut because it's one of those hollow balsa-wood doors. I want to open the door to slam it shut again, but I know that would be weird.

Breathing the fresh night air feels good too. I couldn't stand the gasoline stink in there.

I take a deep breath. I need to get inside and fill some pages. That will make me feel better. Turn on some *Die Hard*. Zone.

I wonder what Dad meant when he said *Last chance?* Oh, who cares. Trying to figure out my parents is like trying to put a tuxedo on a squirrel: difficult, dangerous, and not worth the photo.

It's dark in the backyard. There are no streetlights on our long, one-lane road and no other houses within sight. But the moon is almost full, and it bathes our sprawling, low-slung new house in a ghostly light. Despite my desire to get inside and warm up, I linger between the hangar and the house and savor the silence.

Even though Upper Shuckburgh is only an hour north of Bethlehem (and nowhere near Lower Shuckburgh, which doesn't exist), it feels like a different world. Sometimes—like right now, when I can't see or hear another living thing—it feels like the moon. We moved here after Melanie died because Mom said our old house had "too many bad memories."

Even though we've been here since the summer, I'm still not used to how quiet and dark the country is compared to the suburbs. Without any streetlights or other houses, the emptiness is a little scary. I didn't know nothing could feel so big.

I look up and I'm amazed by how many more stars I can see here. Another thing I don't think I'll ever get used to. It's like looking through a telescope. A riot of diamond-white pinpricks crowd the sky, some actually twinkling like in a goddamn nursery rhyme. I follow the curve of the Milky Way, the stars clustering in a band that runs across the sky, from the big hill on the left of our house to the Blue Mountain range on the right. It makes me dizzy, like I'm riding a cosmic roller coaster, and I look back down at our house to steady myself.

The wind picks up, and I catch the faint cinnamon whiff of dead leaves. It reminds me of the spiced cider Melanie and I always used to get at Scholl Orchards. The association arrives unexpectedly, and grief blows in on that cold wind too as I realize I won't be going to Scholl's this year. It's too far away to bike from here, and I bet Mom won't drive me. "Too many bad memories."

I'm so cold that my arms are starting to shake, but I don't want to go inside. An irrational voice—I know it's irrational, but it sounds very sensible and convincing at the moment—suggests I never walk back into that strange new too-empty house. It whispers a dark promise: If I can figure out how to let go, the autumn wind will lift me up to the stars, where all these problems will look small. Cotton-ball clouds. Model-railroad towns.

If such magical thinking is possible anywhere, it's here. The laws of logic hold no sway in Upshuck County.

CHAPTER 2

I CLOSE THE DOOR OF MY ROOM QUIETLY, HOPING that Mom won't realize I'm back inside. I've had just about all the talking and touching I can handle tonight. Yuck. What I need now is the cleansing fire of *Die Hard* and the calming waters of my notebook.

My room is the only bedroom on the ground floor, which makes it easy to sneak in and out, especially because there are no squeaky spots in the floors and all the door hinges are freshly oiled. Our house is brand-new, built to order, but Dad got carried away and made it a little too big, I think. We don't have enough furniture to fill it, so every room feels kind of empty. Wide swaths of eggshell-white wall stand bare, with nothing but a painting of the seaside centered over a love seat.

My phone buzzes in my pocket, and I see a text from PJ to me and Jake: Hey, wanna study for a biology exam tonight? I have a new method I want to try.

"Study for a biology exam" is the code phrase we use when texting, just in case one of our parents sees our phone. And while I am intrigued to see what PJ's "new method" is—last week we tried using spray paint instead of house paint, and it was a disaster—I'm in no mood to socialize tonight. I write back Thanks, but I'm not in the mood and see that Jake has already replied Whatever, which could mean yes or no; it's hard to say.

I step over a cluster of cardboard boxes and pull a warmer sweatshirt from the pile of clothes in my closet.

Even though we've been in the new house for six months, my room looks like we just moved in today, all my stuff still taped shut in cardboard boxes. Sometimes when I get bored, I arrange the boxes into ancient architecture, like Stonehenge or the Great Pyramid. My junk can be preserved for eternity like King Tut's treasure. The only thing I need is my laptop. It sits balanced on top of a stack of boxes, facing the only piece of furniture I need, Melanie's old easy chair.

When we moved out of our old house, all of Melanie's stuff—her clothes; her Chronicles of Narnia books; her purple stereo, which she played the *Les Misérables* soundtrack on over and over again—got shoved into heavy-duty trash bags and tossed out on the curb for the garbage truck. All her furniture got thrown out too, left on the curb next to the garbage when the moving guys lifted the rest of our furniture into the big yellow truck.

But for some reason the movers didn't throw out Melanie's easy chair. It's a boat of a recliner, nasty orange corduroy with a lever on the side that makes the footrest pop out. It was originally down in the den, but we moved it into Melanie's room when she first got sick so she'd have someplace comfortable to rest and watch TV.

Whatever the reason, the easy chair got moved with the rest of our furniture to the new house, and my parents didn't realize until they found it sitting in the living room. Mom actually screamed when she saw it. She told Dad to get rid of it immediately, but I said I could use it in my room. I'm not sure why I said that, since I knew it would upset Mom.

But I also knew that I couldn't stand seeing Melanie's chair sitting on the curb with the rest of the trash. I pictured Dad putting a smelly trash bag on the seat, old food in the bag leaking gross trash juice onto the chair. The garbage men drive up and toss her chair into the truck, where it gets buried in trash, old diapers, banana peels, and truck oil. Then they toss the chair into some stinky dump, mountains of dank garbage crawling with rats. The chair sits by itself at night in the rain. Wearing down. Decomposing. Slowly becoming trash itself.

No way, no how, no sir. I couldn't do it. I mean, I understand why Mom hates to see Melanie's chair. Looking at it kind of bums me out sometimes too, but it would bum me out even more to get rid of it. I'd see the empty spot where it used to be.

But of course I didn't tell Mom any of that. I just told her it's a comfortable chair, and I needed one. Which is also true. Maybe the last true thing I can remember telling my parents, ha.

I pass the full-length mirror propped against my closet door and notice for the millionth time that my sleeves are dangling over my hands. I have narrow shoulders, so I always have to roll my sleeves up. Even though I'm sixteen, I look younger, and I think it's mostly because my sleeves are too long and my glasses are too big. I roll my sweatshirt sleeves up, take my glasses off, and stand up in a way that feels totally unnatural but which is probably just a normal, healthy posture. I look a little better, but mostly because everything is blurry with my glasses off.

I tear myself away from the handsome stranger seducing me with his eyes, put my glasses back on, and open my laptop to play *Die Hard*. The familiar fanfare of the Fox Searchlight opening credits fills the room, and I prepare to do the same thing tonight that I've done every night for the past year: sort of watch John McClane single-handedly battle a high-rise full of terrorists and try to save his failing marriage at the same time. Most nights I fall asleep with a pen in my hand before the SWAT team even shows up, but some nights—more and more lately, I'm sad to admit—I'm still wide-awake and writing while John and Holly, bloody but smiling, limp into Argyle's limo together while "Let It Snow" plays on the soundtrack.

I feel for John. He didn't ask for this shit, and neither did I. I lift the seat cushion of Melanie's chair to reach for my notebook and discover that tonight is going to be different.

Because my notebook's not there.

I quickly scan the floor around the chair, but it's not there, either.

There's a moment of cognitive dissonance as I stare at the empty spot under the cushion, the absence as surreal to me as a melting clock, while I'm trying to understand this impossible image.

I always put my notebook under the cushion when I'm done each night—it's the most secure spot in my room, since I usually end up sleeping in the chair. It's the only place I hide the notebook, and I *always* hide it.

On the screen behind me John McClane's 747 lands at LAX with a screech of tires. The *whoosh* of jet engines fills my head as I toss the cushion aside, searching around inside the chair, thinking the notebook *could* be wedged in the crack where the back of the chair meets the bottom but knowing it's too big to fit there. It's a five-subject spiral-bound, for chrissakes. I pop the footrest and drop to my knees to look under the chair, but the notebook's not there, either.

I'm about to flip the chair over and tear off the upholstery when someone clears their throat in front of me, and I look over the top of the recliner to see Mom and Dad standing in my room, glaring down at me. Apparently our home's non-squeak floors and well-oiled doors are just as useful for parents sneaking in as for kids sneaking out.

I can feel the sweat standing out on my forehead as I brush the hair out of my eyes and tap the space bar to pause the movie. I turn back around to face Mom and Dad and in my smoothest retail voice say, "Hello, parents. May I help you?"

A pained smile is stretched across Dad's face, but Mom is serious as an undertaker. She's still wearing the purple sweater she had on when I got home from school, nervously twisting the chain of the small gold cross around her neck. By this time of night she's usually in her nightgown, ready for bed.

Mom looks at me with weary disappointment, and even though she's way shorter than me—Mom sometimes shops in the girls' department at Macy's—that look makes me feel small. I'm definitely in trouble for something, but it's hard to guess what, because there are so many options! Do they know I'm still hanging out with Jake? He hasn't been allowed over since Dad caught him stealing beer. Oh shit. Do they know I've been sneaking out? Maybe we should've picked a more believable code phrase than "study for a biology exam."

But it turns out I have made a much graver mistake than choosing a weak code word.

The good news is I know where my notebook is.

The bad news is it's in Mom's hand.

She holds it out like a snake that could bite, although it's just a seemingly harmless, well-used spiral notebook. It has a red cover with a thick blue rubber band wrapped around the middle, and I'm very, very thankful that rubber band is keeping the notebook shut. I am less thankful for the numbers 11/7/18 written on the cover in black Sharpie, because they're the reason I know my parents are going to open it.

For a long time I kept the front of the notebook blank. But one night at the end of summer, I had just finished writing my pages, had filled *twice* as many as usual, in fact, but I still didn't feel good. Didn't feel the temporary relief I usually got after filling a long section.

It was the night before my first day at the new school, and I was remembering how Melanie and I always used to stay up late going through our school supplies and comparing class schedules. She was two grades ahead of me, so I would ask her about the teachers I was going to have, ask if she had had them before and which ones were tough. I was always nervous and she'd calm me down, but now I was sitting in her chair in this empty room that was supposed to be mine, writing a bunch of bullshit in a stupid secret notebook. I felt silly. What was I doing? I couldn't even remember the point.

So I reminded myself.

I paused *Die Hard* and searched through my boxes until I found one with ART SUPPLIES written on the side in Mom's perfect script, then dug a Sharpie out and wrote 11/7/18 real big on the front of the notebook.

I felt much better right after I did it.

But I do *not* feel much better now, because if I had left the stupid cover blank, I bet Mom would've thought it was just a normal school notebook.

As usual, she seems to know what I'm thinking. "You *know* I don't like you sleeping in that chair. It's bad for your back. I was cleaning the blankets up this morning and putting them on your bed when this tumbled out." She points at the notebook. "I thought it was just a normal school notebook, but then I saw the date on the front." She laughs, a dry, humorless laugh. "I thought, 'Oh, that's today's date!' But then I noticed, no, it's not. The year is different." She taps the 18. "It's last year. It's the day before Melanie died."

Well, fuck me.

I do a slow clap, but its intended snarkiness is diluted because I'm so nervous that I miss my hands on the first clap. "Well played, Detective." I hold my shaking hand out. "Now, can I please have my notebook back?"

Mom pulls it away from me. "What's inside here, Kirby?"

"You mean you didn't look?" *Yeah, right.*

"I don't *want* to read your diary, but—"

I scoff, "It's not a *diary.*"

"Oh no? It's not? Then you won't mind if I read it." Mom starts, slowly and dramatically, to slide the fat rubber band up, and I plant a foot on the seat of the easy chair and reach over the headrest to lunge for it.

I almost tip the chair over. "Give it back! It's mine!"

Mom yanks the notebook back and her eyes go wide, like I'm a dog that just snapped at her.

"Whoa!" Dad says. "Calm down, tiger!"

"You have no right!" I yell, standing up on the seat of the chair and pointing down at them. "You have no right to invade my privacy!"

"Invade your privacy? Invade your privacy?!" Mom looks around for the invisible audience I must be telling this joke to. "We've given you nothing *but* privacy since Melanie passed away."

Jesus, I wish they'd stop saying that.

Mom sees me scowl and softens her tone. "Kirby, we hardly see you. You come home from school and go right to your room. You never talk to us—"

I spread my arms in shock. "I'm talking to you right now!"

"You know what kind of talking I mean, Kirby. We used to be a family. But now, now . . . when you talk to us at all, you talk to us like we're your . . . your *roommates* or something."

Mom is getting worked up, and Dad puts an arm around her shoulder. He doesn't like it when Mom gets upset. He gives me a stern look. "It's not healthy, Kirby."

I'm still standing on the chair and I feel silly, so I climb down.

"You're *drifting*," Mom says. "Ever since Melanie died—"

"Jesus," I interrupt, "will you please stop saying that?"

Mom's head snaps up, and she looks at me the way she did in the kitchen, when she asked if I hated Dad. That alert expression once again reminds me of a hunting lioness, and it makes me nervous because it seems to see so much.

She finishes with steel in her voice. "You're drifting away from us, and I don't know how to fix it. But I know that it starts with us *speaking* to each other. You go to school in the morning, and when you come home you lock yourself in your room and maybe, if we're lucky, you say five words to us all day."

I can't deal with this shit. "I've got five words for you right now." I count them off on my fingers. "Get. The. Fuck. Out." I count my four fingers, then flick up the fifth. "Please."

My parents don't flinch. Sad, but not surprised, they regard me like a puppy who just pooped on the carpet.

Mom checks her watch, then looks at Dad, who shrugs. "Okay, well, I guess we're done here." She points the notebook at me like a judge's gavel. "Whether you believe me or not, I haven't read your notebook yet. But believe this: *I will*. I'll give you until tomorrow after school to think about it. If you're willing to sit down and talk with your father and me—a *real* talk, an *honest* talk, about whatever it is that's clearly going on up in that head of yours—then I'll give you your diary back. Unopened."

"It's not a diary," I grumble.

"Fine. I'll give your *whatever you want to call this* back." Mom's face twists in pain, but she swallows the anger. "And if you don't want to talk, that's fine too," she says lightly. Big scary smile on her face, she raises my notebook over her head. "I'll read this cover to cover. I'll sit down with a bag of popcorn and mark my favorite parts with a highlighter."

Mom and Dad turn and walk out my door, but halfway out Mom spins around so violently that Dad grabs her high on the arm, like she's a drunk he's holding back from a bar fight. Tears stand in her eyes as she hisses at me. "I've lost one child. I *won't* lose another."

As soon as the goon squad leaves, I text PJ.

Actually, you know what, I would love to study for biology tonight. Final exam, mothershucker.

CHAPTER 3

THE CRISP NIGHT AIR HITS MY FACE AS I STEP OUT
the garage's side door. It will take PJ and Jake a half hour or so
to walk from their respective houses, but I decide to head down
to the circle early and wait for them there. Better than going
crazy building the Great Wall of Cardboard in my bedroom.

I pull my jacket hood up and stomp my feet on the gravel
beside the back porch. I should be quiet—I usually sneak out
silently, pausing every few seconds to listen for my parents
upstairs—but tonight I just grabbed a couple cans of spray
paint from the garage and stomped out the back door like I
was leaving for school. I don't care if my parents hear me, and
I don't care if Dad notices the spray paint is missing. I can't
possibly get in more trouble than I'm already in. I brim with

the cavalier confidence of a condemned man, sprinting up the scaffolding steps past a sign that clearly says NO RUNNING.

Still, the night holds greater horrors than my parents. So instead of turning on my flashlight, I put it in my backpack with the spray paint and wait for my eyes to adjust, watching the grassy field and hangar behind the house slowly emerge from the dark like a Polaroid developing. Clouds are covering the moon, so it's pretty dark.

It's colder than it was earlier, so I tuck the bottom of my pants into my black boots. I'm sure it makes me look like a paratrooper, but whatever. I'd tuck my pants in once we got to the farm anyhow. The mud and cow shit can get so deep that one night it sucked the shoe right off my foot and I had to hop home on a soggy sock.

I can see the electric fence at the far end of our property now, which means my eyes have adjusted as much as they're gonna, so it's time to roll.

I head down our long driveway. Our house sits a little back from the road, which stretches left up a big hill and right down to a crossroads and then on over a stone bridge and into the woods that lead to the base of the Blue Mountain, a pretty little ridge that's visible now only as an absence of stars. During the day the range does indeed look kind of blue, which I can't explain because it's covered in normal green trees, a pleasant hump in the carpet of forest.

All around our house are cornfields, barren after the harvest. Across the street the plowlines in the dirt trace the contour of the hill like a topographic map, and I just barely spot three dark silhouettes racing over these geometric lines, disrupting the order of the even rows. A chaotic force of nature defying man-made order.

I freeze in the middle of the driveway and hope that the horse dogs are heading toward their barn down the road and not over here, toward my delicious boy flesh. The dogs rarely cross the street into our yard, although the few times they have were memorable indeed.

As they tear down the hill, their paws seem to fly above shadows that ripple over the rutted rows. I breathe a shaky sigh of relief as I trace their trajectory and see that yes, they're heading toward the only other "house" on our street, the big gray barn that's probably filled to its rotting rafters with the bones of deer and drifters. A strong fall wind blows down off the Blue Mountain, scattering stray corn husks into the dogs' path as they disappear through a gap between the barn's big front doors, hanging askew on their tracks.

I wait a few seconds to make sure the dogs don't come back out. Shit. Should I cancel the mission? I've never seen the horse dogs out at *night* before.

For the first time I wish I really *was* studying for a biology exam.

I first saw the horse dogs a couple of days after we moved into the house in Shuckburgh, at the beginning of the summer. The trees and grass were Instagram green, the air filled with the high hum of busy insects, the corn tall and waving like an ocean across the street. Mom and I were on the front porch, lugging in cardboard boxes from the U-Haul. I put a stack of boxes on the porch and was standing up when I saw three horses trotting in the open pasture behind the barn.

"That's weird," Mom said after I pointed them out to her. "There's no fence. Does the farmer just let the horses run wild?"

As though they heard us—which they probably did; I swear those bastards have supernatural hearing—the closest horse swiveled its head in our direction and then started galloping toward us. The other two followed close on its heels, and as the horses got closer, we saw that they weren't horses; they were dogs.

They were dogs the size of horses.

Each of the dogs was a different, unsettling mix of breeds mashed together and inflated to grotesque proportions.

The lead dog was some kind of greyhound mix, with long legs that made it look particularly horselike. Its body rippled with lean muscles, and its tongue lolled out as it pulled ahead of the pack.

The second dog was a kind of Doberman mix, triangular ears, mottled brown and black, running with military precision.

The third dog lagged at the back of the pack, laboring to run under its burden of muscles. It was the scariest of the three, a mastiff mixed with a Volkswagen mixed with a heavy metal drummer. It was solid black, and even in the bright summer sun it seemed to spill darkness onto the field around it. Its head was square with short ears that poked forward like devil horns, its broad face split by an eager grin of sturdy teeth.

Mom dropped the box she was holding, and something expensive-sounding broke inside. She grabbed my arm and pulled me into the house. The greyhound and the Doberman stopped short at the edge of the road and paced back and forth, digging up the dirt and biting the air as they glared at us, but the mastiff kept running across the road, practically tearing up the asphalt, and didn't stop until it was right on our porch. It didn't bark, but merely looked at Mom and me as we peered out through our new front door's window. The sticker was still on the glass, and I wondered briefly if it was shatterproof. A dog can't leap through glass, can it?

The horse dog didn't seem angry anymore, though. It sniffed around our porch, sniffed the box Mom had dropped, then peed on the leg of our new porch glider, marking its territory. Then, before it left, it looked at us through the window again, this time for longer, as though it were memorizing our faces. Then it huffed and ran back across the street, the other two dogs pulling into formation behind it as they ran in a tight pack through the open door of the falling-down barn and disappeared inside.

It had marked us.

We were on their turf now.

I turn around to head back into the house when I see that the light is on in my parents' window and decide that, actually, I'll take my chances with the dogs. As long as I'm quiet, I should be fine.

Just then my phone buzzes in my pocket.

I shield the light of the screen as I read PJ's text: there in 15. When I look back up, I'm gripped by the certainty that I see something move in the shadow of the barn. I imagine the moon sliding out from behind the clouds just in time for me to see the dog's gruesome grin as I try to run but trip and fall onto my hands and knees, placing my tender neck at the perfect biting level. None of that happens, of course, but every moment my straining eyes conjure new shapes from the darkness that evaporate a moment later.

Pull yourself together, man! If John McClane can defeat fourteen terrorists and make it home in time for Christmas dinner, I can sneak past a couple of dogs.

I have a method for getting down to the bus stop each morning, and since it works then, it should work tonight, too . . . I hope.

I turn right and leave the driveway, cutting across our yard toward the line of pine trees that run parallel to the road, past the barn, and down to a small circle of trees about fifty yards from the stop sign.

I tiptoe behind the line of trees. As I pass the barn, its weathered gray boards glow through the gaps in the branches, and I can feel its malevolent presence reaching out to me from the dark gap between its crooked doors. I hold my breath until I pass it, then fast-walk the last hundred yards downhill, into the sanctuary of the circle.

I let out the breath I was holding for the past minute and admire the cluster of stars captured in the oval of pine boughs above me. The circle is a dense copse of pine trees with a nice hidey-hole in the middle, just big enough for three people to meet in. I used to call it "the copse," because that's what it is, until Jake got angry at me and said, "Get the fuck out of here with those bullshit French words," so now we just call it "the circle."

I check the time on my phone. Almost midnight. Jake and PJ should be here soon.

The floor of the circle is covered in a soft carpet of the needles shedded from the pine trees, and I lie down on them, enjoying their springy softness and the night's silence for about two seconds, until I remember the reason I snuck out tonight in the first place.

How the hell am I going to get my notebook back? My heart rate picks up as I realize I probably *can't* get it back. I just don't see how.

Which means my parents will read it. Or I'll have to talk to them, "a real talk," whatever the fuck that means. I'm *drifting*—is that what Mom said? What does that even mean? Did it occur to them that maybe I don't want to talk to them because they're lame? Why does everything have to be about Melanie? They're obsessed. It's unhealthy.

Well, whatever touchy-feely song and dance they want me to go through, I'm not gonna do it. I wonder how bad it would be if I just let Mom read the notebook. I mean, what I wrote isn't that bad . . . is it? I actually can't remember. Most of it was written from the middle of a fog at around three a.m., and I started a year ago. It feels even longer than that.

I can't remember all its content, but I certainly remember the night I found the notebook.... Yes, I do ... the night Mom and Dad came home from the hospital and told me Melanie was gone. I lay on my bed and tried not to move or think, to will myself into a coma, but I couldn't do it. So plan B: I screamed into my pillow until my throat was raw. Nobody came in to stop me. I tore my room apart, punching holes in anything punchable, then stormed into Melanie's room to wreck it, too. I think at the time I intended to tear all her clothes in half, one by one, as messed up and random as that sounds, but as soon as I walked in and smelled her scent and saw all her things, the strength spilled out of me and I collapsed face-first on her bed.

I couldn't really breathe, and I was hoping I might smother to death. But then I realized I was getting snot all over her comforter, so I sat up on the edge of the bed and wiped my nose, and that was when I noticed the untouched stack of new school supplies still left on her nightstand.

I hid the notebook under my mattress that night. I don't know why, since there wasn't anything in it yet. I didn't start writing in it until the next night. That first night I'm sure I wrote some seriously fucked-up stuff. I was pretty raw, and I hadn't yet found my *groove*, wasn't using *Die Hard* to make it easier. Those pages are bad, no doubt. I don't want anyone seeing those, especially Mom and Dad.

Thinking about it makes me feel sick.

I squeeze my eyes shut so hard that little lights dance on the back of my eyelids, and that's when I hear it. At first I mistake the sound for the grinding of my teeth, but then it gets louder and I open my eyes and sit up. I cock my head to listen for it again, but the wind kicks up and for the moment the sound is drowned out by the rustling of the pines around me.

When the wind dies, the sound is back, louder now, and I can clearly hear what it is.

Angry and low and moving toward me, it's a deep animal growl.

I've always thought of the circle as an oasis of safety from the horse dogs, but it's only a ring of trees; the dogs could enter it as easily as I do and just as easily chew my legs off. The growling approaches warily from the direction of the road, and I look around desperately for a weapon, but there aren't even any rocks on the ground.

I remember the heavy flashlight in my bag and fumble with the zipper to try to get it out, but it's too late; the growl climbs to a howl that turns my spine to ice, and the dog leaps through the trees, a huge shape crashing through the branches, scattering needles and knocking me onto the ground. I scream and try to push it off me, its hot breath on my face as the dog laughs and says, "I'm a monster! I'm a monster and I'm gonna eat you! Yum, yum, yum, yum!"

I shove PJ off my chest and roll onto my knees. "You asshole!" I throw a handful of pine needles at him as he rolls around laughing.

Jake enters the circle with the cool elegance of a model

stepping onto a New York City runway, the moonlight shining off his perfectly slicked-back hair. His full lips are pursed into a frown as he brushes needles off his peacoat and draws a dark purple scarf up around his chin.

Jake looks down at PJ and me like we're a couple of nitwits, which I guess we are.

PJ is laughing so hard he's practically hyperventilating, stopping every now and then to growl at me again.

"Rar! Roarrr!" He hooks his fingers into claws and grabs my leg as I stand up and kick more pine needles at him.

Jake stares at me without blinking, his heavy eyelids half closed, an expression that always makes me feel like a bug under a magnifying glass. Jake's eyes are an arresting shade of green, almost spearmint, so large and wide-set they look like alien eyes designed by a special effects team. He has the cold good looks of a fashion model and constantly wears that expression of robotic detachment models have. It makes it hard to read his emotions—although you could flip a coin and guess, since he really has only two moods: bored or angry.

Right now he's bored. Jake sighs. "You two are the lamest nerds I've ever met."

"It must be pretty embarrassing for you to hang out with us," I say, "huh?"

"Hell yes. Why do you think I'm sneaking out under cover of darkness like this?"

"I thought it was 'cause you're a dangerous man on a dark errand."

"Ha," Jake says. "That too."

Jake, PJ, and I are all in tenth grade at Upper Shuckburgh High School, but we met before the school year started, over the summer, just a couple of days after we moved into the new house. I guess it's surprising that we clicked so quickly after meeting. We're all so different—PJ is silly and nice, and Jake is serious and cruel—but we all live within walking distance of each other, and our town is so rural, there were hardly any other kids to hang out with over those endless, muggy summer days.

It's amazing how boredom can bring people together.

I think one thing we have in common, which I didn't notice until the school year started, is that none of us fit in with the other kids at school. Jake because he's mean, me because I'm the new kid, and PJ because he's weird.

Case in point: I reach down to give PJ a hand up from his laughing fit and notice that he's dressed like a ninja. He's got the whole getup, all black: hooded face mask, loose cloth jacket and pants tied with a belt, and cloth booties that wrap around his calves. I shoot Jake a glance, and he returns one that confirms, *Yes, I know.*

PJ pulls his mask down and pushes back his hood, his thick hair bristling up all cockeyed, a goofy grin on his friendly face.

PJ's real name is Pablo Jaramillo, but that's way too long, so everyone calls him PJ. He's the only Puerto Rican kid at our school (Shuckburgh is not the crossroads of the world), which might be hard for some kids, but not PJ. He's so kind and fun that nobody gives him a hard time. You'd have to be a real ass-hole to make fun of PJ.

Jake is a real asshole. He nudges me with his elbow. "How do you like PJ's pajamas?"

"Hey, PJ . . . ," I begin.

"Yes, Kirby?"

"Where'd you get the, uh . . . ninja . . . clothes?"

He takes off his backpack, which is big, the kind hikers use, and tugs on the loose ends of his belt, tightening the knot. "At the dojo," he says, like that should be obvious. "Didn't I tell you I'm taking ninjutsu?"

"You did not. And yet I am not surprised."

"What's ninjutsu?" Jake asks, already bored with this con-versation. "Some kind of weird sex thing?"

"No," PJ says, completely missing the insult. He never notices when people are being sarcastic. "Ninjutsu is the ancient Japanese art of stealth and deception."

He crouches and moves his hands in hypnotic patterns.

"*Stealth*," he whispers. "*Diversion.* Melting into the shadows and disappearing without a trace."

Jake pulls a pack of cigarettes and a Zippo from the inside breast pocket of his peacoat. The lighter has a bald eagle clutch-ing an American flag on it, the kind of tacky shit that doesn't fit Jake's style at all, but his dad is a long-haul trucker and always returns from his trips bearing insane gifts like this: do-rags with skulls on them and Confederate-flag beach towels. Jake flicks the Zippo open with a flourish that must've taken hours to master and lights his cigarette. "I wish you would disappear without a trace right now," he mumbles.

PJ waves Jake's cigarette smoke out of his face. "Well, if you want me to, I certainly could—oh!" He freezes and looks over our shoulders, toward the edge of the circle behind us. Eyes wide, he waves nervously. "Hello, Mrs. Burns."

Crap! Jake and I both spin around—but my mom isn't there.

Heart racing, I turn back around to yell at PJ. "Geez, PJ, you scared—"

But PJ is gone.

He's disappeared.

Jake and I look around the circle, but PJ is nowhere to be seen.

I hear a whisper, but I can't tell where it's coming from. "Deception . . ." PJ emerges from the pine trees on our left.

I do my famous slow clap, nailing it this time, and Jake sighs and throws his cigarette at PJ, who deftly catches it and then brandishes it at Jake like a tiny sword.

PJ dances around, jabbing the cigarette at Jake. *"En garde!"*

Jake ignores PJ. His hair fell down over his face when he spun around, and now he smooths it back, trying to hide any evidence that PJ startled him. Jake's hair is shaved to the bare skin on each side, but it's long on top, combed back in an oily straight wave like he's a 1920s bootlegger or something. It looks cool, but no matter how hard he tries to keep it in place, at least one long dark lock always slips down around the edge of his face. Although that looks cool too.

PJ is still feinting and jabbing at Jake with the cigarette, Jake still studiously ignoring him, when I feel a sudden change in the air, that feeling of electricity that charges the humid summer night right before a bolt of heat lightning strikes down, and I know Jake is about to have an episode.

I try to get between them to stop it, but PJ is completely unaware of the danger he's in and sings, "Taste my blade!"

Jake reaches under the tail of his coat, into the back pocket of his slim slacks. "Taste mine," he offers blandly, whipping out a knife of his own, a real one, whose blade slides out of the handle in a deadly smooth arc as Jake swings his arm forward, the blade clicking into place with a solid *snap!*

Jake looks at PJ, his mouth compressed into a line as thin as the blade, his whole body a weapon yearning to fulfill its purpose.

"Whoa, Jake!" I yell, taking a quick step away from him, knowing how in these moments he acts on reflex and will fuck up anything within fucking-up range.

Even Captain Oblivious gets the message. PJ freezes, cigarette held out in one hand, the other hand above his head in a sort of flamenco fencing pose.

Jake steps toward PJ with the knife held at chest level. It's big, a serious outdoor knife. The handle is matte black, with an American flag on it and a notch for your index finger.

"My dad brought it back for me from a haul he took down to South Carolina last week," Jake says conversationally, hefting it in his hand. "They're hard to get around here because technically it's a gravity knife."

Jake presses a button on the handle, gives his wrist the slightest snap up, and the blade pivots back into the handle, then a quick snap down and the blade swings out again as slick as a snake flicking its tongue. The blade is short but thick, with a wicked curve near its tip and small grooves along the sides that look like they're designed to funnel blood in a specific way. It's the kind of knife a Navy SEAL could fight a shark with, but I'm not worried anymore, because that feeling of static electricity is gone from the air. Jake has terrified the two of us, and that's enough violence to satisfy his craving for now.

PJ is still frozen with Jake's cigarette extended, and Jake leans toward it and puckers his lips. PJ carefully places the cigarette in Jake's mouth as Jake shuts the knife and slides it back into his rear pocket.

I let out a shaky breath, and Jake flashes me a movie-star smile, a Hollywood vampire showing off his fangs for the camera.

Jake can be pretty goddamn charming when he wants to be. He reminds me of a stray cat that used to come around our house in Bethlehem. Silky gray, graceful and sleek, she'd twine herself around my legs, rubbing her cheek against my ankle until I reached down to pet her. She'd let me pet her, loving it, purring like an idling engine—until she'd randomly decide we were done and without warning would turn around and bite the shit out of my hand.

Every day that cat would bite me—and I'd *still* pet her the next day.

Jake sidles up and slides an arm around my shoulders,

shaking me in a manly half hug. He's always in a good mood after he does something violent.

"You need to relax, Kirby. You worry too much." He starts talking in a high, whiny voice. "'I'm scared of the horse dogs. I'm scared Jake's gonna stab PJ. I'm scared of whatever the fuck.'"

I pull my phone out. "Right now I'm scared the sun's gonna come up before we get to the farm. You assholes done sword fighting?"

"Not yet," PJ says. He turns to face Jake, claps his arms to his sides, and bows stiffly at the waist. "Now we're done."

I check my phone. It's midnight, which is the perfect time for our unholy rituals. Late enough so that we won't run into any cars on the road, but not so late that we won't be able to get back before the sun creeps up over that little Blue Mountain range on our right. Also, we still have school in the morning, and I'd like to get a *couple* hours of sleep.

"Are you guys ready?" I ask. "Want to see the farm?" Jake and PJ crowd around on either side of me, looking down at the phone. I pull up Google Maps and zoom in on the satellite view of a long dirt road that runs down to a couple of buildings on the edge of a field. I tap a little fenced-in area between the biggest building and the field. "That's the pen there, on the edge of the pasture. I think that's where the cows will be. It doesn't look like they have serious fences, and the barn and pen are away from the main road, so we won't be visible. Oh, and also!" I reach down to grab my bag and shake it, the spray paint rattling inside. "I got some new spray paint. I know the last time we tried spray paint it didn't work out so well, but . . ."

Jake and PJ exchange a mischievous look.

"What?" I ask.

PJ smiles. "We won't need those. I've got something in my bag too. Something even better." He kicks his big hiker's bag with his ninja booty. I can't tell what's in the bag, but it looks full.

"What is it? What do you have?" I ask.

Jake smiles too, which is rare enough that now I'm really curious. "Wait till you see what the karate kid brought. I mean, it probably won't work, but if it does, it's gonna change the game."

"What is it?" I ask again, but Jake and PJ both just smile at me. Their moods align as rarely as the sun and moon, and I read this eclipse as a sinister omen.

PJ pulls his ninja mask up over his mouth and lowers his hood, leaving only his brown eyes exposed. They twinkle with delight.

"You'll see."

CHAPTER 4

WE LEAVE THE SHELTER OF THE CIRCLE, AND THE rich smell of Jake's smoke drifts over to me on the wind. PJ tightens the straps on his big book bag and its mystery load. "What's our course, Captain?"

I consult the map on my phone and stretch my arm out in front of us like a weather vane. "Thatta way," I say, pointing downhill, luckily away from the horse dogs' barn.

We creep along the side of the road, toward the stop sign. The night is utterly silent. No traffic noise, because of course there's no traffic. During our whole walk I'll be surprised if we see a single car.

We pass the stop sign, and the road makes a hard left into the woods and up over an old stone bridge that crosses a little stream, but Jake, PJ, and I can't take the bridge because we'd have to make a left turn, and that would break our rules.

"Goddammit," Jake swears, vainly grabbing onto a slim branch that breaks off in his hand as he slips down the muddy bank. "The bullshit begins already."

We have a rule about how we walk to the farms: We have to walk in a straight line. Or as close to straight as we can, anyhow, taking into account impassable objects like trees, the inexact measuring capabilities of our own senses, and PJ's dubious assertion that "your left leg is shorter than your right, so if you try to walk in a straight line long enough, you'll actually go in a circle."

I learned about straight-line navigation from flying with Dad. Pilots call it "as the crow flies," but since the three of us aren't flying, PJ and I call it "as the penguin walks." Jake simply calls it, "Better. None of that road bullshit."

As usual, Jake's eloquence cuts to the heart of the matter. Not only is walking straight to the farm quicker than walking along the winding country roads, but it's more *fun*. We hike through cornfields and sparse forests, and every now and then we have to wade through a stream or fight through a patch of brambles.

One very memorable time our path led right through an old farmhouse. PJ and I agreed that this qualified as an "impassable object" and tiptoed around the side, but when we looked back, Jake wasn't behind us anymore. When we got to the front of the farmhouse, there he was, walking out the front door and stepping onto the porch, closing the screen door behind him like he lived there. He was munching on an apple, which I guess he grabbed from the kitchen. It scared me pretty bad. We have to keep an eye on Jake. There's no such thing as an impassable object to him.

The moon still hides behind the clouds, making it hard to see, especially as we climb up the other side of the stream bank and into thick forest. Dead leaves crunch loudly under my boots. I'm glad we're far away from the horse dogs' barn.

I look back at PJ and Jake, but only PJ is there.

"Where's Jake?"

PJ jerks a thumb over his shoulder. "I think he's under the bridge."

I walk back to the edge of the bank, and sure enough, I see the glowing red tip of Jake's cigarette and hear the echo of him tossing rocks around in the shallow water under the bridge.

"Jake!" I whisper-shout. "Jake!"

He doesn't answer me, but after a couple of minutes of cursing, he splashes over and accepts my hand as he struggles up the bank.

"Did you find it?" I ask.

Jake scrapes the mud off his shoes on the edge of a rock. "No," he replies angrily. "I could've sworn I had something stashed under there." He squints at me suspiciously. "You didn't take it, did you?"

"No, Jake, I did not drink your troll booze. Jesus." I turn and stomp back through the woods. Jake can be so infuriating sometimes. He hides bottles of booze all over the countryside—bottles that his dad won't notice are missing, either because they're three-quarters empty or are rarely used alcohols like Campari or mint schnapps—and every time he can't find one he thinks somebody stole it. I imagine the farmers' confusion each spring when they till their fields, the dark fertile soil parting under their plow to reveal airline bottles of Jim Beam and Rumple Minze.

After a couple of minutes of walking in silence we step over a low wall of stacked fieldstones and into—big surprise—a cornfield. No matter where you are in Shuckburgh, you're always near a cornfield, and like the one across from my house, this one is just dirt now, the corn harvested before the weather turned cold. We walk on top of the rows, the dirt hard as rock in the cold, stepping over the ruts and kicking through piles of dead cornstalks. I'm glad there's no corn; pushing your way through cornstalks slows you down. Also, if I'm being honest, it spooks me. The slightest breeze makes the stalks rub against one another and creates this creepy whispering sound. Walking through the narrow rows, you can't see what's on either side of you, and I always imagine murderers and monsters hiding just on the other side of the swaying rows. God, I wish something would swoop out of the darkness and take me now. It would save me the horror of having to face my parents in the morning.

"Are you okay, dude?" PJ trots up next to me.

I am very not okay, but I tell PJ, "Yeah, I'm fine. Why?"

"I don't know. You haven't said anything since we left your house."

I wish I could tell PJ what's wrong, but not only do he and Jake not know about my notebook, they don't even know about Melanie. They don't know I have—had, whatever—a sister. When we first met I didn't mention it because dead siblings is sort of a heavy subject, but then after that there never seemed to be a good time. And now that I've waited this long, I almost feel like I'm intentionally lying to them. The reluctance I initially felt has turned into fear that they'll find out some other way.

We hit another low fieldstone wall, the other edge of the cornfield, and PJ and I clamber over it. Jake is trailing behind us, as usual, probably searching for buried treasure.

"I'm fine," I lie to PJ again. "Honestly, I'm just thinking about what you could possibly have in that bag."

Anytime someone begins a sentence with "honestly," you know they're lying, but PJ trusts everyone. "Ah!" He brightens. "Well, don't waste your time thinking. You'll never guess."

We climb up a massive hill covered in knee-high grass, and I guess the moon must come out from the clouds on the other side of the hill, because all of a sudden its crest glows silver with moonlight.

"We're going to pass the housing complex next to Delps Road, right?" PJ asks me.

"Well, I think that based on our current route we're going to walk past it on our left—but before you say anything, the answer is *no*."

"I don't know what you're talking about," PJ says, immediately starting to drift left.

"Dude, you do this every time, and I've told you before: That's cheating! A straight line is a straight line! You're not allowed to change course like that, especially not for something this stupid."

"Who's changing course?" PJ asks innocently, slowly leaning farther left. Then he drops his book bag, and it rolls downhill a few feet to our left. "Oh shoot. I dropped my bag!" He runs over to pick it up and then continues walking, ten feet left of where he was before.

Jake lags behind us. "What are you girls fighting about?" he calls.

"PJ wants to walk past Vern's house again."

"No, I don't," PJ says. "Oops. I dropped my bag again!"

Vern is a cheerleader in our grade who PJ has a crush on. She's the most unbelievably hot girl I've ever seen in real life. Watching her do normal things like take her books out of her locker makes me feel like I'm watching a movie. I expect a Transformer to break down a wall at any moment. Realistically, PJ has absolutely no chance with Vern, but of course PJ has never let reality stop him before.

"PJ!" I whisper-yell. "You are desecrating the sanctity of our night rituals!"

"What? I can't hear you!" he straight-up yells from so far to the left that I can barely see him.

At the top of the hill we hit the aforementioned Delps Road, a smooth paved road that runs along the edge of a small housing complex, a little slice of the suburbs plopped incongruously in the middle of the farmland. They actually have streetlights here, for God's sake! A dozen crummy lampposts and a couple of porch lights, but still, it's Las Vegas compared to the rest of Sucksburgh.

PJ is down the road fifty feet to my left, at the edge of the housing complex. He waves from a circle of yellow under one of the streetlights before disappearing into a row of neatly trimmed hedges running behind the houses.

I smell something awful and look down at my feet to find a dead possum squished on the side of the road. Oh man. Poor little guy. His head is flattened, blood and brains spread over the road like a dark flower. Roadkill is common in Shuckburgh, not because there's a lot of cars, but because there are a lot of varmints.

Jake stops next to me and nudges the possum with his toe. "Do you think he's all right?"

This is a classic Jake joke: both mean and not funny. I make a mental note to file it away in the *Big Book of Jake Jokes* that I'm editing. Here's a sample joke:

> *Q: Why did the chicken cross the road?*
> *A: Because fuck you, that's why.*

I point at the housing complex. "PJ's spying on Vern again."

Jake shakes his head. "That kid is weird."

"Says *the kid* who buries booze like he's a pirate."

Jake cocks back a fist to punch me in the nuts, but I turn sideways and raise one knee to block him. Instead he pushes me so I stumble back and step into the possum's guts.

"Ah! Crap! Dude, c'mon!"

Jake walks ahead of me, and I hurry to catch up, shuffle-stepping as I try to wipe the fresh possum off my shoe.

We enter the hedges where I saw PJ go in and tiptoe across a couple of backyards until we find him peeking around the side of the shed behind Vern's house, a nondescript split-level with tan vinyl siding.

Even though PJ is obsessed with Vern and talks about her nonstop to me and Jake, lurking behind her shed is the closest he's gotten to talking to her. It's weird. He goes to these insane lengths to be *near* her, but he won't actually *speak* to her. He even joined the football team, as their mascot, just so he could be closer to Vern while she's cheerleading.

All of PJ's scheming is building up to asking her to the Fall Fling dance, which is next week. He's been planning all these different crazy ways to ask her out, like hiring a skywriting plane or hijacking the school's PA system during the Pledge of Allegiance. Although I don't think it matters how PJ asks her. Since they've never talked to each other even once, the answer's gonna be *no,* followed by *who are you?* and probably also *why are you dressed like a ninja?*

Jake and I both think this backyard lurking is creepy, but PJ thinks of it as research and always pulls out his little notepad to write down observations. He has the notepad out now, scribbling intently.

I take a knee beside him and crane my neck around the corner of the shed. "How's the case going, Detective?" I ask.

"Good," PJ says. "I noticed they have geraniums planted behind the house, so I'm going to get a bouquet of geraniums when I ask Vern out."

Jake and I look at each other.

I grab PJ's arm. "C'mon, Sherlock, let's get moving. We're almost there."

Jake and I walk out from behind the shed and cross through the middle of Vern's backyard. PJ lingers a few feet behind us, looking at the house, when suddenly the back porch light flicks on, flooding the backyard with blinding light. At first I assume the light is set on a motion detector, like many of the backyard lights in the neighborhood, but then I hear a sliding-glass door open and my heart jumps into my throat.

Someone steps out of the back door, onto the porch maybe ten feet away from us.

Jake and I duck behind a lone rosebush, which is barely big enough to shield us from view, but PJ is a few steps behind us and has absolutely nothing to hide behind. He's in full view of the house, a spotlight trained on him.

PJ drops to his knees, curls up into a little ball, and kneels there motionless.

I hold my breath and peer between the branches of the rosebush. I can't see the person on the porch well because they're backlit by the spotlight, but it looks like a girl. I guess it must be Vern. She walks to the edge of the porch and leans on the banister, her face turned up to the stars.

She seems to search the night sky for a minute, then looks

down and surveys the backyard. Her gaze passes right over PJ curled up in a ball. Finally, after what feels like forever, she goes back inside and closes the sliding-glass door. The light flicks off, and PJ uncurls like some strange nocturnal animal. He squat-runs toward us, does a little ninja roll, and joins Jake and me behind the shrub.

"I was pretending to be a rock!" PJ whispers excitedly. "I was pretending to be a rock and it totally worked!"

"That's fantastic," I say. "Maybe you can pretend to be a rock when we get arrested for trespassing."

"I probably could," PJ says earnestly. "You know what? I bet I could."

We resume our straight-line navigation, which leads us through the backyards of the few remaining houses on this side of the complex. When we pass a large rock in one of the yards, Jake points at it and says to PJ, "Look, another ninja."

Jake joke!

Parting the shrubs at the edge of the housing complex, we step into farmland so suddenly that the housing complex feels like it was a mirage. I enjoy this fantasy and intentionally preserve it by not looking back over my shoulder.

I don't know why, but it reminds me of a station wagon my parents used to have when Melanie and I were kids. It had a seat which was turned backward, facing out the rear window. Melanie loved sitting back there, but I didn't like it. It made me carsick to ride backward. When I asked her why she liked it so much, she looked at me like I was the dumbest little brother in the whole world. "Because," she said, "it's *exciting*." She pointed out the back window in front of us. "You can see where you've *been*." Then she turned around and pointed out the front window, up where Mom and Dad were sitting. "But you don't know where you're *going*. At least not until you get there."

I love Melanie, but I gotta disagree with her on this one. I'm not interested in looking at where I've already been. Forward ho, I say, and preferably in a straight line.

I run the rest of the way down the muddy hill and stop at a field full of tall corn. Jake and PJ are already waiting for me at its edge.

"What the fuck is this?" Jake asks.

"Corn," PJ says.

Jake tries to smack PJ, but PJ dodges him with a quick ninja head bob.

"Why isn't it harvested?" I wonder. Even in the dark we can see that the corn is dead, the orderly rows slumped and bent like an army of zombies standing at ragged attention. A breeze picks up, and a murmur of dry whispers rises from the field.

A shiver crawls up my spine. "Ugh. Creepy corn."

I reluctantly take the lead as we enter the field single file. The corn is over our heads. The stalks are weighed down by the cobs, and because the rows are all cockeyed and falling down, I have to push the crackling stalks out of our way.

Decaying corn shucks brush against my face like mummy hands. "Ugh. This sucks. Who's the lazy-ass farmer that owns this field?"

"Yeah, it's weird," PJ says. He's lost in the corn somewhere behind me, but I hear a rattle as he pulls an ear off one of the stalks. "The cobs are still on. The farmer just never harvested them, I guess."

"Fascinating," Jake says, disgusted. He pushes past me, slashing at the stalks like he's breaking trail in the jungle.

We stumble out of the field of dead corn to find a small road that disappears around the bend of the big hill we just came down. We pause on the shoulder to catch our breath and pull dead cornstalks out of our shirt collars. I'm going be itching for days. I hope no corn bugs crawled down my shirt.

I consult my phone and see that the farm is just on the other side of the road, down a dirt driveway whose mouth leads down through a break in the skeletal trees.

The wind shifts, and I can smell it now, the rich, disgusting scent of cow manure. It's an eager odor that crawls up your nose and then slides down your throat, seeking your core. I've heard that, of all the evil man-made chemicals destroying the environment, nothing has done more to dissolve the Earth's ozone layer than cow farts, and I believe it. They have physical weight. If you filled a bag with cow farts and threw it in a pond, it would sink like a stone.

PJ inhales deeply. "I love the smell of cow manure in the moonlight."

Jake agrees. "It smells like victory."

I look left and right down the road, then back the way we came. For some reason, it seems familiar. Have I been here before? I look around, but it's hard to see in the dark.

One thing that definitely seems familiar is that, ominously, there's another dead possum squished on the side of the road here. Jake points at it and asks, "How'd he get here before us?"

Knock-knock. Who's there? *Nobody is here, and I have a gun. Go away.*

I point to the break in the trees, and Jake and PJ follow me across the road.

The dirt road leads downhill, and it's so narrow that it's really just a driveway, albeit a long one. Old trees with knotty limbs arch over the driveway, making it feel like we're descending underground through a tunnel. After a few twists and turns, the driveway levels out and ends at an old two-story farmhouse with a wraparound porch. I keep an eye on Jake, just in case he gets the urge to stroll inside and make himself a cup of coffee. The three of us pause behind a big oak and look carefully at the windows to make sure all the lights are off before creeping past the house to the barns behind it.

It's a small farm, just two barns and a chicken coop, and they're all run-down in a way that makes me think whoever owns this place is the same person who owns the field of unharvested corn we just trudged through. Splintery fences surround a scrubby yard of overgrown grass. A couple of rusted cars sit on blocks like the skeletons of ancient beasts.

The larger of the two barns is in the back and is connected to a small pen bounded by a two-tier wooden fence. The mud around the pen is thick and reeking, heavily mixed with manure;

it's grosser than most cow pens I've seen, and most cow pens are super gross.

"Geez," Jake mutters. "Even for a shit hole, this place is a shit hole."

The grubby pen is empty—there are no cows in it—but a gate at the far end stands open, leading to a large, grassy pasture bounded by an electrical fence. From far out in the pasture, moos drift to us like the horns of ships passing at sea.

It's time.

When Jake, PJ, and I met each other over the summer, we instantly felt there was a special connection between the three of us. That our trio held mysterious potential. Even Jake, who is not prone to philosophizing, noted at the time (as PJ was in the middle of demonstrating how you could achieve a mild high by holding your breath until you nearly passed out) that "the three of us should start a band or something."

The feeling was unanimous, but since none of us played any instruments, we agreed that we'd have to focus on the "or some-thing."

A couple of days later, at the first sleepover at my house, PJ told Jake and me about an activity he'd heard whispers of online called cow tipping. Supposedly, some kids in the country figured out that since cows sleep standing up, if you sneak up on them at night, you can tip them right over.

We didn't know if anyone was really doing this or not, but the idea of sneaking up on a large herbivore under cover of darkness and doing something illegal ignited our imaginations. Finally, here was an activity we had all the resources to do: cows, arms, and stupidity.

Tipping cows seemed a little mean, though—couldn't they get hurt? Jake didn't care, of course, but PJ and I did, so we came up with a humane variation: cow *painting*. We would sneak up on the cows and paint them as they slumbered. The cows around Shuckburgh are primarily white; they're large, shoulder height—a perfect blank canvas for rural delinquency.

That very night we filled a whole spiral notebook with ideas. Our minds reeled with the possibilities. "We can paint one to look like a zebra!" PJ suggested. "We can paint them all camouflage so the farmer won't be able to see them!" I said. We'd paint subversive slogans on them like MEAT IS MURDER and WHO WATCHES THE WATCHMEN?

That weekend PJ and Jake spent the night at my place again, and we put our plan into action. After my parents fell asleep, we snuck out to the garage and grabbed a couple cans of house paint along with rollers and brushes. Then we crept outside, cutting across the moonlit fields as quietly as we could while lugging paint cans, toward a cow farm that PJ knew about near his house.

When we got to the farm, we discovered the first of many flaws in our plan.

The cows were not asleep.

The cows were wide-awake, and the whole herd turned their broad, bored faces to us in unison as we sloshed up to their pen through the ankle-deep mud.

Second, although cows are not especially nimble, they had a surprisingly effective evasion system: For every step *toward* them we took, they calmly took one step *away* from us. Once we walked into the pen with them, they wouldn't let us get closer than about twenty feet. We tried running after them, but it was impossible to run in the quagmire of mud and manure in their pen.

Aside from a few small splashes of paint PJ was able to flick onto the cows, our first night of cow painting was a total failure. But failure didn't deter us. We had nothing but time. About once a week we'd sneak out and try again, tinkering with our methods, using different strategies and mediums. Spray paint seemed like a good idea, but the sound of the paint spraying out of the nozzle scared the cows and caused a stampede that almost killed us. We tried wearing black-and-white clothes to "blend in" with the cows and fool them. One time we even climbed up onto the roof of a barn and tried pouring paint onto the cows below. But so far none of our methods had worked.

Cows may be dumb, but apparently they're not as dumb as we are.

Which is why tonight I am very interested to see what secret weapon PJ has in his backpack. It feels like Christmas morning as I ask PJ, "All right, Mr. Ninja, what's in the backpack?"

"Please," PJ says. "My *dad* is Mr. Ninja. Just call me Ninja." He pulls a pair of empty two-liter soda bottles out of his backpack and hands them to me, and it's still Christmas morning, but now it feels like I just unwrapped a pair of socks.

I turn them over in my hands. "Oooookay. What are these?"

"Those are empty soda bo—"

"*Yes, I know they're empty soda bottles, PJ,* but how are we going to paint the cows with them?"

"Well, the bottles need to be filled with water," PJ says. "Fill them about three-quarters full. There should be a spigot around here somewhere. Maybe behind the barn?"

"Okay . . . and then what?"

"And then we fill the water with this." PJ hefts two big containers of Kool-Aid powder out of his bag: cherry and blue raspberry. "We use the water to mix concentrated batches of Kool-Aid, and *then*"—he sets the Kool-Aid down and pulls two big Super Soakers out of the now empty bag—"fill these guns with the Kool-Aid. We're not going to paint the cows. We're going to *dye* them."

Jake can see my mind is blown. He throws his hands up in a simulated explosion. "Boom!"

"My God," I gasp. "PJ, you're a genius."

PJ gives a dismissive wave. "Aw, I'm blushing. You can't see it under the mask, but I'm blushing."

I take the empty soda bottles and walk behind the barn to look for a water spigot or a hose. There has to be something for washing out the cow pens and such.

The grass is high and filled with scrubby weeds, so it's hard to see down near the ground, where a spigot might be. There are pieces of junk, empty beer cans, and wooden boards hidden in the grass, and I trip a couple of times. I'm so focused on looking down that I almost walk into something hanging from a tree only a few feet in front of me.

I hear a buzzing sound, smell something rank, and look up to see a mutilated deer carcass hanging by its feet, strung up from a tree branch by a chain. I almost walk right into it in the dark, and I lurch back and step onto an empty beer can with a loud *crunch*. I'm eye level with the deer's chest, which is sawed wide open from its crotch down to its neck. The wound gapes obscenely. The guts have been scooped out, exposing red muscle and white ribs, bright and saturated with color even in the dark. The inside of the deer seems to be moving, and as I lean closer, I see it's flies crawling around inside the chest. The deer's head is still attached, the soft tan fur of its throat so smooth and untouched that it looks like a stuffed animal, one that some nasty kid has ripped all the stuffing out of.

I'm about to throw up, but I close my eyes and the nausea passes.

When I open my eyes, I don't know why, but it suddenly feels very important that I look in the deer's eyes. I can't see them because the deer is hanging upside down, its head swaying gently a few inches off the ground.

I drop the soda bottles and get down on my hands and knees in the prickly grass, but I still can't see the deer's face. A cold breeze blows through my jacket as the deer's body twists in the wind. I grab the antlers and tilt the head up so it catches the moonlight, immediately feeling disrespectful as I bend the neck at an extreme angle.

The deer's eyes are as lifeless as black marbles, the only light there two pinprick reflections of the moon.

There are thorns in my palms and a spider crawling inside my pant leg as I let go of the deer, and the tree branch creaks under the deadweight. I almost knock over the bucket of black blood under the swinging body as I lurch away, sick to my stomach again. I lean down with my hands on my knees, taking big gulps of fresh cold air.

After a couple of seconds I feel steady enough to walk back to Jake and PJ and tell them to find some water on their own. I pick the soda bottles up from where I dropped them, and there, snaking through the grass, is a hose.

When I walk back with the full soda bottles sloshing heavily in my arms, Jake and PJ are at the perimeter of the electric fence, surveying the empty pasture beyond it.

Jake sights down the barrel of the squirt gun like it's a sniper rifle. He sweeps the farmyard before stopping at me with a little *click!* of his tongue. "What took you so long?"

"Nothing," I say, handing PJ the two bottles. "Here you go."

PJ pours as much Kool-Aid powder into the water as he can while still keeping it a liquid. Then we pour the concentrated Kool-Aid into the two Super Soakers and carefully funnel it into a couple of water balloons as well. Jake and I take the guns, and PJ gingerly places the balloons into his book bag and hoists it onto his back.

We then consider the electric fence that stands between us and the pasture.

The same way jewel thieves become experts on safes, we three brave cow painters have become experts on electric fences. There are various wire configurations—single wire, double wire, the rare triple wire—and voltages ranging from mildly unpleasant to nearly lethal. Some fences don't even have current running through them. At one point they did, the cows got shocked, and now they think it's still live.

However, the electric fence we're looking at now is *definitely* live. It's so alive I'm afraid it will reach out and grab us. It has not one, not two, but *four* wires, all thick gauge, wrapped around white porcelain insulators on every third post. Just seeing those insulators tells me there's serious voltage in this fence, but I can also *hear* the electricity humming through the wires, a low pitch I feel in my molars.

I'm about to suggest, *Maybe there's a gate somewhere*, when PJ takes a running start and jumps over the fence, clearing the top wire easily and landing lightly on the other side. Jake casually threads himself between the two middle wires, avoiding them by only an inch or two. Then they both turn and look at me, surprised to see I'm still standing on the other side of the fence.

I've never touched an electric fence, and I never want to. Jake touched one on purpose once, because he wanted to know how it felt. He stood there shaking for a second, then tore his hand away.

I asked him, "What did it feel like?" and his answer was succinct: "Bad."

Young Ben Franklin waves impatiently at me now. "C'mon, dude," Jake says. "Stop being such a baby."

I toss my squirt gun over the fence to PJ, then get down on my hands and knees and crawl *under* the fence, through the mud and shit.

Jake and PJ laugh in disbelief. "Dude," Jake says, "what are you *doing*? You're getting covered in shit!"

"I know, I know." I crawl underneath the bottom wire, chest pressed into the mud and poop. This close to the ground, the smell is incredible. For the second time in less than five minutes, I almost throw up. When I stand up on the other side of the fence I can feel the clammy stripe of muck running down the front of my shirt, pressing cold against my skin.

Jake and PJ laugh so hard they have to hold each other up.

"It's fucking stupid!" I yell, waving at the fence. "Why would you put up a fence like that? Who do they think is going to break in here, Hans Gruber?!"

"Who?" Jake laughs, trying to catch his breath.

"*Die Hard*!" Sometimes I forget that not everyone has seen it a million times like me.

"Whatever, dude," Jake says, still laughing.

PJ tosses me my squirt gun and I almost drop it because my hands are slippery with poop. "The fence isn't to stop people from getting *in*," PJ says. "It's to stop whatever's in here . . . from getting *out*."

He and Jake go "Ooooooooh!" and wiggle their fingers at me, trying to be scary.

I give my Super Soaker a single brisk pump, like I'm cocking a shotgun.

"I ain't afraid of no cows."

We walk in the direction of the moos. I'm careful to avoid cow patties, especially since the soles of my shoes are the only part of me that isn't covered in shit yet.

The pasture is wide and tranquil in the moonlight, a welcome respite from the grubby farmyard. It's so vast that we walk for a couple of minutes without seeing any cows, and I start to wonder if their ghostly moos are just the wind, but then the herd slowly emerges from the darkness ahead of us.

The cow is not a beautiful animal, but it does have a rustic majesty, a natural dignity intensified by the moon glow the herd is bathed in. Of course that dignity is undermined somewhat by the fact that cows fart so often and so loudly that it sounds like someone clapping their hands. A whole herd farting together sounds like an appreciative audience begging for an encore.

When we get within twenty feet, a few cows on the outside of the herd notice us in their bored, uninterested way. They glance at us while chewing and flick their tails, generally ignoring us. But then our next step passes the magic distance, and the nearest cows slowly lumber away from us.

This is as close as they'll let us get.

"Okay," I say, pumping up my Super Soaker and aiming it at the nearest cow. "Let's see if this works."

I squirt the cow's side, a short burst that leaves a long blue line on its white flank.

The cow flinches, and for a second I'm worried that it will start running and we'll have another stampede on our hands. I recall how far the run back to the electric fence would be, and I'm not sure if we could make it without getting trampled.

But then the cow just snorts, looks at me with bored indifference, and goes back to munching the grass under its feet.

It works. *It works.* My God, it actually works.

None of us say anything, because we don't want to spook the cows, but PJ grabs me in a rough hug and whispers, "YES!"

I feel the same thrill of invention that I imagine the Wright brothers must've felt taking flight at Kitty Hawk, or Neil Armstrong felt stepping onto the moon. Mark my name in the annals of Uppity Fucksburgh and erect a statue here of me covered in cow shit, doing a fist pump.

Jake squirts some cows with his water gun, and I squirt a few more, and they all react the same way: They notice, but they don't really mind. PJ lobs a water balloon at one cow and it *does* mind that. The cow practically jumps and then trots off, deeper into the herd. Luckily, it's near the edge of the herd and doesn't set the others running, but after that we stick to the squirt guns just to be safe.

The dye works great. The colors look desaturated, like all colors do in the moonlight, but we can still see them dark and clear against the cows' white fur, and I know in the light of day they will be Technicolor bright. The dye is way better than paint, I realize, because it's also nontoxic. After they stand out in the rain for a couple weeks, it'll just wash out!

The squirt guns leave long, loopy splashes of color. After a half hour of painting, the herd looks like an LSD trip. Jake is able to handle his gun with the greatest degree of accuracy and manages to shakily write EAT ME on one cow. I try to paint one cow like an American flag, and it sort of works, in an abstract, Jasper Johns kind of way. Will my American-flag cow spark a political debate that forever changes our nation? Probably.

The cows really don't seem to mind that we're squirting them. They don't love it, but I guess they're used to getting hosed down by the farmer every now and then. They're basically ignoring us, just munching on the grass, but then suddenly all of them lift their heads in unison. The whole herd pauses like that for a moment, then trots away alarmed, deeper into the pasture.

What spooked them? The herd's sudden absence makes me feel exposed. The pasture is wide open, the night sky stacked with heavy clouds.

I turn to look at Jake and PJ, who are similarly confused.

"What was that about?" I ask, but then Jake's gaze shifts past me, over my shoulder. I turn around and see, cresting a hill on the horizon, the moonlit silhouette of a lone cow.

Behind me, PJ gives an appreciative whistle. "That's a big cow."

The big cow pauses on the summit, as though it knows how good it looks standing in front of the low moon like that and wants to give us a moment to admire its stature. Then it rears back, kicks its front hooves in the air, and gallops down the hill toward us. Fast.

"That's no cow," PJ says. I turn to reply to him, but he's not behind me anymore. He's tearing back toward the fence at a full sprint. A split second later Jake mumbles "shit" under his breath, drops his squirt gun, and runs for the fence too.

My brain says, *Kirby, you should run too*, and yet I cannot.

I'm transfixed by grim fascination. The big cow approaches with surprising speed, and as he reaches the bottom of the hill, now on the pasture proper with me, I see with my own eyes that PJ is right indeed; this is no cow. The beast drops its massive head like a bulldozer lowering its shovel, and moonlight glints dully off wide, curved horns. Their ghostly whiteness reminds me of the bright ribs inside the deer carcass, and something about this connection at last unsticks me. I turn and run even though in the pit of my stomach I feel it's too late.

As I run, I suck cold air into my lungs, and they tighten up, the beginning of an asthma attack. My left foot goes straight into a cow patty and comes out clean, minus the shoe. I'm running off-balance, limping a little and tripping every time my unshod foot steps on a rock or a sharp stick, which is every single step.

Faintly at first, but growing louder every second, I hear the bull closing in behind me. Its breath is a terrifying wet chugging, like a locomotive made of meat. I do not turn around to look. I focus in front of me, searching the dark horizon desperately for the electric fence.

For a few frantic seconds I don't see the fence at all and fear I might be running in the wrong direction, *deeper* into the field, but then I see the white porcelain insulation knobs floating in the dark. A moment later the fence itself emerges, bobbing up and down in my vision, farther away than I'd like it to be but still, possibly, close enough to reach before I get trampled. PJ is already on the other side, hopping up and down madly and waving at me to *come on, come on, hurry up!* Jake reaches the fence and leaps over it headfirst, like he's diving into a pool.

The bull is closing in. I can tell because in addition to its heavy breathing I hear a disturbing new sound: the deep drum of pounding hooves.

I'm not going to make it.

The fence is still about twenty yards away, an impossible distance. Even worse than the distance are PJ's and Jake's faces, twisted into masks of terror as they back away from the fence. I've never seen Jake look scared, and the expression on his face right now could best be described as "steeling yourself to watch your friend die."

PJ yells, "Hurry! Hurry! Hurry!" and jumps up and down. He throws his backpack toward me over the fence, trying to hit the bull, I guess, but instead it lands in front of me and I have to jump over it and I almost trip.

I can't run any faster.

A second later whatever was in the backpack splinters loudly as the bull tramples it under his hooves behind me— much closer behind me than I expected.

I run faster.

Jake and PJ back away from the fence.

I feel the bull's weight behind me, its gravity so profound it pulls me toward it like a black hole. Its pounding approach shakes the ground under my feet, and although I'm not close enough to jump over the fence, I jump anyway, because if I wait one second longer, I'll be skewered on its horns.

I leap headfirst, like Jake did, and at the top of my arc, time seems to slow down and I see everything with superhuman clarity: the thin strands of wire wound together to make the electric fence's cables, the rusted screws that fasten the insulators to the metal fence posts, the individual blades of grass on the other side of the fence, the side of safety, so close. But I can also see that, indeed, I was not close enough to jump, and I'm not going to sail over the top of the fence. Instead, I'm going to land smack in the middle of it.

My head and shoulders luckily pass through the second and third wire, but my stomach lands on the middle wire, my body stuck halfway through the fence.

An irresistible current sweeps through my body, contracting all of my muscles, even the tiny ones in my face. My toes curl tight. My whole skeleton is united in one single vibration, a tuning fork struck by God's hammer.

I must black out for a second, because the next thing I know, from a great distance I hear PJ yell, "Ah! It stings!" and then I'm looking up at the stars, PJ and Jake each holding one of my arms and dragging me away through the mud on the other side of the fence. They let go of me and I try to stand up, but I can't feel my legs and I immediately fall onto my ass. The best I can manage is to teeter into a sitting position, and when my vision clears, I'm looking up at the bull.

He's right on the other side of the fence, so close I can smell him. He's as big as a car, but his sheer animal presence makes him seem bigger, a building that's about to fall on us, the Leaning Tower of Pisa. His massive head is eye level with Jake and PJ, who are standing, and he snorts softly as he stares at us with dull eyes that I'm surprised to see have long, beautiful lashes.

Steam rises off his black skin in the moonlight as we all contemplate one another in silence. Now that we're on the other side of the fence, he doesn't seem angry at all, and after snorting and staring at us for a couple of intense seconds, he turns around with surprising lightness and trots back into the pasture, disappearing into the darkness.

Once he's safely and definitely gone, Jake gives him the finger and PJ giggles nervously, a brittle edge of tension under his laugh.

I sit in the mud, my whole body aching, an unpleasant tingling radiating out from the spot on my stomach where the electric fence fried me. I'm wheezing badly. I try to slow down my breathing and relax before the wheeze turns into a full-blown asthma attack. I want to grab the inhaler in my back pocket, but I'm sitting on my butt right now and I still can't quite feel my legs.

I reach up to PJ. "Can you give me a hand, PJ?"

PJ starts clapping. "Bravo! Bravo!"

"No, I'm serious. My legs are numb."

"Oh! Sorry." PJ reaches down, grabs my outstretched hand, and hauls me up. I totter on legs that feel like wooden stilts.

"Are you okay?"

"Uh, yeah," I say. "I think so. Just give me a minute to catch my breath."

Just then the farmhouse's porch light flicks on, and a man steps out the front door brandishing the distinctive silhouette of a shotgun. "Who's out there?!" he hollers.

"Shit," Jake grumbles, and runs for the driveway. PJ grabs my hand and tries to drag me along, but he drops it and breaks into a sprint when I have trouble keeping up. "C'mon, dude!" he yells over his shoulder. "Run!"

"I can't!" I yell, but then the man steps onto his front lawn and points the shotgun into the air. A shocking *BOOM!* shatters the night, and suddenly I can.

As I stumble toward the road, I notice with dread that we'll have to run past the farmhouse to get to the driveway. Jake and PJ both bolt past the farmer, but luckily, he seems reluctant to leave the circle of light on the porch. I think he can't see us very well. He keeps yelling, "Who's out there?! Who the hell is out there?!" He cocks the shotgun and fires it into the air again—*BOOM!*—and I jump and lose my stride, almost tripping.

Another light flicks on upstairs in the house.

Jake and PJ are already out of sight, probably halfway up the driveway by now.

As I pass the farmhouse, two more guys run out the farmhouse's front door. The first one is taller and stumbles down the porch steps. The second one is shirtless, and he does not stumble at all; he leaps from the top porch step and lands in the yard, carrying a big flashlight whose beam bobs up and down as he pumps his arms. I catch just a glimpse of him over my shoulder as he passes the farmer with the shotgun and leaves the porch's ring of light.

He's fast.

I won't be able to outrun him. It's the bull all over again, but there's no electric fence for me to hide behind this time. I aim for the driveway anyhow, knowing it's my best bet.

The flashlight beam bounces up and down behind me, casting my shadow huge and stretched on the trees overhead.

Behind me the old man yells, "You better run!" and then Mr. Stumbles, talking to the shirtless guy, I guess, hollers, "Don't you hurt no one, bro!"

I'm at the base of the driveway where it slants up to the road, the last little barn and pigpen to my right. *If I can just make it to the road, maybe I can lose him.*

But a second later I hear fast breathing behind me, and a strong hand grabs my shoulder and spins me around. The flashlight shines in my face, blinding me. I close my eyes and swipe at the light, surprised when, instead, my fist connects with meat and bone. I yelp in shock as the flashlight goes tumbling, its afterimage dancing in my vision as the shirtless guy stumbles back. His butt hits the wooden fence and he flips backward, feet in the air, falling into the mud of the pigpen with a curse and a *splat*.

I run up the dirt driveway until I get to the road, where PJ and Jake are waiting for me. I try to tell them, *Keep running, there's a guy chasing me*, but I don't have enough breath to talk, so instead I grab their sleeves and drag them left, down the road.

We jog without saying anything for maybe five minutes, until I physically can't run anymore. I need my inhaler.

Up ahead, a small covered bridge crosses a creek. I point to it and we slide down the muddy bank and underneath the bridge. I pull my inhaler out of my pocket and collapse heavily onto a large, flat rock. I greedily suck on the inhaler, my breath making a thin, high *wheeeeee* sound, which is very audible in the quiet under the bridge.

PJ looks at me, concerned. "Are you gonna be all right?"

I nod *yes* and try to relax. My knuckles throb. Did I just punch someone in the face? The implications start to sink in. I stare at my feet, one blue Converse and one sock that's so muddy it's completely brown. Why am I wearing only one shoe? When did that happen? I'm having trouble putting all the pieces together.

The stream trickles under the bridge. Jake looks around until his eyes settle on me.

"Can you stand?" he asks.

"Uh, I think so," I say. "I think I'm all right."

"No, no," Jake says. "I mean stand up right now."

I stand up shakily, and Jake shifts the big rock I was sitting on. He pulls a half-empty bottle of triple sec out from under the rock and doesn't bother wiping the dirt off before unscrewing the cap and taking a big slug. He smacks his lips appreciatively, then claps me on the back.

"Man. What a night!"

CHAPTER 5

LIKE A FIRE AT A PAINT FACTORY, WAKING ME UP IN the morning is a three-alarm job.

The first alarm is a little digital clock that sits on the cardboard box beside my laptop. Its insistent beeping sounds like the beat from a tiny dance club: *bap, bap, bap, bap, bap!* but I barely hear it through the fog of my dream.

"Where's that beeping coming from?" the other sky riders ask as we pilot our dragons through the volcanic clouds over Mordor.

It feels good to fly. I haven't done it in so long, I forgot the feeling of lightness. I squint my eyes against the hot wind and look down at the rocky plain below, where a herd of rainbow-colored cattle runs. Ahead, the tower of Barad-dûr rises dark in the distance, but instead of the Eye of Sauron, the numbers "7:45" glow red at its pinnacle.

The beeping stops and I drift back to sleep, pulling my dragon's reins and doing a lazy wingover into the soft mists of slumber.

But a minute later the second alarm goes off, louder than the first, and I wake up with a jerk that knocks the comforter off my legs.

Alarm number two is an old-timey brass clock, the kind with two bells on top and a little hammer that swings back and forth between them like a maniac. It sits on top of a box all the way across the room, so I can't turn it off without getting up. Any normal, average sleeper would get up at this point and admit defeat. But I am a pro. I pull my comforter back on and without getting out of the easy chair *or* opening my eyes, I take the pillow from behind my head and throw it at the clock, knocking it over.

But now I hear the third and final alarm stomping downstairs to my room.

Mom.

I'm pretty sure I can't stop her by throwing a pillow, although I'm sorely tempted to try it this morning.

I'm so tired, it seems like I fell asleep only a couple of minutes ago. It's frigid outside my warm blanket cocoon. I can feel it on the tip of my nose. I hunker deeper into the comforting warmth of the easy chair. *Die Hard* is playing softly. It's the part where Ellis says, "Hans, bubby, I'm your white knight." I put it on loop last night right after I took a scalding shower and collapsed into my easy chair. I actually did a little writing too, even though I didn't have my notebook. I just wrote on some pieces of paper. It was better than nothing, but I couldn't really get in the zone, couldn't disappear the way I usually do. I couldn't stop thinking about Mom having my real notebook, and the fear kept yanking me back to the present. After writing on the paper, I tore it up and flushed the pieces down the toilet.

I pry my eyes halfway open. Morning light squeezes around the edge of my window blinds. I quickly close my eyes again as Mom strides into the room, because I know what she's about to do: She yanks the blinds up, and blazing sunlight fills the room. Even through my shut eyes, the light lances straight into my brain.

With the bored showmanship of a magician who has been doing the same trick for years, Mom pulls all the blankets off me in one quick swoop.

Abracadabra!

The bedspread is gone, but the sleeping teenager is still curled up in his easy chair!

Oohs and aahs from the audience. Scattered applause.

Cold crawls up my bare legs. I keep my eyes shut and curl into a ball like an armadillo being attacked by a crocodile. I remember PJ's ninja skills and think, *I am a rock. I am a rock.*

Mom closes my laptop, then considers me and sighs, an overworked machine letting off pressure. She must love me an awful lot, because instead of dumping me out of the chair and beating me with a newspaper, she takes another calming breath and pats my head.

"Look, honey," she says, not unkindly, "I'm sorry if we scared you last night."

I keep my eyes closed and don't say anything. *I am a rock.*

Mom's tone hardens. "Have you thought at all about what we discussed?"

Have I thought about it? Is she kidding? It's *all* I thought about after we got back from cow painting. It's the reason I filled eleven pages of loose-leaf paper instead of just falling asleep last night.

But I keep my eyes closed and don't say anything. I am a rock. A sleeping one.

Mom sighs and I think she *might* actually tip the chair and beat me with a newspaper, but instead she sighs yet again, a long shaky breath like she's about to start crying. She pats me on the head again, maybe just a little too hard.

"C'mon, honey, you're going to be late for school." She sounds even more tired than I am. On her way out I hear her pause as she passes my closet door. "Ugh," she says. "What is that smell?"

My eyes pop open. *That smell* is the cow shit all over the clothes that I wore last night. I put them in a trash bag and buried them under the rest of the clothes in my closet, but even a mountain of cotton cannot contain the toe-curling stench of cow shit.

Mom looks at me for an answer, and I peer over the back of

the chair and kind of shrug as if to say, *I'm a teenage boy. There are a million different things in this room that could be causing that smell.*

After Mom leaves I ooze out of my chair like my bones are made of pudding. My legs are basically useless. Here's the problem with running for your life: You never have time to stretch beforehand.

Luckily, I don't have far to walk. I stumble to the little bathroom attached to my room, but as I open the adjoining door, I accidentally bump my right hand on the doorjamb. My bruised knuckles flare with pain, the skin swollen and scraped raw. Oh, that's right. I punched someone in the face last night. I remember running for the woods. Being blinded by the flashlight. Striking out in fear, trying to hit the light.

I grab my glasses off the back of the toilet tank, sit down on the seat, and flex my fingers experimentally. It hurts. Boy, I must've really nailed that guy. I wonder who he was. Some farmer, I guess.

I'll have to hide my bruised hand from my parents.

The list of things I'm trying to hide continues to grow, but neither the dirty clothes in my closet nor the scraped skin on my knuckles worries me as much as the red notebook hidden somewhere in my parents' room.

Just the thought of it makes my stomach go light, like I'm falling. I imagine my parents sitting me at the kitchen table as they read my notebook in front of me. The sad, disappointed look Mom will give me; the long, boring lecture Dad will recite earnestly as he leans close to my face and puts his hand on my shoulder.

I'd rather walk barefoot over broken glass.

I turn on the cold water and hold my bruised hand under the tap. As the water runs, I pull my shirt up and look at the spot where the electric fence caught my stomach, expecting to see a scar or something, but there's nothing there. There is, however, a nasty purple bruise on my hip bone, I guess from when I hit the ground after Jake and PJ dragged me off the fence.

I glance up at myself in the mirror above the sink and then do a double take. I look rough. There are bags under my eyes, and my hair is a tangled bird's nest. At the end of *Die Hard*, when John McClane is all beat up, the scars and stubble look cool and rugged.

That is not how I look right now.

I just look like crap. I hate to admit it, but I'm not tough-looking. One time I overheard our pediatrician tell Mom I had "the body of an artist," which is insulting, accurate, and also a weird thing for a doctor to say. "Well, Mrs. Burns, I have good news and bad news. The bad news is that he has the flu. The good news is that your son has the sneeze of a poet!"

I try a rugged smile, the kind John McClane is so good at, but I can't quite pull it off, mostly because of my gross teeth. Little veins of brown and tan run through them, like my smile is made of fine marble.

I was only three the first time Melanie got leukemia, and

the doctors used me as the donor for a bone marrow transplant. But they didn't realize that the anesthesia for the operation, if used on kids my age, will discolor the enamel on their adult teeth when they come in.

Mom keeps telling me that they'll pay for veneers, but I always say no. She says she wants me to get them because it will look nicer, but I think she doesn't want to be reminded of Melanie every time I flash my candy-corn smile. I've sort of fixed the problem myself by not smiling anymore.

I don't like the look I'm giving me, like I'm about to ask myself to dance. I know what I'm about to say, and I wish I could stop because it's so fucking stupid, but my reflection appears beyond my control.

"Happy anniversary," the spooky kid in the mirror says.

Oh shit, my hand is freezing! I can barely feel it. I turn the cold water off and examine the damage on my knuckles, which are less swollen, but of course still missing just as much skin.

Mom knocks on the bathroom door, and I jump. "Are you up?"

"Well, I'm in the bathroom. So . . . yes, I'm up."

"Okay . . ." She sounds doubtful.

"No, Mom, I'm not up. I'm sleepwalking." I start to snore loudly.

"Okay, okay. I'm sorry." Mom pauses, then adds, "Breakfast is ready. Don't let it get cold." Mom acts like cold food is inedible. If she made ice cream for breakfast, she'd still say, "Hurry up. Don't let it get cold."

Even though I took a shower last night, I need another one.

Partially because I was marinated in filth last night and partially because it'll help my muscles feel better. I turn the shower on as hot as it will go and wait for the water to warm up. Since we use well water, it takes a bit. I yawn. I wonder how Jake and PJ feel right now. I bet not half as bad as I do. Jake seems impervious to pain, and PJ just doesn't mind.

Do I have any tests today?

What day is today?

You know what day it is.

This is going to be a long day.

While the water runs, I take my clothes off and catch a glimpse of my scrawny chest and my dumb face in the mirror. I take off my glasses and everything gets blurry.

Huge improvement.

CHAPTER 6

MY ACHING LEGS FEEL LESS LIKE STILTS AFTER I take a hot shower, and I walk upstairs to the kitchen without limping too much. Mom's washing dishes at the sink, and Dad's at the table eating breakfast and reading the paper. Everything looks normal, but I feel a weight in the air. A pressure. I don't know if it's because of Melanie's anniversary or my notebook.

Our kitchen is really two rooms, a kitchen and a little dining area divided by a wraparound counter that Mom loves to call an "island," as though the kitchen is so large that it can only be described in geographic terms.

The dining area has a sliding-glass door on the back wall that looks out into the field behind our house, and the orange glow of sunrise fills the room with warm light. I'd think it was pretty if I wouldn't rather be flying my dream dragon over the burning mountains of Mordor.

The kitchen is Mom's domain, and as such, a land of mystery to me, full of wonders I do not understand. For instance, we have a big dining room off the kitchen, but we never use it. Instead we cram around the little table in the second half of the kitchen.

Mom is up to her elbows in suds, another thing I don't understand. She washes the dishes before putting them in the dishwasher. Why? Is she trying to impress the dishwasher? "This is how you clean a bowl, robot!"

A glass cabinet dominating one wall is full of china dishes that we never use because they're "too nice."

The laws of logic hold no sway in Upshuck County. Whatever. I just come here for the food.

Dad is sitting at the little table in the corner dining section of the kitchen (the "breakfast nook," as Mom calls it), eating the only breakfast I've ever seen him eat—Grape-Nuts with sliced bananas—and reading the paper with an expression of intense concentration.

Dad is dressed for work, a sharp navy-blue suit, a white shirt with his green striped tie tossed over his shoulder so he won't get any food on it. His jacket is draped over the chairback and his shirtsleeves are rolled up so he won't get any food on them, but I can see there's already a small glob of banana on his shirt.

Dad looks up from the paper as I walk in. "It lives!" he says.

"Ha-ha." I open the fridge. I'm not sure what I'm looking

for, but an escape pod or a fireman's pole that leads to the center of the Earth would be nice.

"How's it going?" Dad asks seriously.

I give him a dirty look over my shoulder. *How's it going?* "What is that, a joke?"

Dad folds the paper shut and holds a hand up in truce. "Hey, sorry. Sorry I'm trying to be nice."

"If you were trying to be nice, you'd give me my fucking notebook back."

Mom drops a dish into the sink with a splash, and bubbles fly everywhere. She looks at me angrily. "Excuse me?!"

Dad pinches the bridge of his nose. "Can we just not, right now? It's a little early." He gives me a stern look that's meant to end the conversation, but then I can see it turn to concern as he notices how bad I look. He seems about to ask if I'm okay but stops himself. Probably because he knows I'll yell, *Am I okay? Are you kidding me?!*

Mom gives a little yelp of alarm. "What happened to your hand?"

Shit. I forgot about my hand already. It's in clear view, grabbing the fridge handle, and I stare at it like it belongs to someone else. "Oh, that? Uh, I hit it. Accidentally."

Mom strips off her sudsy gloves to examine my knuckles, still scraped and red.

"You hit it?" she repeats doubtfully.

Dad peers across the top of the island, a soldier peeking above the trenches.

"Yeah," I say. "I hit it on the wall. Accidentally."

I'm sure Mom thinks I punched the wall because I got mad or something. Good. Better than her thinking I punched a farmer after fleeing a crime scene.

I turn my attention back to the chilly sanctuary of the fridge. "Where's the soy milk?" I'm lactose intolerant, so regular milk makes me explode.

Mom allows me to change the subject. "Sorry, honey, we're all out. I'll pick some up later today. But your breakfast is on the table."

"Can I take it with me? Can you make it into a sandwich?"

Mom looks at me, confused. "I don't understand why you never eat breakfast."

Dad's reading the paper again. "You've gotta eat, bud. You're a growing boy." He seems to remember something and puts the paper down. "Oh, by the way, Kirby, have you been taking rocks out of the flower garden?"

"What? No . . . Rocks?"

Dad looks doubtful.

I push my case. "Why would I take rocks?"

Dad shrugs. "I don't know."

Mom says, "You promise if I make you a sandwich, you'll eat it on the bus?"

"I will. I will. I'm just not hungry right now." I hope she can't hear my stomach rumbling.

"Okay." Mom sighs. She pops two slices of bread into the toaster to make the sandwich. I lean against the counter and stare at the china cabinet, filled with plates that are too nice to use, the rising sun reflected in its glass.

"While you're waiting for your sandwich," Mom asks, "would you like a banana smoothie?"

Sometimes I wish my parents were more neglectful. Is that a weird thing to wish for? If they smoked a ton of weed, or were absinthe connoisseurs, that would be perfect. I'd like them to be lazy enough to forget about me every now and then. Give me a little space. *Not ransack my room searching for private notebooks.*

I just want a little privacy, but they always have to pry. They even sent me to a psychologist one time, to get him to pump me for information.

My first day back at school after Melanie died I got a little overwhelmed. All her friends kept telling me how sorry they were, looking at me with sad puppy-dog eyes, trying to hug me. One girl gave me a *framed photo* of Melanie! What the fuck?! You think I don't remember what she looked like? I threw it in the trash in front of her.

Halfway through the day I hid under a table in English class, and when a kid asked me what I was doing, I screamed in his face.

I'm pretty sure one of my teachers—or a couple—called my parents and told them what happened, and the next evening they made me go to an interrogator—I'm sorry, *psychologist.*

The shrink's office was decorated like a swanky bachelor pad. He was lounging in a chair made of bent wood and leather that probably cost more than a TV. He looked like someone who went to smooth jazz festivals. He stood up and shook my hand and looked right into my eyes, which made me uncomfortable. His hand was soft, his eyes deeply calm. I assume his serenity was supposed to put me at ease, but instead it bugged me. *People are coming to you because they're upset. Could you not look so super not-upset?* There was a box of tissues on the low-slung coffee table between our chairs, which I thought was presumptuous.

He closed the door behind me, and as soon as he lowered himself into his Norwegian chair and crossed his legs, I told him right off the bat, "Look, asshole, I don't have anything to say to you. I'm only here because my parents are forcing me."

I was hoping to rattle him, but it didn't work. He spread his hands calmly and purred in his deep NPR voice, "That's fine. I totally understand how you feel. But I want you to understand, even though your *parents* are the ones who brought you here, this session is just between *you* and *me*. Anything you tell me in this room *stays* in this room."

I was not impressed. "Well, that will be easy, because I'm not going to say anything to you *in this room*. So, you know, you can just, uh . . ." I realized I didn't have anything else to say and that I was already talking more than I had intended, so I just trailed off.

He gave me a small smile like I had complimented his sweater instead of telling him to fuck off. "Okay. If you don't want to talk, we don't have to. You can just wait here in my office until your parents pick you back up."

He pulled a deck of cards out of a small drawer in the low coffee table between us and placed them in the center. "Would you like to play, or would you prefer we just stare at each other?"

We played poker for the rest of the hour. I tried to get him to play for money "just to make things interesting," but he said he'd get in trouble. *You're damn right you'd get in trouble*, I thought. *I'll take you to the cleaners. Come on, dude, bet me a couple of those phony diplomas on your wall.*

The next week my parents forced me to go back to the psychologist again. When I stomped into his office, he already had the deck of cards out on the coffee table, shuffled and ready to play. He didn't ask me about Melanie or anything else. The only question he asked before we spent the next hour playing poker in silence was "Would you like to cut the deck?"

Every now and then he'd glance at me with those deeply calm eyes and give me a tepid smile, like *he* was the one whose parents were forcing him to be there. It kind of drove me crazy. His face was so hard to read, I could never tell if he was bluffing. I guess it makes sense that a psychologist would have a good poker face. Their whole job is keeping a straight face while clients tell them insane bullshit.

The third week when I came back, we played cards again, but after a couple hands I was so bored I mumbled, "I don't even know why I'm here. My dumb parents think I'm crazy or something."

The psychologist put his cards down very carefully, like

they were made of glass. Then he leaned back in his chair and regarded me seriously.

"Why do you think they think that?"

And just like that, my resistance crumbled. I started talking, a little at first, but more and more as we continued to meet, because it felt so good. Sometimes I'd even tell him things I didn't realize I was thinking until I heard myself say them. God, it was such a relief.

After a couple of weeks I even worked up the courage to tell him about my notebook and the experiment I was doing with it. This was the secret I was most nervous to tell him. I know that when someone dies, it's *normal* to be sad and to miss them. But what I was doing with my notebook . . . Well, I wasn't sure if it was normal.

I was starting to like Mr. Smooth Jazz, and I was worried that when I told him about my nightly ritual, his poker face would crack just a little, and beneath it I'd see what he really thought of me. That I was crazy. Or maybe just stupid. He might even *laugh* at me.

Luckily, he didn't do any of those things, and when he didn't, when he simply asked, *Why do you think you're doing that?* I was so relieved that I couldn't even answer him. I just cried. It wasn't sad crying. They were tears of pure relief.

He waited while I wiped my face on my sleeve, then asked again.

Why do you think you're doing that?

It was the only time I asked him to pull the cards out again. "C'mon, Doc," I said. "Let's make it interesting. I'll bet you my mom's car, and you can bet me that chair."

I was blindsided when, a month or so later, he began our meeting by quietly announcing, "Well, Kirby, this is our last session."

I didn't realize how much I had come to enjoy our weekly talks until he told me they were stopping. Maybe this was some kind of reverse psychology trick to get me to tell him some *really* deep stuff?

"But wait. I've got more to tell you," I bluffed. "I've got some really crazy shit in my brain that I haven't told you about."

He shook his head. "Kirby, all the feelings you've told me about are completely normal. You're grieving, and that's good. The business with your notebook." He shrugged. "I think you know why you're doing it, even if you're not ready to admit it. And someday soon, I hope, you *will* be ready."

That sounded like good news to me, so I couldn't figure out why he was looking at me so seriously. "So . . . I'm cured? You'll tell my parents I'm not crazy?"

"Yes, I'll tell your parents you're not *crazy*." He hated that word, and spit it out with a hint of disgust. "But as for the rest of the things you and I discussed . . . I told you the first day we met, everything you've told me in this room will *stay* in this room."

He was still giving me that significant look, but I wasn't following him. "Oookay, sooo . . ."

"So you need to talk to your parents. This whole time you and I have been talking, how many of the things you've told me have you also told your parents?"

I was beginning to think I might not miss him so much after all. I looked down at my shoes and tried to ignore him, but the office carpet was the same cool gray as his eyes.

"You don't mind talking to me because I'm nobody," he continued. "This room is nowhere. It's just more words written in a notebook that nobody will ever see. And it's fine. In fact, it's healthy—*for now*. But this isn't the end of your therapy, Kirby. It's the beginning." He gave an embarrassed smile. "This is going to sound cheesy, but it's also true: Today is the beginning of the rest of your life, and you need to start *living* it. It's the only way forward."

Mom met me in the waiting room and talked to the psychologist a little bit by the reception desk. I couldn't hear what they said, but when she walked over to me, she looked hopeful.

Pulling out of the parking lot, she tried to hide her optimism as she asked me, "So . . . what did the psychologist say?"

"Nothing much." I looked out the car window at the cookie-cutter houses passing by. "He said you guys were wrong. I'm not crazy, so there's no point in me going to therapy anymore."

It was not the answer Mom wanted.

We drove the rest of the way home in silence.

A year after Melanie's death, my parents are still trying to do the same thing that psychologist did. Just wait me out. They think that if they're patient, eventually I'll cheer up. Or open up. Or something—honestly, I don't know what they want from me.

But I know they're gonna be waiting a long time.

I'm plenty cheery now, and also I don't have anything to talk about.

If there's one thing I learned from that psychologist, it's how to keep a good poker face.

CHAPTER 7

MOM ALWAYS WRAPS MY EGG SANDWICH IN TINFOIL.
I slide it into my left front jacket pocket as I walk out of the
house onto our front porch, the hot little bundle pleasantly
warm against my stomach. I hope I actually get to eat it today.

It's not as cold as it was last night, but it's still cold enough
that I have to zip up my jacket. The sun peeks over the Blue
Mountain ridge, painting the treetops orange and green above
the sleepy blue foothills. The field across the road lies in the
mountain's shadow, a dark plain under the lightening sky.

I put down my book bag and stoop to pick a few rocks out
of Mom's currently dead flower garden. I put the biggest rocks I
can find into my right front pocket, leaving it unzipped for easy
access, then spread the remaining gravel around with my toe.

Right before I left the house, Mom gave me a significant look and said, "We'll see you after school," as though warning me not to leave the state between now and then. The thought has certainly crossed my mind. If I had a passport and a false mustache, I probably would.

I shoulder my book bag, walk down our driveway, and turn right, following the same path I took last night, sneaking toward the circle and the bus stop that cruel fate has placed on the corner directly across the street from the horse dogs' farm.

This is my life.

This. Is. *Sparta!*

I hate sneaking to the bus stop every morning. It's a nerve-racking process that I've broken down into five levels of ascending danger, much like the US military's DEFCON system.

DEFCON 5: I sneak behind the screen of pine trees and hide in the circle. The stop sign is out in the open, so I wait until I hear the bus coming, then dart the twenty yards to the stop sign at the last second. This works about four days a week. However, if the horse dogs see me before I reach the circle, I move up to

DEFCON 4: Throw rocks at the dogs. This doesn't scare or hurt them, and my aim is so bad I couldn't hit them if I wanted to, but the dogs think it's some kind of game and will chase the rocks like I'm throwing them a ball. I thought this was cute until I saw them pick the rocks up and crush them with their jaws.

The rocks only work on the greyhound and the Doberman, though; the mastiff ignores the rocks and stays locked on me, so if the mastiff rounds the corner of that big gray barn, I increase the alert level to

DEFCON 3: Throw my egg sandwich at the mastiff and hope he finds that more appetizing than my tender boy flesh.

Luckily, DEFCON 3 is the highest alert I've reached, because DEFCON 2 would be *fight a pack of wild dogs with my bare hands*, and DEFCON 1 would be *hope I give them indigestion*.

One time I made the mistake of telling Jake about my DEFCON system, and he stared at me in utter disbelief.

"So wait," he said. "Every day you have to avoid getting attacked by these dogs?"

"Technically, twice a day. But yes."

"Just kill them," he said.

I was shocked. I couldn't tell if this was a Jake joke or not. "Uh . . . I don't think I want to do that."

"Okay, if you want to be a total wuss about it, you could call the cops or the SPCA or whatever. Show these fuckers who the dominant species is. Do *something*."

But we *did* try something.

A couple of days after we moved in, Mom and I were pulling out of the garage in our car when the Doberman ran up our driveway and leapt directly onto the hood of the car. Claws squeaking on the metal hood, slobber flying all over our windshield, barking like a maniac.

Mom screamed and slammed on the horn with both hands,

but that just made the dog angrier, barking and biting the windshield wipers. It didn't jump off the hood until Mom started slowly driving again, and then it hopped off and ran back to the farm across the street, disappearing into the high corn. When we got out of the car at the Shuckburgh Corner Store, we found a big dent in the hood.

That afternoon Dad went over to the farm to talk to the horse dogs' owner, although we had never seen any people across the street and the dogs' behavior certainly didn't indicate that they were anyone's pets.

Mom and I watched nervously through our front door window as Dad knocked on the trailer, a sad little pair of deer antlers nailed above its aluminum door.

A skinny guy holding a beer answered. Dad talked to the guy for a while, but I could tell he wasn't making any headway because he started waving his arms and poking the guy's chest. The skinny guy didn't seem to care. He sipped his beer and adjusted his baseball cap like Dad was selling Girl Scout cookies.

The skinny guy said something final and closed the door. Dad stomped back over to our property, and Mom and I stepped aside hastily as he slammed the front door behind him.

Mom asked, "Well . . . what happened?"

Dad laughed, a tense, edgy laugh he only does when he's trying not to flip out, like when we're lost on a long car trip. "Well, I told that guy he needs to control his dogs. And he said . . ." Dad laughed again and shook his head. "He said *no*."

"No?" My mom repeated the word like it was in a foreign language she was trying to learn.

"Yep," Dad confirmed. "He said, 'I don't have to leash my dogs. They're farm dogs.'"

Now when the horse dogs attack the car, Mom just beeps the horn and goes "*Shoo! Shoo! Scat!*" like it's a fly on the hood and not a two-hundred-pound killer canine.

It's amazing how quickly people adapt to bad situations. To you it seems crazy, but to me it's just another Friday.

I'm three-quarters of the way to the circle, out of sight of my house and too far to run back, when I hear a distant bark.

I tighten the straps on my book bag in case I have to run, and I look between the branches at the big gray barn across the street. The walls are made from splintery wood that *used* to be painted red, maybe a hundred years ago, but since then, wind and rain have worn it to a ghostly gray with only flecks of red, like bones that have been picked clean. One of its two massive front doors rusted off the hinges and is held crooked to the other with a chain, so I can see the darkness inside. As the sun comes up, the gloom is striped with bars of light where there are gaps in the boards.

One of the shadows moves.

"DEFCON four." I sigh and pull the rocks out of my pocket. As I jiggle the reassuring weight of the rocks in my hand, I creep sideways toward the bus stop like a crab, never taking my eyes off the approaching wraith.

Still just a shadow, it heads toward me, trotting for a moment before it breaks into a run.

I hope it's the greyhound. He's fast, sure—he easily keeps pace with the few cars that drive up our road—but he doesn't like to cross the road.

The dog runs through a bar of sunlight from a hole in the roof, and I can see the Doberman's shiny brown-and-black coat. The Doberman doesn't give a shit about the road or any other man-made barrier. He runs silently, as single-minded as a guided missile.

I cock my arm back to throw the rock, but then the greyhound rounds the far corner of the barn.

I barely have time to think, *Oh shit*, before a deep, mournful bay announces the arrival of the mastiff, lumbering from the tree line behind the farm. The other dogs circle back to join him, nipping at one another like happily deranged maniacs, before wheeling and charging toward me in formation, bone and meat united in grisly purpose. They howl in unison, and their meaning is clear: *WE WEAR NO COLLARS. WE HEED NO COMMANDS.*

"Dammit." I drop the rocks and pull the egg sandwich out of my pocket. "I was hungry."

I'm dead meat. I'm dog food. I'm John McClane perched on the edge of Nakatomi Plaza's roof. I have only one move left.

I lob the egg sandwich like a hand grenade, and it lands in the middle of the road. The mastiff scoops up the sandwich without slowing down and shakes it in his jaws like he's trying to break its neck. He paws at it in the road, trying to get the tinfoil off.

The other two dogs try to snatch a bite, but the mastiff growls, picks the sandwich up in his mouth, and runs back to the trees. The Doberman and greyhound chase him, nipping at his ankles as they disappear in the shadowy woods.

The street in front of me is suddenly empty. The only evidence that the dogs were there at all are the distant growls I can barely hear over the pounding of my heart.

Then I hear another sound, a low mechanical hum.

The grind of gears downshifting.

I run toward the stop sign and arrive, panting, just as the school bus pulls up. The door swings open, and Granny gives me a funny look as I climb the stairs. Our bus driver is probably ninety years old, but she looks older. She's little and wrinkly like an ancient elf. She hates that we call her "Granny," but I don't even know her real name.

She blinks at me behind the lenses of her sunglasses, the huge square ones that only old people and futuristic bounty hunters wear. I must look shaken up, because she asks me in her high, creaky voice, "Are you all right?"

"Yeah," I lie. "I'm fine."

CHAPTER 8

MY STOP IS EARLY IN THE BUS'S ROUTE, SO ONLY a few kids are sitting on the bus as I head toward my seat in the back. All of them have headphones on, either sleeping or staring out the windows like zombies.

I still don't know most of the kids on the bus too well, but I at least know their names: Jeff Albanese; Katie and her sister Avalon; this weird kid who looks like his mom uses a soup bowl to cut his hair. I pass Liam "Spags" Spagnaletti, sleeping with his head tilted back against the green plastic seat, mouth wide open, just begging for some bully to drop a bug in his mouth.

I walk all the way back to my usual spot, last seat on the left, across from Trey. He too is sleeping, folded up in his seat like a beach chair, legs wedged against the back of the seat in front of him, knit hat pulled over his eyes.

The bus pulls away from my stop, gears grinding noisily, and bumps down the road into the woods. I look out the back window and watch the horse dogs' farm disappear around the bend.

On my school bus, as on most, the cooler you are, the farther back you're allowed to sit. The two last seats are the most coveted, but the fact that I sit back here has little to do with how cool I am and a lot to do with how early I get on the bus and how few cool people I have for competition. PJ is on the bus too. He sits with me, but his stop is the last one before school, so we don't sit together for long.

The only time I can't sit in the back is if Mark Kruger is on the bus. Mark is not only cool, but he's also tough, *and* he's a senior, a triple whammy that guarantees him platinum-plus back-seat status.

Mark is real country: He eats homemade deer jerky from ziplock bags and dips chewing tobacco on the sly during class, spitting the juice into a disgustingly full Yoo-hoo bottle when the teacher isn't looking. He's on the football team, but he doesn't dress like a jock. He wears work boots, flannels, Carhartt jackets. A scar runs from his left ear up to the part in his hair, on which no hair will grow. PJ and I have had a few discussions about how he got that scar, and our most likely guess is that he got it while wrestling a twelve-point buck to the ground with his bare hands.

Mark is rarely on the bus. He usually drives to school,

something only a couple of the older students do. At the end of the school day I often see him climbing into his rusted pickup outside the vo-tech, a separate building behind the high school where some of the seniors like Mark learn how to do plumbing or electricity or other trades like that.

Mark also isn't at school a lot of mornings because this is the fall, and fall is deer-hunting season, so he comes into school late.

Yes, that's right. Here in Whatthefuckburgh, deer hunting is a valid reason to skip school.

Teacher: You have to come into school today to learn how to read, write, and do arithmetic. Also to learn history and chemistry.

Student: I can't. I have to kill an animal instead.

Teacher: Oh, okay. That's more important. You can learn about the forces that govern society and order our universe some other time. Someone needs to teach those deer a lesson too.

I don't have a moral objection to deer hunting. I eat animals every day. I don't think that hunting is immoral. I just think it's *rude*.

The bus winds its way through the pleasant countryside of Shuckburgh, springy suspension bouncing over the roads' many bumps and holes. The back of the bus may or may not be the coolest, but it is undoubtedly the bumpiest.

This morning it also seems to be the smelliest. I notice a foul stench and assume it must be manure still stuck somewhere on me from last night, but this stench is different from manure.

Manure is robust and lively. This smells more like . . . decay.

Trey is still sleeping, so I reach across the aisle and nudge him. "What's that smell?"

He doesn't pull his hat up above his eyes, but he points down to his book bag. "It's my bag."

Like a fool, I lean down and take a big whiff of his bag. The stench is so bad I rear back immediately. "Ugh! Is it full of shit?"

Trey smiles and pulls his hat off, revealing a disturbing twinkle in his eye.

"Dude, you won't *believe* what's in my bag. Wait till we get to school. I'll show you then."

Well, it's nice to know I have *that* to look forward to.

Trey doesn't care that I'm revolted. He doesn't care about anything. He treats teachers and adults as if they're kids like him. This makes him come across as cool and confident, but honestly, I think there's something wrong with his brain. He always has this crazed look in his eyes, and I'm pretty sure he cuts his own hair, because one day half his head will be shaved, and the next day it will be dyed green, and then a week later it's all gone. His two front teeth are huge, like a rabbit's, and there's a gap between them wide enough to slip a penny through, which he does sometimes as part of his "vending machine impersonation."

I lean back in my seat and look out the window. Trees blazing with yellow and red leaves slide past. Even though I miss Bethlehem, I admit that the countryside has its charms. The ride is relaxing, a nice way to ramp up to the day and get ready for class.

I'm excited for English today because we're going to be discussing *Lord of the Flies*. I used to be a voracious reader; I could burn through a book in a day, no problem, if it was a good one. I especially liked adventure—the Sherlock Holmes mysteries, Jack London, wolves and spaceships and swords and shit.

But I haven't read many books since we moved. I don't know why. I guess I've just been busy with the move and all and getting used to the new house. How empty it feels. I suppose I devote most of my reading time to watching *Die Hard* now, ha. I only read *Lord of the Flies* because our teacher Ms. Hunt forced us to, but boy am I glad I did, because it was great (even though it *did* cut into my *Die Hard* time). It's about an airplane full of elementary school kids that crashes on a deserted island. Some of the boys try to establish a civilized society, but of course that doesn't last long. After a couple of days they're bashing each other's brains in with rocks and offering bloody sacrifices to a pig head on a stick: the Lord of the Flies. Ms. Hunt sort of hinted we might have a pop quiz about it today. No problem. I'm ready.

Across the aisle, Trey's asleep again, his head bobbing up and down in rhythm with the bus's gentle motion. We bump over a one-lane bridge that is only about a foot wider than the bus and have to slow to a crawl before dipping down the other side and speeding up again. The farms give way to the natural tangle of woods. I like the sound of the engine, deep and calm. I put my headphones on but don't play any music.

The bus starts to fill up. Nobody I know too well.

We pass the housing development on Delps Road and Vern floats onto the bus, radiant as a sunbeam. She's a walking Instagram filter, perpetually backlit, light streaming through her long blond hair. There must be a football game tonight, because she's wearing her cheerleading uniform—a short black dress with a bold orange *S* on the chest—under a cropped white jean jacket. She struts down the aisle and sits a few seats in front of me. She glances at me for a second as she sits down, and my heart hiccups.

The bus breaks from the dark woods into bright morning sunlight. My head is leaned back on the seat, bumping pleasantly, and I'm almost asleep when the view out the window looks familiar to me. A big hill slopes up and beyond sight above the top of the window, and I notice it's filled with unharvested cornstalks.

Hey, that's the hill we walked down last night!

I stand halfway up to look over the seat backs and out the windows on the opposite side of the bus. The bus slows down, and I realize why the farm looked familiar to me last night: The bus drives past it every day. This is Mark Kruger's stop.

I'm still tired, so the pieces fall together very slowly in my mind. I can almost hear them clicking as they slide into place like falling Tetris shapes.

This is Mark Kruger's stop.

The bus grinds to a stop, and Granny swings the big silver handle that opens the bus doors.

That means that the farm we painted last night is probably Mark's.

Mark climbs the bus steps, the top of his camouflage baseball cap slowly rising into view.

That means I probably punched Mark Kruger in the face last night.

Mark walks down the aisle toward me, his left eye black-and-blue and swollen shut.

Correction: I definitely punched Mark in the face last night.

I grab my bag and scramble out of my seat.

Mark looks out of place on the school bus, his hands stuffed into a beat-up Carhartt jacket, trudging down the aisle like he's headed to pull a double shift at the steel mill. Hat pulled low over his serious face, he glances up at me indifferently before looking back down at his boots.

But a second later he looks up at me again, suddenly interested, and his one eye that isn't already swollen shut narrows shrewdly. I quickly stuff my right hand in my pants pocket to hide my scraped knuckles. If I didn't look guilty before, I sure do now.

I'm still standing in the aisle, so I quickly sit down in the nearest seat, realizing only once I sit down that I'm sitting right next to Vern. I jostle her, and she scoots away from me, toward the window.

"Hey!" she says. "What are you doing?"

I don't want Mark to notice me any more than he already has. I try desperately to act casual.

"Oh, nothing. I'm just, uh . . . Big game tonight, huh?"

This question catches her off guard. "Uh, yeah?" She smells

fantastic, like honey and flowers. "Yeah, we're playing Lehigh. The Fightin' Game Hens."

"Ooh. The Game Hens," I say, searching my suddenly blank mind for football terms. "Killer . . . defense."

"Yeah," she says, starting to get a little annoyed. "Uh-huh."

Mark stares at me as he walks past, and I expect him to grab me by the neck and shout, "IT'S YOU!" But a moment later he's already passed by and taken my old seat in the back across from Trey.

"Well," I say, sliding out of Vern's seat. "Good luck at the game!"

"Thanks," she says, relieved that I'm leaving.

The bus starts rolling again as I hurry toward the front. Granny sees me running up the aisle in her rearview mirror and yells, "No standing while the bus is in motion!"

"Sorry!" I sit in the seat directly behind her. If I could sit on her lap, I would. I very badly want to turn around to see if Mark is looking at me, but I know that if he *is* and he sees me looking over my shoulder, it'll make me appear even more suspicious.

I wish I still had my egg sandwich. This is DEFCON 3 for sure.

The kid with the soup-bowl haircut is sitting in the seat across the aisle, and he stares at me blankly.

"What are you staring at?" I ask him.

He doesn't say anything, but he doesn't stop staring at me either, so I scooch down in my seat and scowl out the window.

It's clear that some great force is at work here, cosmic

powers aligning for the sole purpose of destroying me. First the bull was sent, then the dogs, and now Mark. Even if I make it off the bus alive, I'm sure a great leviathan, like the whale that swallowed Jonah, will gobble me up during swim class.

Despite my hopes that a freight train will broadside the bus and end the terrible suspense, I'm still alive a couple of stops later when PJ gets on the bus. He's surprised to see me sitting up front. For my part, I'm surprised to see he's wearing a tuxedo. He's also holding a big, evil-looking warthog head under his arm, but that's normal, part of his Iron Pigs mascot costume.

"Why are you sitting up front?"

"Why are you wearing a tuxedo?"

The bus pulls away. "No standing while the bus is in motion!" Granny yells at PJ.

PJ sits down next to me, the warthog head on his lap.

Our football team is called the Iron Pigs because Shuckburgh used to produce a lot of pig iron. It doesn't anymore. All the steel plants closed down a long time ago, putting the whole town out of work. I'm pretty sure most of those people never got another job, or at least not a good one, because the bus passes a lot of tumbled-down trailers and rusted pickup trucks on the way to school.

But, silver lining, at least the steel industry's glorious legacy lives on in our football team's stupid name.

At the beginning of the school year PJ wanted to join the football team so he could be closer to Vern, but he didn't want to have to tackle anyone, so instead he decided to be the team mascot, as in, the guy who runs around in a costume at the games. That wasn't a position that was currently filled, or that even existed, but PJ thought it would be fun and nobody had the heart to tell him no.

He's gotten really into being the mascot, even writing his own chants for the crowd to recite at games.

PJ tried to buy a giant pig head at the costume store, but he couldn't find one that he liked, so instead he made one himself out of papier-mâché. The result was a terrifying creature, more boar than pig, more monster than boar. When he proudly showed Frankenswine to Jake and me, we recoiled in horror.

Massive tusks framed its mouth. Brown pipe cleaners bristled from its sloping brow. PJ was thrilled with the result, so I tried to break it to him easy. "That pig is . . . awfully hairy," I said.

"That's not a pig," Jake said, *not* trying to break it to him easy. "It's a warthog. Look at the fucking tusks, you idiot."

Since then PJ has been trying to get the football team to change their name to the Iron *Hogs*. He slips the modified name into the cheers he leads at the football games, but so far it hasn't caught on.

Never quick on the uptake, PJ doesn't notice that I'm terrified about Mark. He points to the orange flower in his lapel and smiles. "A geranium! See? Just like in Vern's garden." He opens his suit jacket so I can admire the lining. "Do you like it? I'm going to ask Vern to the Fall Fling. I finally figured, what the heck. I'll just—"

I cut him off. "That's fantastic. Listen: The farm we painted last night?"

"Oh yeah, that was great! I've been thinking of ways we could make the water balloons work and thought that maybe if we warmed the water up, it wouldn't shock the cows quite so—"

"That was Mark Kruger's farm."

PJ stops, puzzled. "Really? How do you know that?"

"Because the bus picked him up right there, and he has a black eye, and he gave me a suspicious look when he saw me."

"Ah," PJ says, "I see." He turns and looks toward the rear of the bus, and I quickly slouch down in my seat to hide my head.

"Do you see him back there?" I whisper.

"Yep."

"What's he doing?"

"Staring at me."

"Crap." I rub my scraped knuckles, incriminating evidence. "What if Mark figures it out? Oh my God, he'll kill us. Or what if he tells on us? What if we get in trouble?"

PJ considers this. "He doesn't seem like the type of guy who'd tell on us."

"I guess you're right. . . ."

"He seems more like the type of guy who'd beat us up."

PJ is right, no guessing about it. I vividly remember the gutted deer behind the barn.

I text Jake, the only person I can think of at school who's scarier than Mark. With Jake on our side, maybe we don't have to worry about Mark. I wait a minute and he doesn't text back, but that's not unusual for Jake. He never checks his phone.

PJ tries to calm me down. "Look, even if Mark is suspicious, how could he know it was us who painted his cows? I mean know for sure?"

"Well, he probably sort of got a look at my face when he was chasing me with the flashlight," I say.

"But not a *good* look, right?"

I remember the way Mark squinted at me as he walked to the back of the bus. If he had really recognized me, I think he would've said something.

"No, not a good look," I concede. "But if he sees my messed-up hand—"

PJ brushes this aside. "Mark is in vo-tech for most of the day, so it'll be easy to avoid him. Just remember to keep your hand hidden, and I don't know. . . . If Mark asks if it was us, we just say no. He doesn't have any proof."

I guess PJ's right. But I don't know. I have a bad feeling. I feel like I'm Sergeant Al Powell, poking around the eerily quiet lobby at Nakatomi Plaza.

The bus passes the Greyhound terminal on the edge of town and turns right at the bottom of Main Street, which runs past the school. It gains momentum because there are no more kids to pick up; it's just a straight shot to school now.

PJ tells me his plan for asking Vern to the dance, but I'm not listening.

"Uh-huh. Uh-huh," I mumble at random intervals. My fear

of Mark is fighting for supremacy with my fear of my parents, and I'm not sure which to be more worried about right now.

PJ finally notices me drifting and changes topic. "Did you have to use your sandwich today?"

"Yeah."

"Sorry about that. Are you hungry?" He pulls a string cheese out of a pocket inside his tuxedo. "Do you want some cheese?"

Even though I shouldn't eat the dairy, I take the cheese and gnaw on it nervously. I know I'll be sorry later, but for now it gives me something to do besides worry.

"Oh, hey," PJ says, pulling his little notepad from his pocket. "I've been working on some new chants for the football team. What do you think of this one? 'Our team has some real big-wigs. Cream cheese tastes good when you put it in figs. We're good at football; we're the Iron Pigs.'"

I stare at him blankly. "Not many words rhyme with 'pigs,' huh?"

"No." PJ frowns. "Not too many."

The bus passes the school on Main Street, then swings into the parking lot in front of the school behind a long line of buses waiting their turn to unload. Streams of students get off the buses at the front of the line, talking and laughing, and slowly merge into the river of humanity that narrows to a bottleneck as it squeezes through the school's front doors.

I cautiously poke my head up over the back of the seat to look at Mark, and sure enough, he's still staring at us, his black eye an ugly ring of purple. He idly scratches the scar in his hair.

I duck back down and ask PJ, "What would a ninja do? What does your ninja training tell you?"

PJ's calm is infuriating. "Well, the tenets of ninjutsu assert that deception and evasion are preferable to combat."

I grab the satin lapels of his stupid tuxedo and shake him. "ENGLISH, PJ. SPEAK. ENGLISH."

"If we want to avoid Mark, we should distract him."

"Distract him? Okay . . . okay . . . how? Do you have any smoke bombs on you?"

PJ pats his pockets. "Not today."

"NO STANDING while the bus is in MOTION!" Granny yells, her voice rising to a shriek.

Someone walks up the aisle toward our seat, and I turn around, expecting to see Mark's fist flying at my face, but instead Trey is standing in the aisle, holding a leash. I smell the awful stench that was coming from his backpack, but it's stronger now.

"Sit down!" Granny says. "How many times do I have to tell you kids?"

"But I gotta let my dog out," Trey whines. "He's gotta pee-pee!" He holds the leash up. Dangling from a dog collar on the other end is a dead raccoon. It's roadkill, big and fat except for the middle of its back, which is squashed flat by a tire track. It looks relatively "fresh," if that word can be applied to roadkill, like Trey might've picked it up this morning while waiting for the bus.

Trey dangles the dead raccoon in front of Granny's face,

which has gone white and slack with horror. "My dog's sick, Granny!"

Granny doesn't know how to react. She shrinks as far away from the stinking carcass as she can. Unable to speak, she reaches out and pushes the silver lever that opens the bus door. Trey skips off the bus, smiling, and tosses a jaunty "Thank you!" over his shoulder.

Everyone on the bus flips out. We rush to the right side of the bus in a gaggle so we can stare out the windows at Trey skipping toward school, dragging the dead raccoon behind him. His "dog" leaves a trail of blood on the pavement, and as Trey begins passing the few kids at the back of the herd filing into school, they start to freak out too.

The kid with the soup-bowl haircut spins around, and it's the first time I've ever heard him talk when he yells the obvious, "That's a dead raccoon!"

We all just about trample one another trying to get off the bus to watch Trey drag the raccoon across the courtyard. We trail behind him as he walks through the crowd, more and more students noticing him, ripples of panic spreading, the pandemonium building into a grisly parade. Kids are laughing, kids are shrieking, cell phones are held above the crowd, trying to get a clear shot to film.

I walk backward for a moment to keep my eye on Mark, but I've lost him.

PJ and I run to catch up with Trey.

PJ asks Trey, "Where did you get that?"

I'm surprised that Trey drops the act for a second, and I'm even more surprised by the real emotion in his eyes. "Found the poor little bastard squashed right in front of my bus stop this morning," Trey says. "I felt so bad for him, I figured I'd bring him to school. Give him a *real* send-off, like a Viking funeral, you know?"

PJ and I do *not* know, but we nod in respectful silence anyhow.

A little, excited kid runs alongside and asks Trey, "What are you *doing*?!"

Trey snaps back into character. He smiles and says, "I'm walking my dog!"

"He's walkin' his dog, he says!" the kid screams in disbelief as the crowd around Trey grows so large that I'm surprised Mr. Hartman hasn't noticed the hubbub yet.

Our school isn't very big, so Mr. Hartman is the only person who's dedicated full-time to security. He looks like an undercover cop from the seventies: thick mustache, brown polyester pants, wire-frame glasses whose orange-tinted lenses are the size of a Camaro's windshield. His loud sports coats are always a half size too small for his barrel chest, like he bought them twenty years ago and refuses to admit that he's gained thirty pounds since then. If he weren't so big and tough, it would look funny.

I hear Mr. Hartman actually used to be a cop, a real cop, which is probably why he takes his current job too seriously. If he catches you running in the hall or using the bathroom without a hall pass, he acts like you're stealing a car or dealing drugs. Dude needs to chill.

He and Jake sort of have a vendetta going. A lot of times when we walk down the hall, Mr. Hartman will surreptitiously tail Jake at a distance. Like he's on a sting. Despite the fact that Jake is constantly breaking the rules, Mr. Hartman rarely catches him in the act, and it drives him crazy.

He always keeps a massive walkie-talkie clipped to a holster on his belt buckle, but since he's the only security person in the school, I'm not sure who he calls on it. The president? He even has a *pair of handcuffs* folded and clipped to a loop on the back of his pants, although you can practically see the cobwebs on them.

Mr. Hartman is standing sentry next to the front doors, thumbs hooked into the waistband of his polyester pants. He notices the crowd laughing and hooting as Trey nears the school's front doors and cranes his neck to see what the commotion is.

"What's going on? What's going on?" Mr. Hartman asks no one in particular. Then he sees Trey dragging the dead raccoon toward the school. His face flushes bright red, and he holds out one meaty hand like he's stopping traffic. He crouches into an action stance, and his right hand cocks down to his walkie-talkie like it's a six-shooter.

"Hold it right there, mister!" Mr. Hartman barks. He points at the raccoon. "What the hell is that?"

Trey stops in the center of the courtyard, right next to the flagpole, and he deserves an Oscar for how sadly he says, "It's my dog, Mr. Hartman. He's *sick*."

Mr. Hartman can't tell if Trey's legitimately stupid or just pretending, so he plays it safe. "Son . . . ," he says as delicately as he can, "that's a raccoon."

Trey looks down at the raccoon in surprise. "Oh my God, you're right!" He lifts it off the ground and starts to swing it over his head like a lasso, building momentum until the leash sticks straight out like a shot put about to be released, the raccoon at the end spinning at a dangerous velocity.

The crowd scatters, a circle clearing around Trey. Kids hit the ground or turn and run for cover. Even Mr. Hartman falls to his knees and puts his hands over his head. *Nobody* wants to get hit with a face full of roadkill.

Trey spins and spins, then adjusts the arc of the raccoon upward and lets go of the leash. The raccoon flies clear over the heads of the crowd and disappears onto the roof of the school.

Mr. Hartman is up like a flash and grabs Trey by the arm. He looks like he wants to kill him as he marches him into the school. The crowd parts and applauds as Trey passes through their midst, a hero on parade. Trey waves with his free hand and blows kisses to the girls.

I turn to ask PJ, *Did you see that?* but he's not there anymore. I look around, but I don't see him anywhere. Is this another one of his stupid ninja tricks?

I'm carried along in the crowd of kids walking through the front doors of the school, and as we walk inside the school, the shift in temperature—from cold, crisp outdoor air to warm, moist indoor air—makes my glasses fog up.

Dammit. Every time.

I step near the wall, away from the flow of students, and wipe my lenses on my shirt. I turn and look back into the front courtyard, out through the glass double doors, the crowd a blur of moving shapes. I put my cleaned glasses back on, and the courtyard snaps into focus.

It's madness, everyone clapping and laughing. I search the crowd, both hoping to see PJ and hoping not to see Mark, but I don't see either of them.

CHAPTER 9

I WANT TO REACH MY LOCKER AND THEN THE safety of homeroom as quickly as I can, but as happens so often in this damn school, I get lost. Even though I've been at Upshuck High for more than two months now, I still get lost all the time. The school's layout is super confusing and is arranged around four large cylinders stood on their ends like fat, short grain silos.

The central cylinder is the school's hub, the main entrance I entered a moment ago from the courtyard before somehow getting turned around. The middle of the cylinder is the lobby, a round, cathedral-like space with rows of lockers lining the periphery. The lobby is so big, the locker rows are broken into different numbered sections, but I can still never find mine. The other three cylinders surround the lobby and empty into this soaring space.

The setup is annoying because 90 percent of the time, to get to your next class you have to walk through the lobby. The middle of the lobby is sheer chaos, all the students crossing to different circles to reach either their classes or their lockers.

This is why many students refer to the lobby as the Thunderdome. (Actually only Jake, PJ, and I call it that, but still, we're hoping it'll catch on with other kids.)

It takes a special talent to pass through this crucible of flesh without getting bumped and jostled and dropping your books, and I've been told that on the first day of school, kids line the edges of the Thunderdome to watch the inexperienced freshmen get mangled in the morning, the busiest time of day.

My first couple of days were pretty rough too, although now I'm able to slip through the crowd with balletic ease, unconsciously in tune with the seething masses around me.

At the far end of the central cylinder are doors that lead to the cafeteria, the gym, the pool, and the long hallway that wraps around the outside of the gym and connects to the science room. The principal's office is at the front of the lobby, right when you walk through the main doors.

Behind the gym, on the far side of the rear parking lot, is the vo-tech, an ugly concrete building with a large steel garage door on the front. On warm days sometimes they roll up the door and you can see students in there working on cars. It's comforting to remember that I probably won't run into Mark for the rest of the day because he's in the vo-tech, so—aside from lunch, gym, and a few other classes—we'll be in separate buildings.

Speaking of classes, where the hell am I? My locker is in the Thunderdome, where I was just a second ago, but somehow now I'm in one of the circles, Circle C. I speed up, looking for the hall back to the lobby, or for PJ, Jake, or (heaven forbid) Mark. I wish my eyes were placed on the sides of my head, like an herbivore, to give me a wider range of vision. I do not need these forward-facing predator eyes. I am prey, buddy, pure and simple.

To prevent students from constantly running into one another as they round corners, each of the circles has one-way traffic, which means you can only walk clockwise. If Mr. Hartman catches you walking counterclockwise around one of the circles, you get written up, and you also have to endure his aftershave, which smells like the blue stuff barbers soak their combs in.

I text PJ, Where are you?

I pop out of Circle C back into the lobby, but now I'm at the far end, away from the main entrance, up near the gym.

The student government is busy decorating the gym for the Fall Fling next week. The walls and ceiling are strung with Christmas lights and strobes and even a big disco ball. Someone yells, "Flip the switch!" The big overhead lights go off and the party lights flick on, and suddenly the gym looks like a crazy dance club. It's impressive, actually. Someone should get the student government to redesign the whole school.

Is that my locker? No. This is Section 13. How'd I skip Section 3?

I think of the cardboard Stonehenge in my bedroom and wonder if the school's odd layout has some secret significance, if perhaps during the summer solstice the four circles align with four constellations in the night sky.

I picture my school in the middle of the night, the parking lot empty and all the windows dark except for one light flickering in a gymnasium window.

The locker room is illuminated by hundreds of candles as Ms. Hunt, my English teacher, and Herr Bronner, my German teacher, strip off their clothes and slip hooded red monk robes over their heads. Mr. Perry, my biology teacher, stands at a locker nearby, still fully clothed.

Ms. Hunt fans the hem of her robe out. "I wish these things weren't wool. This is the summer solstice. Why can't we have cotton robes?"

"We are not to question the will of the Old Ones," Herr Bronner intones in his ruined baritone.

"The Old Ones didn't buy the robes," Ms. Hunt counters. "The home ec class made them. And there's nothing in the Sacred Scrolls of Za'aal that says we have to sweat our balls off while we open the portal to the Darkness Beyond the Stars, is there?"

Herr Bronner shrugs. "None can know the mind of Za'aal. So it is written, so it is true."

They hang a small pouch of baby teeth around their necks,

then turn to Mr. Perry, still dressed in his normal clothes.

"Ron, do you have the totems?"

"What? Oh yes, yes." He hands them each a live frog, which they carefully put into their pockets.

Ms. Hunt gestures for him to hurry up. "Ron, get dressed. What are you waiting for?"

"Oh, uh, nothing. I was just gonna, uh . . ." Mr. Perry opens his locker and pulls a towel out. "I'm gonna take a blood shower. You guys go ahead without me."

"The Shower of Blood comes *after* the opening of the Dark Portal," Herr Bronner says. "So it is written in the tablets of Nardorock—"

"No, yeah, I know that. I just like taking one ahead of time too. I was playing tennis earlier today, so I'm a little grimy. You two go ahead without me." He bows slightly. "Glory to Za'aal, until the Old Ones rise."

Ms. Hunt and Herr Bronner exit the locker room, and Ms. Hunt jerks a thumb back toward the door. "Ron's shy," she whispers to Herr Bronner. "He doesn't like taking his clothes off in front of other people."

Herr Bronner raises an eyebrow. "But we will all be nude during the Orgy of Evil."

Ms. Hunt shrugs.

They glide down the hall that connects the science room to the Thunderdome, their bare feet silent, and enter the Thunderdome. After lighting a torch, Ms. Hunt lifts the pulsing green flames against the gloom and looks around the darkened circle. "Okay, so let's see. . . . We're meeting the rest of the coven in the Central Cylinder dungeon, which is through a locker in Section Three, which is . . . that way?"

Herr Bronner points in the opposite direction. "It is *that* way. I think."

"Okay, right, so we walk around the circle this way to the main hub, and then—"

"No, we cannot walk that way. That is *counter*clockwise. We must always walk along the path of the clock. So it is written in—"

Ms. Hunt throws her torch. "Oh, FUCK where it's written! I hate this damn school! WHERE THE HELL IS SECTION THREE?"

A girl with long black hair stares at me like I'm crazy. "Yo, dude, chill out. You're *in* Section Three."

The first bell rings, the one that means there's ten minutes until homeroom. I snap back to reality, and there's my locker, right in front of me.

The black-haired girl squints at me suspiciously. "Are you all right?"

"Yeah, I'm fine," I reply, and she seems to believe me, until I follow it up by bowing a little and saying, "Glory to Za'aal, until the Old Ones rise."

My locker smells like a pool because my swim trunks are hanging on a hook in the back. I know I should take them home at the end of the day, but I always forget to bring a plastic bag to put them in. I have swim class twice a week. It replaces gym on Wednesdays and Fridays, so I'll have it today. Even though at first it seemed like a weird class, I enjoy it now. Luckily, it's my last period of the day, so I don't have to sit in school all day with wet hair. Otherwise I would definitely *not* enjoy it.

I hang my backpack on a hook inside the door and grab the books I need for the first three periods today—German, art, and English—before checking my phone. Neither PJ nor Jake has written back yet, although Jake gets like this sometimes. He just doesn't check his phone. I think he's the last person left on Earth who doesn't check his phone every two minutes.

PJ is probably already in homeroom. All the teachers are strict about not letting you use your phone once the second bell rings, but our teacher, Mrs. Zimmerman, is especially zealous. There are a couple of different homeroom classes, but PJ and I are in the same one, and he sits right in front of me. I won't see Jake until art class, though.

People are closing their lockers, heading to class. Everyone is still buzzing about Trey and his raccoon. I overhear a passing kid say, "I heard it was a *poodle*, not a raccoon."

Pretty soon kids will be saying it was a bear.

The second bell goes off, which means five minutes until homeroom, and as though the bell is a starter pistol, the cheese stick PJ gave me on the bus hits my lactose-intolerant system like a kick in the stomach, and my guts clench with an audible gurgle.

I have sixty seconds to reach a toilet.

I run through the Thunderdome's turbulent eye toward the

nearest bathroom, knocking students aside and dodging a pack of cheerleaders who are stapling paper foliage to a bulletin board outside the boys' room.

There's only one guy in the bathroom, standing at a urinal, and he gives me a startled look as I rush into the nearest stall and slam the door shut. I sit on the toilet just in time. The Old Ones are rising today, glory to Za'aal.

I can hear the guy washing his hands. Then the bathroom door slams open so hard it hits the wall, and someone says, "Get the fuck out of here." The voice sounds familiar, so I peer through the crack between the door and the stall.

It's Mark Kruger.

But he's not alone. Tommy Richter and Rob Klein, two goons who are friends with Mark, enter behind him, and—oh God, no—*Tommy is dragging PJ behind him.* Tommy is the biggest kid in school—heck, he's the biggest *person* in school aside from Mr. Hartman—and he lifts PJ off his feet as he drags him into the bathroom. Opposing football teams call him the Richter Scale in hushed tones. As he passes, I see a flash of the orange-and-black Iron Pigs jersey he always wears, and then Rob brings up the rear, an evil dwarf, holding PJ's mascot head, which is almost as big as he is.

My pants are still down around my ankles. Nowhere to run, I quickly pick my books up off the floor and lift my feet so they won't see I'm sitting in the stall. Legs up, arms full of books, I balance on the toilet seat in the most uncomfortable yoga position ever.

I peer through the door crack, trying to see them, but the group moves farther into the bathroom, out of my line of sight. I can still hear them clearly, though, a few stalls down, next to the sinks, their voices echoing off the tiles.

A scuffle and the squeak of sneakers as someone is pushed. PJ yells, "Hey, c'mon!" but is cut off by a sound like someone punching a pillow. PJ goes "Oof!" as someone slams him against the wall.

Mark's voice is tight with fury. "You and your friends think you're pretty funny, don't you? You think you can fuck with my old man just because our farm is so shitty already, huh? 'Oh, it's the Kruger Farm. Nobody cares if we mess that place up,' huh? 'It's already a piece of shit,' *huh*?"

When PJ responds to Mark, I almost don't recognize his voice. First because it's a frightened wheeze, but second because he's doing something I've never heard him do before: He's lying—and he's not doing a very good job of it.

"Hey, look, no!" PJ says. "We didn't mean to . . . I mean, I didn't . . . uh . . . I don't know what you're talking about!"

"We found your book bag in the pasture, dipshit," Mark says. "It had your name written inside it. At first I didn't realize it was you because it said 'Pablo Jaramillo.'" Mark mangles the pronunciation. "But then I checked Facebook and saw your stupid face. The same stupid face I see before you put that pig head on at games. Fucking dumbass."

"How could you betray our team like this?" Tommy asks,

genuinely wounded. "How could you do this to a fellow Iron Pig?"

"Tommy, shut up," Rob squeaks. Rob is half Tommy's size, but he makes up for it by being twice as mean. He has a high voice that he tries to make sound tougher by speaking with a very thick, very unconvincing New York accent.

A sound like someone punching a pillow again, another *ooof!* from PJ that makes me flinch and almost spill the books off my lap. My legs are shaking, still sore from all the running last night. I don't know how long I can hold them off the floor with all these books on my lap.

I know I should help PJ. I should yell or something, but my pants are around my ankles. I haven't even wiped yet!

Also, I'll be honest, I'm not in the mood to get beat up.

"There were three of you last night," Mark says, voice low and angry. "I saw you running away. One of you fuckers clocked me. Was it you?"

"It was *not* me," PJ says.

"What's your friend's name? The kid you were sitting with on the bus? Was it him?"

"Who's that?" Tommy asks.

"I don't know," Mark says. "Big glasses, kinda skinny. New kid."

"His name is Kirby," Rob says. "He's in my English class. Fuckin' nerd."

A sharp slap, and PJ yelps again. Then another punch.

"Who was with you?" Mark demands.

"Uh . . ." PJ wheezes. "What?"

Rob laughs, a high giggle like an evil chipmunk. "Maybe we have to ask him in Spanish," he says. "Maybe BJ don't speak English."

He speaks it better than you, I think.

"It's PJ, not BJ, and I *absolutely* speak English," PJ says. "And look," he adds hastily, "we're sorry. Honestly. I swear we weren't trying to hurt your dad's farm. We were just . . . messing around."

Mark sighs, frustrated. "I'm sorry. Honestly. I swear I am *not* messing around, and I want to know: Who the fuck was with you last night?" He switches tactics, talks to PJ like they're buddies. "Help me out here," he says reasonably. "I got three beatings to hand out, and I need to know who gets them. Otherwise I'll just give all three to you, Pedro."

"Pablo," PJ corrects him, right before getting hit again.

"One of 'em could've been that burnout psycho, what's his face . . . Jake," Rob says. "He's always hanging around with them."

"I guess." Mark sighs. "Probably."

An uncomfortable silence descends while all three contemplate the unappealing prospect of tangling with Jake. The lull is broken by the bathroom door creaking open. Rob barks, "Bathroom is closed!" and whoever it is leaves.

Another punch. My legs are shaking so bad I'm afraid Rob will actually be able to *hear* my knees knocking together. I can hold them up for *maybe* another minute.

"Hey," Rob chirps. "I have an idea. Check this out. I grabbed it on our way in here."

"Oh, dude!" Mark says. "Dude, you are fucked *up*."

PJ inhales sharply and then speaks in a rush. "Okay, yes, it was Kirby and Jake with me."

Mark, Rob, and Tommy all burst out laughing.

"Holy shit!" Mark laughs. "Oh my God, you folded so quickly."

"Dude's shitting himself!"

"Good thing he's already in the bathroom, huh?"

They have a good long laugh about this. Then Mark says, still laughing and out of breath, "Fuck it. Let's do it anyway. I wanna see what happens. Tom, take off his jacket and roll up his sleeve."

They laugh even louder, and there's a quick scuffle that sounds like PJ trying to get away. Rob squeals, "Hold him!" and Tommy grunts with exertion. Then the bathroom is silent except for PJ's panicked panting.

"Now," Mark calmly explains, "don't yell, or I'll put one in your forehead."

There's a quiet but crisp *chunk!* and PJ screams in pain.

"I told you," Mark says, annoyed. "Shhhhhhhh."

There's another *chunk!* and PJ whimpers quietly this time.

Chunk!

Chunk!

Chunk!

The sound is familiar, and after maybe the fifth time I realize why.

It's the sound of a stapler.

They're punching staples into PJ's arm.

Finally PJ can't hold it in any longer and cries out in pain, "Look, I said we're sorry! Honestly, please stop!"

"All right, fine. We're done," Mark says. "Go to the nurse and tell her you had an accident or something. You're so goofy they'll probably believe it. If you rat on us, I'll tell on you for fucking up my dad's farm. That's probably a crime, right?"

"Vandalizing," Rob says. "Trespassing."

"Cow hurtin'," Tommy suggests.

"Tom, shut up," Mark says reflexively. "Also . . ." There's another *chunk!* and PJ yelps quietly, like a broken dog. "Also, if you tell on me, I'll hunt you down like a varmint with my thirty-aught-six. Bitch got a hundred-yard scope."

I watch Mark, Rob, and Tommy stride past the stall crack's narrow strip of vision and out of the bathroom.

"Where'd you get that stapler?" Tommy asks out in the hall.

"Dude, shut up," Rob says, barely audible as the door swings shut behind them.

PJ sobs quietly and mutters to himself, "Ah, shoot, my *flower* . . ."

Somehow my legs are still up, and I try not to make any noise at all, but I'm so focused on keeping my legs up that I don't think about my stomach and it gurgles—*loudly*—amplified by the bathroom's perfect acoustics.

A rustle as PJ turns around. "Hello?" he says uncertainly. He pauses. "Is someone in here?"

I hold my breath.

I feel like such a creeper, but I can't let PJ know I'm in here.

I don't want him to know I just sat here with my pants down while he was being tortured. I can apologize later, but not now, like this.

PJ turns the sink on, and I breathe a quiet, *very* quiet, sigh of relief. I guess he starts pulling the staples out, because I hear him mutter, "Ow! Shoot . . . Ow! Drat . . . Ow!" This goes on for a minute or two. Then he turns the sink off and pulls a couple of paper towels from the dispenser. He sighs and walks out.

When the door finally creaks shut behind PJ, I drop my feet and books with a groan of relief, pins and needles racing up my thighs.

Behind the relief follows a wave of shame. The kind of wave you see in disaster movies, skyscraper tall, poised to wipe out an entire coastal city.

I wonder if I could flush *myself* down the toilet.

I know I couldn't have stopped PJ from getting stapled—I'm no John McClane; hell, I'm not even *Ellis*—but I could have at least stopped hiding in the stall after Mark left. I could've helped pull the staples out.

PJ *did* rat on me, but I would've done the same thing in his place. Heck, I would've given up Jake and PJ way before the stapler came into play.

I wipe, flush, and leave the stall, but I don't leave the bathroom because I'm afraid I might bump into PJ in the hall. A pile of orange geraniums are scattered across the tile floor, one sad, soggy blossom floating in a urinal.

Crap, I realize. *PJ's in my homeroom too.* I'm going to see him again in, like, two minutes anyhow. How am I going to lie to his face and act surprised when he tells me what happened?

And what am I going to do about Mark and those guys?

I briefly consider calling Mom and telling her I'm sick. I could fake a stomachache, go to the nurse's office, then head straight home from there. But going home is the only thing I can think of that's worse than getting mauled by the Office Depot Suicide Squad.

CHAPTER 10

I SNEAK INTO HOMEROOM LATE, BUT NOBODY notices. This early in the morning, everyone has their heads on their desks or buried in a book—even Mrs. Zimmerman, who's at her desk over by the windows, reading. PJ is slumped at his desk in front of mine, head in his hands. His tuxedo is rumpled and missing the geranium from its lapel, but I'm relieved to see that he doesn't have a Frankenstein-like row of staples circling his forehead.

As I walk past his desk, PJ looks up at me and my stomach flips. I feel like there must be a neon sign over my head flashing GUILTY, GUILTY, GUILTY, but I try to smile at PJ as naturally as I can while I slip into the seat behind him.

Mrs. Zimmerman finally notices me and purses her lips

like she just licked a lemon. "You're *late*, Mr. Burns."

"I know. I'm sorry."

Mrs. Zimmerman dramatically pulls out her roll-call notebook. "I'll change your mark from absent to present. *This* time."

I bow like the queen has just saved me from the executioner's ax. "Thank you, Mrs. Zimmerman."

I pull my art history book out of my bag, open it to a random page, and pretend to read.

PJ and I are on the far side of the classroom, away from Mrs. Zimmerman, but we still can't really talk. Homeroom is a quiet period, like a short study hall.

PJ half turns around in his seat, pretending to check his bag under the desk, and whispers to me, "Mark and some guys jumped me in the bathroom and beat me up."

My tongue feels like a dead slug in my mouth as I say, "What? Oh fuck."

"Yeah." PJ shoots me a stricken look. "They *stapled* me!"

"Stabled you?" Despite feeling like a creep, I think 'stabled' is a pretty slick ad-lib on my part.

"*Stapled*," PJ whispers. He shrugs off one arm of his suit jacket. Underneath, a row of double red dots are bleeding through the white sleeve of his dress shirt.

Seeing them makes me feel so awful I don't have to act at all when I moan, "Fuuuuck."

Mrs. Zimmerman looks up from her desk. "Did you say something, Mr. Burns?"

"No, ma'am."

"I'll tell you more after homeroom," PJ whispers. "But Kirby, we're in big trouble." He buttons his jacket back up and faces the front of the classroom.

I stare at my open art history book. A Hieronymus Bosch painting leers back up at me, a nightmarish landscape of tiny naked people being tortured. Some are getting tossed into a fire that's broken through a fissure in the Earth. One dude is upside down, getting flayed by a man with the head of a pig that is almost as scary as PJ's mascot costume. Some people are dancing, oblivious to the destruction around them, or perhaps—even worse—fully aware. In the corner, a naked man is being eaten alive by dogs. It's a pretty accurate depiction of my day so far.

I flip through the book until I find Van Gogh's *Sunflowers*.

Much better.

I feel bad for PJ, but at least he's in the clear now. He already got his beating—er, stapling. What office supplies will Mark use to mutilate my virgin flesh? Will he pour Wite-Out in my eyes? Post-it Note my asshole shut?

Mark's in vo-tech most of the day, so I guess I don't have to worry about bumping into him until lunch or gym or something like that. But Rob and Tommy are both sophomores like me, so I could bump into them at any time.

I've never been beat up before, so I don't know what it'll be like. The only injury I've ever had was years ago, when I was eight, back when we lived in Bethlehem. I was skateboarding down a friend's driveway and fell. I landed weird on my right leg, it bent back at a painful angle, and I went down hard on my ass in the street. I tried to stand up, but the leg wouldn't take any weight. A white-hot ball of pain grew in my thigh, blotting all rational thought from my mind. Someone was screaming. It was me.

My friend ran over, terrified. "What's wrong? What's wrong?"

All I could manage to say was "My leg! My leg!" I was afraid to look at it, and when I finally did, my worst fears were confirmed. The leg was bent back at an impossible angle, my knee bulging strangely, a knob of bone pushing the skin near my knee, trying to poke out.

Dimly, I was aware of my friend running inside to get help, and while I was lying in the street alone, a redheaded kid I had never seen before ran out of a house across the street.

He hopped around me. "What's wrong? What's wrong?"

"My leg is broken!"

"No, no, no," he said, very concerned. "Don't say it's broken. If you *think* it's broken, then it *will* be broken."

The pain was so distracting, I could barely think about what he was saying. "What?! Are you crazy? Look at it!"

A few more neighbors ran out of their houses. A small crowd formed around me, everyone asking, "What's wrong? What's wrong?"

I cried, "My leg's broken!! My leg's broken!!"

"No, it's not!" the redhead told everyone. "It's not broken. Don't say it's broken," he told me again, "or it *will* be!"

"CAN SOMEONE GET THIS ASSHOLE OUT OF HERE?"

Dad was at work, but a couple neighborhood dads carried me to the back of our station wagon, and Mom drove me to the hospital faster than I have ever seen her drive before, swerving and running stop signs while, stretched out in the back seat, I wailed like an ambulance.

The doctors discovered that, yes, indeed, my leg was broken. To be exact, the *femur* was broken, which—I don't mean to brag—is the largest bone in the human body. They put me in a body cast from the waist down, which meant I couldn't leave my bed for two whole freaking months! I couldn't even hobble around on crutches or anything. I just had to lie in my little yellow bedroom, looking for ways to kill time.

I watched TV and read books all day, straight through into the night. I didn't just kill time; I murdered it. I talked to friends on the phone. I did crossword puzzles. I played video games. It was fun for the first couple of days, but after that I started to go a little crazy. It was rough. But then, suddenly, after three weeks of not leaving my room, something strange happened—I stopped being bored. It was like I had been addicted to stimulation, and, after a traumatic withdrawal process, I had come out the other side clean, no longer a slave to excitement. After all, what are drugs but an artificial form of stimulation? Now I was even free from the need for *natural* stimulation.

Time got slippery. I couldn't tell the difference between two minutes and two hours. I could fill a whole day watching the square of sunlight from my window move around the room. I was an oak tree for whom the passage of decades felt like mere seconds.

My mind expanded to fill the void the world had left. No longer held in the grip of time, I traveled freely, visiting old memories and imagining new futures. I submerged myself in the water of time and felt my body dissolve. This lack of desire, was it happiness? Or was this what death felt like?

The whole thing was a weird experience, but the weirdest part of breaking my leg was that Melanie started actually being *nice* to me.

I hate to admit it, but Melanie didn't like me. Mom always tried to make me feel better by reminding me that lots of older sisters don't like their younger brothers, but still, I think Melanie disliked me more than average. One time Dad wanted to take a picture of the two of us, and he had to pay her a dollar to put her arm around me.

We were in my parents' bedroom, and I must have been pretty young, because my eyes were level with the top of their bed. As Melanie haggled with Dad over the price, I tried to ignore the embarrassment by focusing on my parents' bedspread, running my hand over the green quilted top and counting the stitches between the squares. Why are the worst memories the ones you remember best? I recall it all with crystal clarity: the silky slip of that bedspread under my hand, Dad announcing cheerily, "Okay, bud, put your arm around your sister!" Melanie looking at me like a bug she was being forced to eat.

But she was nice to me when I broke my leg. Maybe she felt bad for me, or maybe she could relate to not feeling well and having to spend lots of time in bed. She brought me books and would sit next to me and watch TV. Every day when she got home from school, she'd sit on the edge of the bed and tell me what had happened that day. It almost made breaking my leg worth it.

One day when Melanie came home from school, she said, "Hey, I brought someone who wants to see you."

It was the redhead. He looked at my cast and whistled, shaking his head.

"I told you," he said sadly. "You shouldn't have said it was broken."

That night while I was lying in bed, the house stone silent and the clock stopped dead on the wall, I wondered if maybe he was right. I mean, I knew he was wrong . . . but what if he was right?

Would my leg still have been broken if I said it wasn't?

Of course I know the answer is *yes, it would still have been broken*, but I can't stop myself from wondering sometimes. From wondering frequently, in fact. And I worry that's proof that the psychologist was wrong and I am indeed crazy.

The scrape of Mrs. Zimmerman's chair alerts me to the end of homeroom—she always gets up to open the door before the bell rings—and as she props the door open, I see Rob Klein standing in the hallway with a guy I vaguely recognize from the football team. I think his name's Jono. He's tall and slim, with feathery red hair and a patch of baby-thin whiskers on his upper lip that he's trying to pass off as a mustache. He looks like the type of guy who is very good at giving wedgies and has gotten that way through diligent practice.

Rob leans against the curve of the hallway, a nasty little smirk on his face. He sees that I see him and smiles wider, exposing tiny teeth with a small gap between each of them, like he never lost his baby teeth and they've just spread out to fill his mouth.

Even though Rob is small, he's dangerous—a Chihuahua with rabies. He's the best insult craftsman in the whole school, and every student is terrified of him. You can feel the tension when he walks down the hallway, everyone he passes praying that he won't notice some small flaw of theirs and magnify it for everyone to see.

Rob understands that what makes a great insult isn't *nastiness*; it's *stickiness*. The most effective insults *linger*. They're words or names that are so specific and memorable that people will repeat them, and this is how they'll spread. It's not just an insult that you get once. It follows you.

On my first day of school at Upper Shuckburgh High, I wore a shirt with subtle—very subtle, I thought—dots on it. Yes, I guess you could call them polka dots. It was a rookie mistake: In high school, you never want to stand out, *especially* if you're the new kid. You want to blend in with the pack, so the predators won't notice you.

Rob noticed that shirt like a lion noticing a wounded wilde-beest.

"Yo, look at this clown," Rob said to his friends. They were big guys, wearing Shuckburgh football jerseys, and they all laughed.

Now, *look at this clown* isn't much of an insult, and Rob seemed to know it, because then he made it more specific, more *sticky*, by saying, "Look at Chuckles the Clown here."

I thought that was still a lame insult, but for the next week—a solid *week*—all the guys on the football team called me Chuckles. Even a couple days ago, months after I thought this had ended, some kid I barely know in my swim class was surprised to learn my name was Kirby. "I thought it was Chuck," he said, confused.

The insult didn't seem so weak then.

Rob didn't just embarrass me; *he took my name.*

So even though Rob's nasty smile is barely higher than Jono's elbow, it makes me nervous.

PJ jerks his thumb at Rob and whispers, "He was one of the guys with Mark!"

I almost say, "I know," but I stop myself just in time.

The bell rings, and everyone stands up and gathers their books to leave.

I moan with dread, and PJ smiles. "Don't worry, buddy. I got this. Grab your stuff and get ready to run. *Deception* and *evasion.* Watch."

As the class slowly files out the door, PJ puts on his Iron

Pigs head and jumps on top of his desk. He squeals like a stuck pig, a terrifying sound he has put hours of practice into being able to achieve, and the classroom turns around to look at him, alarmed.

Standing atop the desk in his warthog head and tuxedo, PJ cuts a commanding figure, a jungle beast out for a night on the town. He does a funny dance and shouts, "Whose defense is tougher than a cement truck?"

Everyone stares at him, too shocked to respond, so he prompts them in a loud stage whisper, "The Iron Hogs!"

"You mean Iron Pigs?" someone corrects him.

PJ puts his hands on his hips. "Yes, okay, fine, *pigs*. Now, whose defense is tougher than a cement truck?"

Two of the guys in our homeroom are wearing football jerseys, and they yell back, "The Iron Pigs!"

Mrs. Zimmerman looks mildly alarmed, but she doesn't tell us to quiet down. I guess she can't be mad at us for having too much school spirit.

"Whose offensive line will leave you awestruck?" PJ asks.

Half the class answers now. "The Iron Pigs! The Iron Pigs!"

"And who will mess you up 'cause they don't give a *shuck*?!"

The rhyme is so stupid, but PJ's enthusiasm is contagious, and the whole homeroom shouts with one voice, "THE IRON PIGS!"

PJ jumps off the desk, lets loose another bloodcurdling squeal, and leads the cheering crowd out the door in a stampede.

"Chaaaaaaaaarge!!!"

PJ and I duck down and run out of the classroom in the middle of the chaos, two rabbits in a herd of buffalo. Through the crowd I catch a glimpse of Rob and Jono pressed against the hallway wall, understandably confused, and then we're around the curve of the circle and out of sight.

One period down, seven to go!

CHAPTER 11

PJ AND I HEAD AROUND THE CIRCLE AND THEN down the stairwell toward the Thunderdome. I'm going to German class in Circle A, and PJ has Spanish in Circle "That's Not Fair; He Already Speaks Spanish." It's like letting me take third-grade English as my foreign language. But there are so few Latinos at old Upshuck High that the school hasn't thought to close the loophole yet.

Along the way PJ tells me what happened in the bathroom with Mark, a story I, of course, already know, because I was two stalls away doing intense toilet-seat yoga while it happened.

However, I notice one interesting difference between PJ's version of the story and what really happened. PJ doesn't mention that Mark found PJ's book bag with his name inside it or that

Mark interrogated him to get Jake's and my names. Instead, PJ says that Mark already knew it was Jake, PJ, and me at the farm because he saw us running past the house and recognized us.

I can tell PJ never lies, because this is such a bad one. If Mark recognized us last night, then why didn't he react when he saw me on the bus this morning? Besides, Jake and PJ were already halfway up the driveway before Mark even ran out of the house; there's no way he could have seen them.

I guess PJ feels guilty that it was his bag that got us in trouble and about giving up our names under questioning. Whatever his reasoning, I'm glad he lies, because it makes me feel less guilty about my own deception. We're all down here in the shit together.

"So, are you okay?" I ask, lightly touching his arm where he got stapled.

"Yeah, I'm fine," he says. "They're just tiny little holes."

Sure, they're just little tiny holes IN YOUR FLESH. No big deal.

"I'm more concerned," PJ continues, "about where I can get a new shirt before lunch."

"You're *more* concerned about that?"

"Well, I still have to ask Vern to the dance, remember? I told you the whole plan on the bus. At lunch, the dance I'm gonna do with the music? You said you'd press play."

I don't even want to get into this right now. "Oh right, of course, yeah."

"I think I can get a shirt from behind the stage," PJ says as we cross the lobby and enter the bustling heart of the

Thunderdome. It's crowded, lines of fast-walking students crisscrossing one another with a natural choreography. "They're doing *Guys and Dolls* this year, so I can probably get a white shirt from the wardrobe rack."

I text Jake again, although you're not supposed to text even in the halls. If Mr. Hartman sees me, I'll be in trouble, but I figure he's probably still wiping dead raccoon off the roof. Heads up, I type. Mark Kruger, Tommy Richter, and Rob Klein are after us. Watch your back!!!

I'm pretty sure he won't respond—or he'll just text back Whatever. Jake's in my art class, so I'll see him then. Besides, Jake can take care of himself. I'd rather grab an electric fence than fight Jake.

I grabbed all the books I need for my pre-lunch classes before homeroom, but PJ stops at his locker between every single class to load and unload weird stuff: Slinkies and cowboy hats and stuffed animals.

We stop at PJ's locker, and I scan the crowd nervously, looking for Rob, Tommy, or Mark. Tommy will be the easiest to spot, since he's a foot taller than any other student and always wears his orange-and-black Iron Pigs jersey. Rob, on the other hand, is so tiny, he could slither right up through the crowd and I wouldn't see him until he was sinking his sharp little teeth into my ankle.

"Do you think I should still ask Vern out today?" PJ asks me as he rummages through his locker. "I don't have my geraniums anymore. Mark threw them in a urinal."

I don't say *I know*. Instead I ask the very reasonable question, "How can you still be thinking about Vern? Aren't you nervous?"

"Well, of course I'm a little nervous," PJ says. "It's a complicated dance. But if you're willing to help out and press play when I give you the signal, then—"

"Not nervous about Vern!" I yell. "Mark! Rob! Tommy! *Death!* Aren't you concerned about the situation we're in here?"

PJ pulls a trumpet out of his bag and puts it in his locker while he considers the question, then shrugs. "Well, I already got stapled, so I think I'm in the clear."

"Well, that's great, PJ. I'm real happy for you. What about *me*? What am *I* gonna do?!"

PJ is getting frustrated. "I don't know. What *can* you do? I mean, you could go to the office and tell the principal that Mark wants to beat you up, but then Mark will say that we vandalized his farm. Which, please don't do that—my parents will be *pissed* if they find out. Also, I'm pretty sure they wouldn't let me hang out with you anymore."

He plops a three-pound bag of Swedish Fish into his book bag and closes his locker, spinning the combination lock with a flourish.

"So that's it," I say. "You just want me to let them beat me up?"

PJ is never serious, so it surprises me when he loses his perma-smile and lowers his voice soberly. "Look, dude, we snuck over to Mark's house and messed with his stuff. You punched him in the *face*."

I try to protest, but he stops me. "I know we were just goofing around, and I know it was an accident. And I know that Mark and those guys are, uh . . ."

He struggles to find a diplomatic way to put it.

"Assholes?" I suggest.

"Yeah." He giggles. "Super assholes. Super-duper *raging* assholes. But they're also bigger than us. And they're meaner than us." He puts his hand on my shoulder. "And they are going to beat you up. I'm sorry, but you can't avoid it."

I think you underestimate my ability to avoid stuff, friendo. I brush his hand off my shoulder as the bell rings.

PJ's smile pops back onto his face. "And, actually, you do have one way to avoid getting beat up."

"What's that?"

"Well, if they fight Jake before they fight you, he'll probably kill them."

With this cheerful thought in mind, I hurry to German class, my ears cocked hopefully for the wail of approaching sirens.

CHAPTER 12

HERR BRONNER IS OUR GERMAN TEACHER, BUT HE
should be a geometry teacher, because his body is a perfect circle.
It's a shape that belts don't work on, so Herr Bronner wears
suspenders, always in a jaunty color like lime green or purple.
Today they're an autumn-appropriate pumpkiny orange. His
curly black hair frizzes high above his friendly face.

Herr Bronner takes roll from his desk, calling out our German
names cheerfully and patting his belly after each name.

"Hans?"

"Hier!"

"Dieter?"

"Hier!"

"Elsa?"

"*Anwesend!*" Elsa shouts.

Elsa's real name is Myka. She's the most motivated student in class—and probably the whole school—so of course she says the German word for "present" instead of the simpler *hier* (which is pronounced just like "here" but with a German accent). Elsa is *aggressively* smart and holds the rest of us slackers in cool contempt.

Myka is head of the cheerleading squad, and today she's wearing a baggy pink sweatshirt over her cheerleading skirt. She's dating Tommy—I see them holding hands in the halls and sitting together at lunch—but they seem like such an unlikely pair, the best and worst students in the school. It makes me wonder if there's something about Tommy I can't see. If he's not as bad a guy as he seems.

I chose German instead of Spanish or French because I heard it was the easiest of the three languages, although I have since found out that is *extremely* incorrect. As evidence, I invite you to compare the German word for incorrect, *unrichtig,* against its Spanish counterpart, *incorrecto.* The only time German is useful to me is when I'm watching *Die Hard* (*Schießen dem Fenster! Schießen dem Fenster!*), which, come to think of it, is every day, so maybe I'm not so dumb after all.

Herr Bronner finishes roll call and folds his hands over his grand belly as he greets us.

"*Guten Tag, meine Damen und Herren.*"

"*Guten Tag, Herr Bronner!*" we reply in something resembling German.

Herr Bronner winces as we mangle his native tongue, then announces that we're going to run some dialogues from the book. We pull out our German textbooks, massive tomes large enough to break a toe if dropped. The cover says *Komm Mit!* which means *Come Along!* and sports a photo of two strangely European teenagers from the 1980s laughing deliriously in front of a castle.

Herr Bronner gamely approaches Liam Spagnaletti's desk. Spags is the worst student in class, seemingly incapable of absorbing even a single foreign word. I think it's funny that Spags has the most Italian name I've ever heard—his name is practically *spaghetti,* for guten Tag's sake—but he's in German class. His German name is Johann, and Herr Bronner addresses him loudly and slowly, like he's talking to a baby. *"Johann, wo wohnst du?"* Where do you live?

Spags is sweating like he's just been picked out of a police lineup. His eyes dart over to Myka, who is examining her perfect blue-painted nails. I'm pretty sure Spags has a crush on her.

"Ah . . . ," Spags begins. *"Ich lebe—"*

"Wohne!" Herr Bronner interrupts. *"Ich wohne."*

"Ja, ja, sorry. Uh, *Ich wohne aus—"*

"Ich wohne in," Herr Bronner corrects him.

This is torture. You live in Shuckburgh, numbnut! *Ich wohne in Shuckburgh!*

"Ja, sorry, uh, *Ich wohne in* . . . uh . . . How do you say 'Shuckburgh' in German?"

"Shuckburgh," Herr Bronner says with a German accent.

"Ich wohne aus Shuckburgh."

"*Ich wohne in Shuckburgh,*" Bronner corrects, with the patience of a saint.

"Right."

"*Nein,*" Bronner says, overenunciating. "*In* Shuckburgh."

"*Ja,*" Spags says, smiling. "Shuckburgh."

Herr Bronner gives up and summons a pained smile. "*Sehr gut, Johann . . . sehr gut.*"

One thing I do like about German class are the weirdly specific sample dialogues our textbook provides. I can't imagine ever being in a situation where I'd say things like, "Hello. My dog would like a haircut, one that emphasizes his tail," or "This sauna is too dry. Can someone throw scented water on the embers?" But the textbook is full of conversations like this:

> Man: Good afternoon. I would like to buy some eggs.
>
> Grocer: Wh at kind of eggs would you like to purchase?
>
> Man: Do you have brown hen eggs?
>
> Grocer: We have brown eggs, but they are from geese, not hens.
>
> Man: Goose eggs are not flavorful enough. I am baking a quiche.
>
> Grocer: Then I cannot help you, but I wish you good luck in your baking.
>
> Man: Before I leave, can you direct me to the nearest tailor?

Although maybe Germans are constantly seeking very specific eggs and getting their pants hemmed. Maybe it's a very different place from here. A whole different country even.

I must have drifted off, because Herr Bronner is staring at me.

"I'm sorry," I ask. "What was the question?"

Giggles from the class. Everyone loves it when they're not the one getting in trouble.

"*Ich habe gesagt,*" Herr Bronner says, "*wo wohnst du, Adolf?*"

I decide to give Elsa a run for her money and show off some German I learned while watching *Die Hard* with the German subtitles on. "*Ich lebe am Rand.*"

Herr Bronner laughs. "You live on the edge?"

"*Ja.*"

"*Nein, Adolf,*" he replies with a hint of pity. "*Sie leben in Shuckburgh.*"

The last fifteen minutes of German are dedicated to working alone in class, and I spend them drawing pictures of Nakatomi Plaza exploding and rereading *Lord of the Flies*. It's pure rugged.

My desk is near the door, and Herr Bronner's desk is on the other side of the room. He's asleep in his chair, snoring like a tuba, so I check my phone under my desk to see if Jake has written back yet. He has not, which is a little odd, but I'll see him next period.

I glance at the clock above the door to see when the bell is going to ring, and I am dismayed, but not surprised, to see Tommy Richter waiting for me in the hallway, his linebacker shoulders so wide he blocks my view of the hallway through the door. Although he's a big guy, he's strangely unhealthy-looking, like if Frankenstein had been made of ham.

For a second I hope, *Maybe he's here to pick up Myka?* But then he leans into the doorway, his face as big and as flat as a tombstone, and draws a finger across his thick neck. It's supposed to be scary, but he sticks his tongue out and crosses his eyes like he's pretending to be dead, and it just looks goofy. When Tommy stands there he's fucking terrifying, but as soon as he moves or talks, he wrecks it.

Jono is with Tommy, and so is some goon I always see sneaking cigarettes behind the gym when we walk out to the buses at the end of the day. The two of them lean into view and make rude faces and mouth curse words at me. *How are they getting to my classes so quickly!?* I guess they're leaving their classes early, or maybe getting a hall pass from the football coach.

My next class is all the way across the Thunderdome in another circle. I don't think there's any way I can avoid these guys.

The bell rings, and everyone gathers their books and walks out. I linger at my desk so I'll be the last one to leave the classroom, so at least everyone in German class won't see me getting my *bütt ger-beaten.*

On her way out Myka sees Tommy waiting in the hall and squeals with delight.

"What are you doing here, you big brute?" She smacks him on the chest playfully. "Couldn't wait to see me?"

"Nah." Tommy points at me, still lingering in the classroom. "I gotta pound this jerk."

"Oh." Myka turns and looks at me, confused, and I give her a little wave. "Okay, well . . . have fun." Myka wanders down the hall.

I'm still at my desk, gathering my books as slowly as possible, moving them from the chair to the desk and back again. Herr Bronner washes the blackboard, his large circular butt swaying hypnotically. Tommy gives me an impatient look and spins his finger in a *hurry it up* motion. "C'mon, dude!" he says in a stage whisper.

I never thought I'd want to stay in German class forever. I was *unrichtig*.

I trudge out of the classroom, and Tommy, Jono, and Cigarettes surround me, like border collies herding sheep. They can't do anything physical right now because we're passing too many classrooms with teachers in them, but they start softening me up verbally while we head toward the stairwell.

"What's up, chickenshit?" Tommy asks, giving me a lazy shove.

"Chicken, chicken," Jono sings in a high voice, before launching into an enthusiastic chicken impersonation, complete with arm flapping. "Buck, buck, buck, buck!" It's startlingly realistic, one of the benefits of living in the country, I guess. Jono bugs his eyes out and bobs his head at me. "Buck, buck, buck, buck-KAW!"

I deserve better bullies.

The other kids give us a wide berth and hurry around us, their pack-animal radar alerting them to danger. We're approaching the stairwell that leads downstairs, and I try to keep going around the circle, because it's safer up here—there are no teachers or classrooms in the stairwell—but Tommy's big hand grabs the back of my collar and flings me toward the double doors. Cigarettes slams the push bar way too hard, banging both doors open, and as soon as we're in the stairwell, Tommy smacks the books out of my hands from behind and they spin across the linoleum. I turn around wearily, and Tommy pushes me against the wall.

"You got a problem, fuckstick?" Tommy says. He gives my face a playful smack. "Huh? You think you're tough?"

Cigarettes stands behind Tommy, providing unnecessary backup. He's nervous, bopping from foot to foot and looking over his shoulder a lot. Jono is still back in the hall, craning his neck around the corner to see if Mr. Hartman or any teachers are coming. He cups his hands around his mouth and continues to do his chicken impression at random intervals. "Buck, buck, buck . . ."

There are fewer kids in the stairwell than in the hall, but those who pass us slow down to watch with the fascination of motorists passing a car accident. Someone yells, "Fight!" and a few kids go with the classic "OOOOOOhhhh . . ."

Cigarettes hurries them along nervously. "C'mon, c'mon, get out of here."

Most kids walk around my scattered books, but a few go out

of their way to kick them farther down the stairs. This hurts more than Tommy slamming me against the wall did.

Tommy grabs my hand, the one with the scraped knuckles, and holds it up. "Oooh!" he says with surprise. "So, *you* were the one who punched Mark last night, huh?" He shakes his head, genuinely delighted. "You like punching people, huh? You wanna fight? Sweet, let's go."

Tommy spreads his legs in a boxing stance, fists up, dancing on the balls of his feet, and starts shadowboxing, throwing vicious jabs that stop only a few inches in front of my face. I can feel the wind from his punches on the tip of my nose, and I shrink back against the wall, too afraid to do anything else.

Now kids aren't just slowing down; they're stopping to watch.

"C'mon!" Tommy barks, throwing punches. "C'mon, let's go!"

"No!" I say, my voice shaking like crazy. "If you wanna hit me, go ahead, but I'm not going to fight you."

Tommy drops his hands and sticks his chin out. "C'mon, I'll give you the first shot."

"I don't want the first shot, asshole. I just want you to leave me alone!"

"Who you calling an asshole?" Tommy asks, spreading his arms in a *come at me, bro* stance.

"Buck, buck, buck . . . buck-KAW!" Jono clucks with disturbing skill.

Cigarettes reaches around Tommy's massive shoulder to push me. "Yo, this dude's a fuckin' weak-ass *coward*."

"Yeah," I agree angrily. "I guess I am."

My sad response makes Cigarettes uncomfortable enough that he stops, but it doesn't slow down Tommy. Tommy is on a roll. He grabs the front of my shirt with his big hands.

In movies I've seen bullies pick kids up off the ground by their shirt collars, but in real life all that does is jack your shirt up so everyone can see your belly button, which is just as awkward for the bully as it is for you.

But Tommy doesn't make that mistake. Although he has a weak *verbal* bullying game, his *physical* technique is strong. He twists my collar so it tightens around my neck, pulls me toward him, and then pushes hard with his legs, slamming me into the stairwell's cinder-block wall again, knocking the wind out of me. The back of my head hits the bricks, and my glasses almost fall off, teetering on the tip of my nose. The world splits in two, the top half blurry, the bottom half sharp, dominated by the big orange *S* on the front of Tommy's jersey.

The Richter Scale looks as big as the bull from last night as he gets right in my face. He has bad acne, and his face is so red and angry that I'm afraid one of his white zits will pop on me.

Tommy glances at my mouth and suddenly recoils. "Ugh," he says with disgust. "Your teeth are fucking *brown*. What, do you brush your teeth with shit?" Cigarettes laughs and Tommy beams, surprised by his rare wittiness.

No, I don't brush my teeth with shit. I donated bone marrow to try to save my sister's life, you big dumb asshole. It makes me so mad, I forget that Tommy is twice my size and about to kick my ass, and I guess that's why I say, "No. I was eating your Mom's asshole last night."

Tommy jerks back like I just slapped him. Cigarettes covers his mouth and tries not to laugh.

Tommy blinks at me, frozen while his tiny brain computes this unexpected data, and his face slowly settles into a hard mask that is not meant to scare me, not meant to look tough—although it does. It's his game face, the look that unconsciously falls over him right before the ball snaps and he knows he's about to cream the defensive line.

All business now, he pins me to the wall with one hand and cocks his other fist back over his shoulder, about to pound me in the face, when Jono rushes into the stairwell, hissing, "Hartman! Hartman!"

Tommy is going to punch me anyhow—he's in the zone—but Cigarettes grabs him by the shoulders and physically pulls him away, down the stairs.

Jono looks up at me from the curve of the stairwell below and sings, "Chickenshiiiiiiiiiit," one last time as he slides down the banister, a dancer leaving the stage of the meanest musical ever.

The crowd of onlookers disperses guiltily as Mr. Hartman lumbers into the stairwell. I'm not sure if I look traumatized or if he can just smell the testosterone in the air, but Mr. Hartman stops and swivels around to appraise the situation.

Nobody is left in the stairwell except us, so he asks me, "What's going on here?"

"Uhhh . . . someone knocked the books out of my hands." I point to my books all over the stairs, although it's hard; my arm feels as wobbly as a noodle. I'm having a hard time behaving normally, adrenaline pounding through me.

"Who?" Hartman demands.

"Uh . . . I don't know," I say. "They were behind me." I'm not sure why I lie. I guess it's just my natural teenage *stay out of trouble* instincts kicking in.

Mr. Hartman sees through me like a screen door and harrumphs loudly. He shakes his head, hoists his belt buckle up, and does a bunch of other things whose only purpose seems to be to burn off excess frustration.

"C'mon," he finally grumbles, pointing at my books scattered down the stairs. "I'll help you pick 'em up."

CHAPTER 13

I'M GRATEFUL THE HALLWAYS ARE EMPTY AS I WALK
to art class. My neck hurts, and so does the back of my head
where Tommy smacked it against the wall. I try to feel if there's
a bump, but I can't tell.

Each classroom I pass, teachers are taking roll call, and the
kids near the door notice me walking past and stare. Their
expressions look hostile, like, *Oh shit, there's that nerd that Tommy
Richter beat up!* But of course it's just my imagination. There's
no way everyone could've heard already. Still, I wish there were
a way I could get to class without having to walk past all these
classrooms. My limbs are still buzzing with unused adrenaline,
and I have to resist the urge to run the rest of the way to class.

I can't wait to tell Jake what happened. Usually, his

over-the-top anger bothers me, but right now it's exactly what I want to hear. He's gonna *murder* Tommy. Tommy thinks he's tough, but he's just fake tough. Jake would never ask, "Do you wanna fight?" He'd just straight-up clock you.

I hope Jake doesn't get expelled. He wouldn't give a shit, but I would. He's my friend—he is literally 50 percent of my friends right now—and I like seeing him in school.

Jake has already gotten in trouble a couple of times this year, and he says that Mr. Hartman and Mr. Braun, our principal, are "out to get him." I don't know if that's true; the type of stuff Jake does, there's no way he *couldn't* get in trouble. For instance, a couple of weeks ago he got suspended for chugging NyQuil in school. He drank so much cough syrup that he fell asleep in class and the teacher couldn't wake him up. I asked him why he didn't get high off DayQuil instead, and he said I was stupid (although it still seems like a valid question to me).

Maybe I'm off the hook now. Maybe, if I'm lucky, Tommy will tell Mark that he sort of beat me up, and that'll be it.

Yeah! And maybe when PJ asks Vern to the dance, she'll say, "Sorry, I'd rather go with your handsome friend Kirby," and we will be crowned queen and king of the Fall Fling. The whole school will stand in a silent throng around our dais, dressed in tuxedos and gowns, as Mark, Tommy, and Rob crawl toward my feet on their hands and knees, begging for forgiveness.

"I'm sorry I was such a jerk," Mark blubbers, choking back tears. "Those cows you painted . . . They were works of art. My family sold them to a gallery for a hundred million dollars, but we don't deserve the money. You should have it."

"I already have the greatest treasure in the world," I reply, squeezing Vern's hand as she beams at me. "Donate the money to the Children's Hospital of Philadelphia instead."

The crowd at the dance bursts into applause. Mark, moved by my Christlike forgiveness, weeps openly. Somewhere in the crowd, I hear Jono's familiar "buck, buck, buck," but it's quiet, chastened, a cluck of repentance.

I open the art room door to the soothing sounds of a string quartet playing from speakers on Ms. Torres's desk. Nobody looks up when I walk in; they're all engrossed in their charcoal drawings, perched on low stools around a still life of exotic fruits.

Ms. Torres sees me, however, and looks at her watch dramatically, like a stage actor emoting so people can see her expression from the balcony. Her clothes look like she's in a play too, dressed for the part of Elderly New Age Artist: short hair dyed reddish purple, dangly earrings with bells on them, and lots of chunky jade jewelry. I don't mean to make fun of her; she's nice, but she's so *absurd*, I sometimes wonder if her persona is an elaborate performance-art piece.

I don't have to worry about Ms. Torres writing me up for being late. She has this teaching philosophy where she only gives positive feedback. For instance, if you're talking in class, she won't say, "Don't talk in class." Instead she'll say, "It would be great if you didn't talk in class." Or she'll ask an absurdly open-ended question like, "Do you think every-one would be able to focus more clearly on their work if you weren't talking?"

Would everyone be able to focus better on their work if I weren't talking? Y'know, who can say? I guess we'll never find out, but it's certainly an interesting question to consider.

Ms. Torres glides over. Her feet hidden beneath a long flow-ing dress, she sails toward me like a ship blown by an unseen breeze, the HMS *Tranquility*. She folds her hands and arches a thin red eyebrow at me. "Mr. Burns. When do you think the ideal time to arrive at art class is?"

Wow. Tough question. "I mean, I guess . . ."

She looks at me expectantly, mouth slightly open.

". . . the beginning?" I venture.

She beckons me into the classroom, everything forgiven. "Grab a board, paper, and charcoal from my desk, then find a seat," she says beatifically.

We're allowed to sit wherever we want in art class because rules are for squares, man. I grab my paper and a smudgy stick of black charcoal and scan the room for Jake. I spot him alone in the back left corner, and he's easy to spot because he's the only person not busily drawing. He's dead asleep, slumped against the wall.

Of course, asleep or not, Jake's always easy to spot, since he's the only kid in Upshuck High who dresses like he's actually in Paris for Fashion Week. Today he's wearing tight black jeans and a white oxford shirt, untucked but buttoned all the way up to the neck. His sneakers are black leather with gold trim, oddly large, some brand I've never seen before.

I asked Jake one time where he gets all these cool clothes, and he said his sister mails them to him from California. Jake is always talking about his sister—how cool she is, how she's studying to be an actress—and it kind of bugs me.

I feel like every time Jake mentions his sister, he's doing it because he knows I'm lying to him, that I used to have a sister I'm not telling him about. I know I'm being paranoid, but I still can't shake the guilty feeling.

I skirt around the edge of the drawing group and sit down next to Jake, who is enjoying the untroubled sleep of a child. In repose, his face looks peaceful and innocent, so different from the hard, guarded expression he usually wears.

I'm sure Ms. Torres has already asked him, "Mr. Grivas, do you think you'd be able to draw better if you were awake?" while he snored at her. Miraculously, his large drawing board is still balanced on his lap, a stick of charcoal resting inside his open hand.

I'm not surprised to see Jake sleeping in class, but I *am* surprised to see charcoal smudges all over the right sleeve of his shirt where it's resting on his drawing. Jake's so picky about his clothes, he sometimes will change into a T-shirt for art class.

Ms. Torres floats around the room, and when she's on the far side, I nudge Jake.

"Yo! Dude! Wake up!"

Jake jolts awake, and the charcoal stick snaps in his suddenly clenched fist.

"Dude, are you all right?" I ask.

"Huh?" Eyes still half closed, Jake swivels his head in my general direction. "Who's that?"

"Remember!" Ms. Torres tells the class from the other side of the room. "Draw the shapes from the inside out! Don't draw the surface. *Burrow inside* and work your way out of the forms."

Jake seems to be working his way out of his *own* form with a struggle.

"Are you drinking NyQuil again?" I ask him.

Jake rubs his large eyes, puffy with sleep, and blinks them open. "Kirby?" he asks, like, *What are you doing here?* He shakes his head, and a long strand of hair falls over his eyes. "NyQuil . . . ? Uh, yeah. Just a little. Got a bad cold." He slicks his hair back in place.

"Did you get my text?"

"Oh, yeah, something about . . . what?"

"The one about Mark! Do you have any idea what's going on?"

"Uh, no. Actually, I forgot to charge my phone last night. It's been dead all day."

Ms. Torres floats up behind Jake and looks at his paper, which is not a drawing of the fruit in front of us, but a wall-to-wall mass of frantic black scribbles, with a big smudge in the middle where his arm was resting.

She inhales suddenly, and the bells on her earrings tinkle as a shiver runs through her. "Wow . . . Jake."

"Huh?"

"Wow," she repeats, walking away.

Jake turns his paper left and right, considering it from different angles. "Does she like it or not?" he asks me.

"I can't tell."

"What do *you* think of it?" he asks, his large eyes two searchlights, more awake now, more like the sharp Jake I love and fear.

"I . . . I don't know."

Jake drops the drawing pad and stretches like a cat, hands over his head and toes pointed.

"It's probably good, then," he says, growing bored. "That's what great art does. It confuses you."

Steve Decusatis sits on the other side of Jake, concentrating very hard on his drawing. It looks great to me, realistic and carefully shaded, but Jake taps the paper with his finger, leaving a black smudge right in the middle, and declares, "As opposed to this shit."

Steve is about to protest, then takes one look at Jake—full lips turned down in a cruel frown, flawless white shirt buttoned up to the neck but smudged all over the arm with black, total *American Psycho* vibes—and wisely chooses to instead move his stool to the other side of the room.

I tug Jake's sleeve and am relieved when, jerking it away from me, he notices the charcoal all over it.

"Ah, what the fuck?" Jake curses, wiping his arm on my shoulder.

"Jake! Focus! Has anybody hassled you today?"

"Sure. Lots of people. Why?"

"No, but I mean, not Mark Kruger or Tommy Richter or Rob Klein?"

"I barely know those jerks. Mark who?"

I fill Jake in on the whole situation: discovering it was Mark's farm we painted last night. The black eye. PJ getting stapled in the bathroom—wisely omitting my toilet-seat yoga—and Tommy roughing me up in the stairwell. I think Jake is going to get angry and say something tough like, *Don't worry about those losers, Kirby. They're all talk. I've got your back.* But instead of angry, he looks positively delighted.

"This is perfect!" he says.

I'm confused. "Do you literally mean *perfect*, or are you saying that sarcastically? Because it doesn't sound like you're saying it sarcastically. And you're smiling really big."

Jake is smiling so wide I can see his sharp canines. He looks around the room to make sure nobody is watching, then slides a knife, the blade folded into the matte-black handle, out of his back pants pocket. There's an American flag printed on the handle. It's the knife he waved in PJ's face last night.

He presses a notch and gives his wrist the slightest flick, and the blade pivots out of the handle smoothly. The blade is matte black like the handle, something I didn't notice last night, and it looks sharp enough and thick enough to gut a shark. Jake sees the alarmed expression on my face and smiles even bigger, exhilarated by my fear. Simply resting in his palm, the blade gives off a dangerous vibration, as though it's a living thing that—at any moment, if the urge gripped it—might jump up and slice the nose off my face.

Jake keeps smiling as I lean away from the knife. "This is perfect because I brought this to school today, and I've been looking for a reason to use it."

I can't tell if Jake's kidding—or at least, like, *half* kidding. Is this another jest I should include in the *Big Book of Jake Jokes*? Or is he actually saying that he's going to stab Mark and Tommy? I remember when I told him about the horse dogs and he replied with a straight face, "Dude, just kill them."

All these thoughts must be playing clearly across my shocked face, because Jake bursts out laughing. He snaps the blade shut with another quick flick and punches me in the arm as he hides the knife in his rear pocket again. "Relax, Kirby. Relax!" He laughs so loudly that one of the kids in front of us looks over his shoulder.

"I'm totally relaxed," I say. "You're not going to stab anyone, though, right?"

"You worry too much," Jake replies, which isn't the same as saying *No*.

CHAPTER 14

JAKE SPENDS THE REST OF THE CLASS CONTINUING to darken his page with overlapping scribbles, while I silently prepare my defense for accessory to murder. "Your Honor, I can't survive in prison. I have the body of an artist and a doctor's note to prove it."

When the bell rings, Jake hops off his stool like a sprinter leaving the blocks. He pushes through the crowd of students ahead of me, no doubt hoping that Rob and Tommy, or maybe even Mark, will be in the hallway waiting for us. When I get out into the hallway a couple of seconds later, I'm relieved to see they're not.

Jake spreads his arms and spins around like a demented Julie Andrews. "Where the fuck are they?"

"I don't know, dude. Somewhere else? I mean, I guess they don't know where all my classes are. Or they don't care. Or whatever."

"Shit," he grumbles, ducking back into the art room. I lean into the doorway to see what he's doing and watch with shock as he takes a big pair of scissors out of his front pocket and tosses them onto a table before rejoining me in the hall.

I can't believe it. "Why did you need the fucking scissors if you already have the—" I look around to make sure no one is listening, then whisper, "The knife?"

"I thought you didn't want me to use the knife," Jake says loudly enough for everyone in the hall to hear.

"I don't!" I hiss. "I don't want you to use the scissors, either!"

Jake rolls his eyes like I'm totally overreacting. He turns on the ball of his foot like a dancer sketching a lazy pirouette and saunters down the hall. "I wanted to see if I could fight two-handed with them," he says. "I saw a guy do it on *Game of Thrones*. Also, I worried that if I had to throw the knife, then I wouldn't have anything left to fight with."

Throw the knife? My God, he sounds serious. Would he be thinking it through this much if he was just kidding?

I hurry to catch up with him. "Look, Jake, are you kidding? You're kidding, right?"

He gives me his most charming smile, a great white shark assuring you that yes, really, he's a vegetarian.

"Jake, look, I don't want to fight. And I don't want you to *stab* anyone!"

"You don't *have* to fight." Jake sighs, ignoring the second part of my statement. "I'll handle all that for you. Kirb, I say this as your friend. . . ." He stops and tenderly lays his hand on my shoulder. "You're a wimp."

I swear, the shoulders of my shirt are going to wear out from all the people tenderly placing their hands on me today.

"Look," I say, "if we can avoid Mark and those other guys for the rest of the day, I bet by tomorrow they'll have gotten tired of all this. I mean, Mark's in vo-tech, so the only time we could conceivably see him anyhow is at lunch."

Jake's big green eyes sparkle. "Ooooh, lunch. I forgot about that. That's *perfect*. We can kill all three of those jerks at the same time."

"No! We can't! We're not *killing* anyone!" But Jake isn't listening. I've seen him get like this before. Once he makes his mind up, there's no swaying him.

One of the first times we ever hung out, after we moved to Shuckburgh but before my parents got suspicious of Jake, Mom dropped me off at his house to spend the night. Jake said, "C'mon, let's go to the drive-in. They're showing *Predator*."

He grabbed a pair of keys out of an ashtray on the kitchen table, which was piled high with newspapers, plates, and random junk. I was shocked at how messy it was compared to our kitchen.

"Wait, there's a drive-in around here?" I asked Jake. "And wait, you have a driver's license?" In Pennsylvania, you can get a learner's permit when you're sixteen, but you can't get a real, full license until you're seventeen. But Jake *did* seem older.

"Sure," Jake said, which I have since discovered is Jake's way of saying *No*.

"Where's your dad?" I asked. "Is he going to be cool with us going?"

"Sure," he said dismissively. "He's upstairs. Sleeping."

This also shocked me. It was only seven p.m.

Jake could see I was surprised. He lifted a big prescription bottle from the pile of debris on the kitchen table and rattled the pills inside. "He's got a bad back," he said. "He has to rest it a lot. Also, he just got back from a long haul, so he's beat."

He tossed the bottle back into the mess and jingled the keys. "C'mon, let's go."

At first I was nervous—I knew Mom wouldn't want me driving with Jake, or leaving the house without his dad's permission—but I was excited because I had never been to a drive-in before. I didn't know they were even still around!

The huge neon sign out front said SHUCKBURGH DRIVE-IN in a looping script, but it looked like the neon had burned out years ago, and of course someone had stolen the *h*, so it read SUCKBURGH. Jake pulled over in the high grass beside it and told me to get out of the car and hide in the trunk, so we wouldn't have to pay for two people.

"Don't you think it'll look a little suspicious," I said, "you driving in alone?"

"You can get in the trunk," Jake said, "or I can put you in the trunk."

Once we parked and I was allowed to get back into the car like a person and not a piece of luggage, Jake grabbed a six-pack of beer from the back seat. He tried to open a bottle, but they had caps, and we didn't have an opener. "Shit," Jake grumbled. "Dad just got me a bottle opener with the stars and bars on it, but I don't know where it went. Well, don't worry. I know a trick." He opened the car door and wedged the edge of the bottle cap against a piece of metal.

"You just wedge this here," Jake said, "and then *whammo!*" He slammed his hand down on the bottle top, intending to pop the cap off, but instead the whole neck of the bottle broke off in a shower of glass and foam that drenched his pant leg.

"Shit." He shook the foam off his hand. "Lemme try again."

Jake tried five more times, and every single time the cap stayed on, but the neck of the bottle itself broke off with a sharp crack.

"No problem," Jake finally said, a dripping, jagged bottle in his hand. "You just have to avoid the sharp edges. Just pour the beer into your mouth from a few inches away." He tipped the broken bottle over his mouth and poured the beer in a golden waterfall that dripped down his chin.

"Ooookay," I said doubtfully. "But what if there are glass shards in the beer? What if we drink little pieces of glass and they cut up our stomachs?"

His retort was elegant and unassailable. "Whatever."

"More like *whatnever*, dude." I laughed.

Jake wiped his chin with the back of his hand. "What?"

"More like what*never*, I said."

Jake stared at me. "I don't get it."

"Like, I would never do that, is what I'm saying. Like, instead of what*ever*, I'm saying—"

"It sounds like you're saying you want to go back in the trunk. Is that right?"

"No, sir."

Jake tossed the empty bottle out the window and grabbed another. "All right, then."

If Jake wants to do something, he *will* do it. So now I have to (1) stop Mark from beating me up and (2) stop Jake from stabbing Mark.

I realize that *not* doing number two would help me accomplish number one, but no matter how much I dislike Mark, I don't want his blood all over Jake's hands. As has been observed multiple times today by both friend and foe, I guess I'm just a wimp.

Jake and I curve around the hall and down the stairs back toward the lobby. In the stairwell, I can already hear the noise of the crowd talking and slamming their lockers in the Thunderdome, a distant roll like approaching . . . thunder. Like a . . . dome . . . full of thunder.

I'm too tired for metaphors.

CHAPTER 15

I HAVE ENGLISH NEXT, WHICH IS IN A DIFFERENT circle, which means I have to cross through the lobby again for the hundredth time today. Jake has study hall back in the circle we were just in for art, but he insists on walking me to English "for my protection."

"You don't have to do that," I protest. "Really. You don't have to walk me to class."

"It's fine, dude."

"Won't you be late for your class?"

Jake gives me a pitying look, like I'm a sucker for letting clocks tell me when to go places.

Jake keeps swiveling his head around, looking for Mark, Tommy, or Rob. What I haven't told Jake is that I know exactly where Rob is: He's in my English class. One reason I don't want Jake to walk me to class is that I'm afraid they'll bump into each other in the hallway, and Jake will fillet him like a fish with his black blade. That little fucker won't stand a chance.

We reach the ground floor of the circle and follow the flow of students moving clockwise around the hallway. Jake's eyes dart restlessly from face to face. A couple of people who meet his stare quickly look away or suddenly become very interested in the conversation they're having.

As we near the lobby, we pass through a section of the hall lined with lockers. The lockers in our school are different colors depending on what circle they're in. These are safety-cone orange. Kids open and close them with a loud *clang*. I want to distract Jake, but I don't know what to talk about. Finally I venture, "PJ is going to ask Vern to the dance today."

Jake continues scanning the crowd as we walk. "Is that why he's dressed like a ventriloquist puppet?"

"Oh, you saw him?"

"Um . . . sort of. Across the lobby." Jake rubs his eyes.

"You all right?"

"Yeah," he says. "Just tired from last night, you know?" We pass a bathroom, and he swerves toward it. "Hold on a second," he says, going inside. "Gotta piss."

I wait for him, standing against the wall and watching people pass. Boy oh boy, what a crummy day.

A couple of minutes later Jake careens out of the bathroom. His face and the top of his shirt collar are soaking wet, like he dunked his head into the sink. He's still clutching a wad of paper towels and wiping his face off as we resume walking. He crumples the paper towels up and drops them on the floor.

"Why are you soaking wet?"

He looks at me like I'm an idiot. "'Cause I washed my face," he snaps.

Okay. I am now officially more scared of Jake than of Mark.

We pass Mr. Hartman in the hallway. He eyes Jake suspiciously, as he should, and follows us as we enter the Thunderdome, posting up outside the principal's office near the main entrance.

The Thunderdome is crowded, kids crossing through the center in pairs or clumps of friends. Happy voices bounce around the vaulted dome above us. Jake and I pass through the chaos, but right in the center of the circle someone bumps into me with their shoulder as they walk past. They hit me so hard that I spin around and almost fall over. My glasses fall off. I bend down to pick them up quick, before anybody steps on them, and when I put them back on, I look up to see who bumped into me.

Of course it's Tommy, with a pack of other guys, including Jono, and they're laughing at me as they walk away.

It's reassuring to know that in a world that's spiraling out of control, there are some things you can always count on.

I stand up and adjust my glasses. Tommy gives me the finger and yells, "Hey, numbnuts, you're dead," then turns around and keeps walking, the crowd quickly separating us.

I think Jake is going to reach into his back pocket and grab the knife, but instead he grabs one of the books out of my hand—*Komm Mit!*, a thick, compact book—cocks his arm back, and yells, "Hey, Richter!"

Just as Tommy turns around, Jake throws the book at him like a pitcher whipping a fastball. Tommy is an easy target, a head taller than everyone else and wide as a barn, and the book soars over the crowd and strikes his nose edge-first. There's a sickening crunch, and a spurt of blood squirts out of his nostrils down the front of his jersey. Tommy screams, "AH SHIT!" and stumbles backward, tripping and toppling into his friends' arms, a mighty redwood felled by a small ax. It happens so fast that everyone around him is confused.

"What's going on? What happened?!" kids yell.

I spy Mr. Hartman jogging over from the principal's office to see what the hubbub is, his firm belly shaking up and down.

Jake tries to push through the crowd toward Tommy and finish the job, but I pull him away. "Mr. Hartman is coming!" I hiss, ducking my head to hide in the commotion. "C'mon, let's go!"

I push and prod him away from the growing mob behind us: Tommy yelling in pain, his voice muffled behind his cupped hands, the crackle of Mr. Hartman's walkie-talkie as he yells, "I have a one-two-three. Possible one-three-seven, over!" and the general hollering of kids.

"Ah God! My nose!"

"What happened? What happened?"

"Did anyone see that?"

"What happened?!"

Jake strains against me like a dog pulling on its leash. "Keep moving; keep moving," I say, pushing him until we're out of the lobby, into Circle C and around the corner, at which point he calms down and walks forward like nothing happened.

"What the hell was that?!" I yell.

"That"—Jake smiles—"was a fastball of righteous justice, *that's* what that was."

"Dude, you're going to get us both expelled!"

"Who cares?" Jake says.

I throw my hands up, framing my face. "Me! I care!"

We're passing classrooms now. A teacher materializes from one and looks at me curiously. My chest tightens. I can't handle all this shit. I'm going to have a fucking asthma attack.

"Relax, dude," Jake says, calm and content now that he got his little fix of violence. He leans into me, waggles his eyebrows, and unsheathes a smile that's keen as a blade. "People are staring."

I'm unable to ditch Jake before I get to English class, and I'm afraid we'll run into Rob outside the classroom, but we don't, and luckily, Jake doesn't look in the door when he drops me off. We arrive just as the second bell rings.

"All right," Jake says, clapping me on the back so hard I stumble. "I'll come back here to get you after my class. Lunch is going to be the tough part. All three of those losers are in lunch. There's no escaping it." His mouth is practically watering.

Escape is the last thing on his mind. Jake is locked on a collision course.

"How about we skip lunch?" I suggest. "I can ask Ms. Hunt if I can stay late to get some help with something, or you could ask Ms. Torres if we can chill in the art room and draw some fruit? She likes you. . . ."

"No, no, no," Jake says, shaking his head. "Uh-uh. We're gonna show these hillbillies who's boss."

"*They* are, Jake! *They* are the boss. I'm an employee. Or, no, I'm an unpaid intern, and they are the CEO of the entire corporation, and I don't want you to stab anyone, please—"

But Jake is already walking away, backward against the flow of the circle.

"Just promise me you won't kill anyone!" I yell after him.

He spins around and cocks his fingers at me like they're guns, grinning as he pulls the triggers.

"Sure."

Rob is already in his seat on the far left side of the English room, near the windows, his short legs barely reaching the ground. He smirks when he sees me, then pretends to sneeze and says "Chickenshit!" at the same time. A few kids around him snicker.

Maybe I *should* let Jake murder him.

Everyone is still settling into their seats. Our teacher, Ms. Hunt, is messing with papers at her desk, a flurry of pretty energy: now chewing on a fingernail, now twisting a lock of her wavy chestnut hair, her every move adorable. Everyone loves her, and half the class has a crush on her. Today her hair is wrapped in one of those tight, complicated braids girls wear if they're riding a horse or doing gymnastics. She pops a pencil into the thick braid as she shuffles through a stack of multicolored three-by-five cards.

Ms. Hunt briskly taps the note cards on her desk. She's young compared to other teachers, so young that sometimes new students mistake her for a senior. It's not just the way she looks, but it's also her enthusiasm.

For instance, every time one of us recites a passage from a book we're reading, she applauds and yells "Bravo!" afterward, like we just put on an entire Broadway show.

It's exhausting being around her, but she's so naive that nobody wants to be the one to rain on her parade. So we try to all behave like the fictional class she thinks we are, perfect students super pumped about school.

I glance across the room to check on Rob. He's looking at me, too, whispering something to the kid at the desk behind him, whose name I don't know. The kid looks at me, shocked, then laughs. It makes me feel rotten. It makes me feel every bit like the new kid that I am.

The weird kid from my bus, the one with the soup-bowl haircut, is sitting at the desk next to me on my left. I have an urge to talk to someone so I feel slightly less unpopular, and *Lord of the Flies* is sitting on his desk in front of him. He has a cool copy of the book with a cover I've never seen before, a blotchy drawing of dense forest vegetation.

I point to the book. "That's a cool cover. Great book, huh?" I'm not just making idle chatter here. I really did like the book. And I have to say, as this fucking insane day continues, I'm starting to relate to the boys on the island more and more.

Soupbowl swivels the full moon of his face toward me and stares.

"I really like the pilot, the one who's stuck up in the trees," I continue. "I thought that part was spooky."

Soupbowl doesn't say anything.

"Did you like that part?" I ask.

He slowly shakes his head from side to side, his eyeballs staying in the same place, an unsettling motion that reminds me of one those cat clocks with the moving eyeballs.

I look past him at Rob near the windows. Now he's whispering to the girl in front of him, a pretty girl who is in my swim class. I think her name is Mary. I've always wanted to talk to her, but I've never found an excuse. She has short, very blond hair and a cute little face like a fox. Whatever Rob is whispering in her ear, it shocks her, because her eyes go wide. She spins her head to look in my direction, and when she sees I'm already looking, she looks away guiltily and bites her lip.

Oh man. I think I'd rather just get beat up than deal with this psychological warfare. I feel my blood pressure rising, and it reminds me of the last time I flipped out at school. As much as I like poker, I'd rather not be sent to a psychologist again, so I take a deep breath and pull myself together.

"She has something special planned for us today."

It's Soupbowl. He's speaking to me.

"She has something special planned," he repeats in a slow monotone, never taking his eyes off me as he nods at Ms. Hunt.

Dude is giving me the creeps. "Uh, yeah. I think it's probably a pop quiz."

"I do not think so," he says. "I think, whatever she has planned, it will involve those desks."

Soupbowl is right; there are three desks lined up at the front of the room, facing the class. On the blackboard behind them Ms. Hunt has written:

LORD OF THE ISLAND DEBATE!
THE SOUND OF THE SHELL!
THEMES:
• CIVILIZATION • GROUPTHINK
• WILL TO POWER • SOCIAL ORDER

Ms. Hunt finishes organizing her cards and briskly raps the rainbow-colored stack on her desk. She skips to the front of the class, next to the three desks, and sings in a champagne-bubbly voice, "Good morning, everyone!"

We all stop talking and face forward like perfect angels, our hands clasped on our desks and our feet flat on the floor. Soupbowl is the only one a little slow to get with the program, giving me one last ominous look before facing forward as well.

Ms. Hunt sits down on top of the center desk, briskly crossing her slender legs under a tweed skirt and placing her stack of rainbow-colored cards on the desk next to her.

"I'm sure you're all wondering what today's surprise could be." She smiles and wrinkles her nose. "Well, I'm *sure* you all remember at the beginning of the book—chapter one, 'The Sound of the Shell'—when Ralph blew the conch to gather all the other children onto the beach."

She holds an invisible conch shell in her hands and presses it to her lips. *"Blap, bla, bla, blaaaaaaaa!"* She smiles at everyone, and we all smile back.

I swear, if you're pretty, you can get away with anything.

"The boys held a vote to decide who should be chief, and Ralph won. Well, today in class we're going to hold our *own* debate to decide who should be chief of the island. Three of you will pretend to be Ralph, Jack, and Piggy."

She spreads her arms across the three desks in front of the class. "The rest of the class will be the boys on the island. We'll have a debate, and then at the end the class will vote on who should be the new chief. This will help us examine the themes of groupthink and social organization that the book explores. And, most importantly, it will give all of you a little taste, maybe, of what it felt like to be with those boys on the island. *Doesn't that sound fun?!"*

It does *not* sound fun; it sounds like three of us will have to speak, unprepared, in front of the entire class. Everyone slumps down in their seats or hides behind their books, willing themselves to become invisible.

Ms. Hunt doesn't pick up on our fear as she claps her

hands and hops up from the desk. "Now, do we have any volunteers?"

We each look around like the person next to us just volunteered.

"C'mon, somebody must want to volunteer! Mary, how about you?"

The fox-faced girl looks around the room, embarrassed. "Uh, sure," she says reluctantly.

Ms. Hunt acts like Mary jumped out of her seat with joy. "That's the spirit! Now, who else?"

Mary tucks a short lock of hair behind her ear as she walks to the front of the class and takes her place behind the first desk on the left.

I'm surprised to see Rob raise his hand next and say, "I'll be Jack."

Of course he'll be Jack. Jack is the wildest of the wild kids on the island. He leads the hunting parties that are obsessed with killing pigs. It's a role Rob was born to play, although I'm still a little surprised *anyone* would want to volunteer for this.

"Fantastic!" Ms. Hunt does an adorable fist pump. "Now we just need a Piggy. He is a *very important* character. Remember, Piggy is the most intelligent boy on the island, the voice of reason, and"—she quickly glances at her top note card—"the symbolic upholder of the conventions of society."

Yeah, he's also a fat, asthmatic nerd who gets made fun of the entire novel until one of the boys crushes him with a boulder. Nobody is going to volunteer to—

From his new seat at the front of the room, Rob points at me. "Kirby wants to be Piggy!"

Ms. Hunt's lively eyes focus on me. "Wonderful!" She claps her hands and waves me up like a game-show host. "Come on up, Kirby."

"What? No, I don't—"

"Then why'd you raise your hand?" Rob asks accusingly. "Ms. Hunt, I saw him raise his hand. I think he's just shy."

What the hell is he doing?

"There's no need to be shy," Ms. Hunt says, beckoning me like I'm a frightened kitten. "It's okay, Kirby."

"I'm not shy. I just didn't—"

Rob pounds his fists on the desk and starts chanting, "Kirby, Kirby, Kirby!" A few kids join in the chant, already swept up in the groupthink of the island.

Ms. Hunt gives me a sharp look and points at the empty desk next to Rob. I'm spoiling her fun. "C'mon, Kirby, get up here. Let's get started."

As terrified as I am to be facing the English class, I have to admit that Mary, Rob, and I are perfectly cast for our roles. Mary is similar to the good-natured, likable Ralph. Rob has plenty in common with the violent Jack. And just like Piggy, I have glasses, asthma, and a huge penis.

Rob gives me a sideways look and winks.

My stomach drops.

"All right, everyone!" Ms. Hunt announces. "Welcome to

the Lord of the Island Debate!" The class claps, and she smiles, pleased with her cleverness. Ms. Hunt turns to the three of us, arranged in front of the class. "Now remember, candidates, you have to pretend you're your character from the book. Keeping that in mind, let's hear your opening remarks. *Ralph*," she says, winking at Mary, "why don't you go first. Class, listen closely to *Ralph's* points and decide: Is this the person you think is best suited to lead you on the island?"

Ms. Hunt sits on the edge of her desk, like cool teachers do on TV.

Mary stands and takes a deep breath. "Hellooo, my name is, uh . . . *Ralph*." She laughs nervously at that, and the class laughs too, which helps her relax a little bit. "My name is *Ralph*. And you should vote for me because I have the seashell. The, uh . . . the *conch*."

Ms. Hunt glances at her note cards. "And what does the conch symbolize?" she asks, leading Mary on.

"Well, it symbolizes society, I guess. The sound of the conch is what brings all the boys together at the beginning." She tucks that rebellious little lock of hair behind her ear again. "The conch is what organizes the boys, and I'm the one who blew the conch, so maybe, if you want to, vote for me?" She shrugs and smiles at the absurdity of this whole theater, and I think, *Shit, I'm running, and even* I'd *vote for her*. Everyone applauds politely as she sits down with relief.

"That was an excellent point you made, Ralph. You were the one who found the conch and first rallied everyone to the beach. A significant contribution to the *social order*"—she points to the words SOCIAL ORDER on the blackboard—"of the island. Jack, it's your turn."

Rob rolls his shoulders and cracks his knuckles, a weasel in a henhouse. He doesn't bother to stand up to deliver his opening statement, simply swivels to address Mary at the desk next to him. He touches her lightly on the arm as he says playfully, "Ralph, thank you *so much* for finding the conch and bringing us all to the beach like this." Mary smiles, and Rob turns to the class. "I agree that organizing all the boys was an important first step to maintaining order on the island." He speaks like a politician, poised and confident. "But I think now we have a graver concern than *order*. . . ." He pauses dramatically. "And that is *survival*. All due respect to you, Ralph"—he nods to Mary—"I'm in charge of the hunting parties that have been providing us with meat. And without meat, we won't be able to survive." He stabs a finger into the desktop and lets this fact sink in, and the class gets so quiet and serious I think they've forgotten that we aren't, in fact, on an island.

Ms. Hunt claps her hands to her chest in an ecstasy of teacherly rapture. "Wow, Jack," she says. "Just wow. Great points." She shuffles her colored cards and shrugs. "I have nothing to add. Piggy?" She looks at me. "It's your turn."

Mary leans down to look at me across the desks, and against my will I feel myself actually giving a shit about this stupid debate. I want to beat Rob. In the book, his character Jack crushes Piggy's head with a rock. It was Rob's idea to staple PJ in the bathroom. I want to beat Rob for Piggy, for PJ, for all the kids who are too weak to stand up for themselves.

No matter how many pigs we kill, that still won't get us off the island. I stand up and open my mouth to say just that, but before I can say a word, Rob makes a loud snorting noise, like a pig.

"SNORT! SNORT! SNORT!"

Mary laughs.

No, the *whole class* laughs.

I look to Ms. Hunt for help and am shocked to see that she's giggling too, although with a reproachful look on her face.

"Now, now, Jack," she chides, wagging her finger. "Piggy didn't interrupt you during your turn, did he?"

"Thank you," I say to Ms. Hunt.

"You're fat," Rob whispers.

"No, I'm not!"

"Piggy *is* overweight," Ms. Hunt offers equitably. "But, Jack, you can't keep interrupting Piggy. He has the conch." She addresses the class. "As you can see, the unifying power of the conch is already dissolving. Does that affect which candidate you think might be the best leader?"

"I'd like to throw into question the entire concept of the conch as a symbol of power," Rob offers.

"Okay, okay, let's keep this organized," Ms. Hunt says, the hint of a frown creasing her pretty face. "We'll do rebuttals later. This is still opening statements. Piggy, what's your opening statement?"

I haven't even given my opening statement yet! I look at the classroom of students facing me, still laughing at me a little.

I see no sympathy there, just relief that *they're* not the ones being embarrassed. I think of Piggy's head, crushed by a rock, the broken glass from his lenses glinting on the ground next to him. I think of Melanie's framed picture shattered on green linoleum tiles, the glass as bright and as sharp as the memory.

"Maybe we don't deserve to get off the island. Hell, maybe we can't get off the island, even if we leave. Maybe we brought it with us. God," I marvel, exhausted right down to my bones. "We're all fucked."

Why is everyone staring at me?

Oh, I said that out loud.

My words hang in the quiet room. Nobody is laughing anymore, their mouths perfect *O*s of surprise.

Ms. Hunt raises her eyebrows, an expectant look on her face, and after a couple of seconds, when I don't add anything else, she frowns and shuffles her note cards. "Oookaaaay," she sings in a tight little voice. "I highly doubt you'll get elected with that attitude." She taps her stack of cards against her desk and tries to regain her enthusiasm. "Okay, those were the opening statements. Now let's begin the questions."

She perks back up as she focuses on Mary. "*Ralph*, how will you get the boys rescued?"

Mary gives me a concerned glance as she stands, and then her face screws up with concentration as she tries to remember the book. "Well . . . I would . . ." She remembers with visible relief. "*Make a fire!* I would make a fire, and then planes or ships could see the fire and we'd get rescued. Also, if I'm allowed to offer methods not described in the book, I suppose I'd also suggest using Piggy's glasses as a reflection device." Mary looks at me again.

"Great idea," Rob says.

Ms. Hunt agrees. "Those are both good ideas, Ralph. Class, notice that Ralph has a concrete plan to rescue the boys and return you to *civilization*." She points at the word on the blackboard. "And, Jack, how would you get us rescued?"

"Personally, I agree with Piggy," Rob says, smiling at me. "Bollocks rescue!" he says in a surprisingly good English accent. He's really getting into character. He stands up—not increasing his height by much—and his high voice rises to a savage squeal as he pounds the desk with his little fist. "Kill the pig! Drink its blood! It's meat that we want. Who cares if a ship sees our fire if we all die of starvation before then?"

Ms. Hunt looks worried about the direction the debate is taking and shuffles through her note cards nervously. "Uh, that's an excellent point, Jack. A strong demonstration of the *will to power* and the importance of survival over *social order*." She turns to me with a *this is your last chance* look. "Piggy," she says slowly and clearly, like Hans Gruber telling Karl to *Shoot. The. Glass*. "Do you have any thoughts on that?"

Rob smiles at me, and I can imagine chicken feathers stuck between his pointy little teeth. I know he's trying to embarrass me, and I've got to pull it together *fast*. "Well," I say, adjusting my glasses and clearing my throat. "Obviously a fire is the best way for us to be seen by passing ships. And while I agree with

Jack that food is *important*, I don't think that sending out hunting parties would prevent us from—"

"Shut up, you fat slug," Rob says to me, impressively recall-
ing a line from the book.

Ms. Hunt shakes her finger at Rob and says, "Rob, this is
your last warning." But her rebuke is drowned out by the class's
laughter. I look to see if Mary is laughing and, thank goodness,
she's not. In fact, she actually looks a little sorry for me, and for
some reason that pity is what tips me over the edge.

I can't believe I have to put up with this shit today of all
days, and I can't believe it's actually bothering me. How dare I
care about something so petty? It's an insult to Melanie that I
should give a shit about anything other than her, and suddenly
I'm not mad at Rob or the class. I'm mad at myself. Furious.

I stand up, and the room spins. My face is so hot, it must
be red as a stove. I try one last time to swallow my anger, but
it won't go down. It sticks in my throat, and an animal growl
comes out of my mouth as I grab the edge of my desk and
flip it over. The metal desk lands on its top with a loud *clang*,
then slides and slams into the front row of seats, which shocks
everyone into silence.

Until a moment later, when they erupt into laughter again,
even *louder* this time and backed by a deep chorus of "oooooohs!"

Welcome to the party, pal!

Ms. Hunt falls off her desk, spilling note cards all over
the floor in a cascade of bright colors. "Stop right there!" She
tries to grab my arm, but Mary and Rob are between us, Mary

staring at me in shock, Rob leaning back with his arms crossed. "Kirby! Stop it!"

I point an accusing finger at the class. "Go ahead and vote for Jack! You animals deserve him!"

Someone yells, "Get 'em, Kirb!"

Ms. Hunt dings the brass bell on her desk furiously. "Calm down, everyone! End of debate! Calm down!"

"You're animals!" I repeat, shaking my finger at them.

"Tell it like it is, fatso!" someone yells.

Rob surveys the havoc with satisfaction, until I turn to him and his smug smile drops. He sees that he's pushed me too far.

I raise my hands toward his neck and he shrinks away, but before I can choke the life out of him, there's a knock on the door, and a deep voice booms, "Ms. Hunt! Is everything all right in here?"

A guilty silence drops as we look over and see Mr. Hartman's imposing polyester frame standing in the doorway. His eyes dart around the room behind his tinted aviator glasses, assessing potential threats. He plants a meaty fist on his hip and looks at Ms. Hunt like he's ready to arrest all of us if she says the word. "Is everything all right in here?"

"Oh, uh, yes," she says like someone waking from a troubled dream. She shuffles an invisible deck of cards before realizing her hands are empty and looks down at the cards all over the ground. She straightens the pleats in her skirt instead. "Yes, we were just having a little . . . debate."

Mr. Hartman must get tired of people constantly lying to

him, but this time at least he doesn't seem to care. Whatever's going on, it's not his problem. "I see," he says. "Well, I don't want to interrupt. I just came to borrow one of your students." His eyes lock on me, frozen in mid-lunge at Rob, my fingers splayed like a killer in an Italian horror film, and holds my German book out, a smear of blood on its spine.

"I think this belongs to you, Mr. Burns."

Komm Mit!

The room seems to spin again.

Rob reaches out and shakes one of my extended hands. "Good debate!"

CHAPTER 16

IT'S BETWEEN PERIODS, SO THE HALL IS EMPTY AS
Mr. Hartman and I walk to the principal's office together. Well,
I walk; he lumbers, breathing through his mouth like a grizzly
bear with a hiker's boot stuck in his throat.

He doesn't try to talk to me, and I'm glad, because if he did
I'd probably start screaming. All these emotions are blowing
through me, and I have to get a hold on them or I'm going to
fly away like a kite. I can feel it.

I picture the beach.

The waves crashing on the shore.

The roar as they land foaming white and the sigh as they
retreat serenely blue.

Far out, beyond the breaking waves, a familiar silhouette bobs up and down and waves for me to join her.

The wind in my head dies down and I remember, *Oh, right. I'm in big trouble.*

This will be my first visit to the principal's office at Upshuck High, although I have met the principal before. Mom and I went to Mr. Braun's office on the first day of school, and he talked to us for a while, welcomed me to the school. He's very friendly. A cuddly grandpa with white puffy hair and an easy smile. He looked at me kindly and said, "I think you'll be very happy here at Upper Shuckburgh High, Kirby." He seemed genuinely nice, but still, that doesn't mean I won't get in trouble.

I hope I don't get expelled. Oh man.

The worst part about getting in trouble is the disappointed looks Mom and Dad will give me after school, the long sanctimonious lecture. Although if I'm going to get in trouble, I suppose today is the perfect day to do it, since I'm already scheduled for a big long shitty heart-to-heart after school. Might as well double down. Maybe if I fuck up bad enough, they'll send me back to the psychologist and I can learn to play pinochle.

I follow Mr. Hartman around the hallway of Circle C and we pass through the double doors into the stairwell, the same stairwell where Tommy threw me up against the wall and Mr. Hartman helped me retrieve my books only an hour or so ago. I guess the memory jogs something in Mr. Hartman's mind, because he slows down and stops on the landing. He looks at me in a searching way, an unusual note of compassion in his gravelly voice.

"Is there anything you'd like to tell me, Kirby?"

He's giving me a chance to come clean.

The problem is, I don't want it. Jake has gotten in trouble so many times at school, if I tell on him now, he'll get expelled. A couple of days ago he got in trouble for carving his initials into one of the biology tables with a dissection knife. "Well, that's strike two," he said as I walked him to the library for after-school detention.

"What do you mean?" I asked.

"I mean one more and I'm out."

"What do you mean, *out*? Like, for good?" I was surprised he wasn't more concerned. To me getting expelled seemed pretty serious.

"Probably," he said. "Whatever. I don't care. I'll just move to California and live with my mom and sister if that happens. I'm sick of this shit hole anyhow."

If I lie and tell Mr. Hartman that *I* threw the German book, I'll get in way less trouble than Jake would. Maybe I could even say it was an accident? I'm pretty sure nobody actually *saw* Jake throw the book. It all happened so fast—

"Hello?" Mr. Hartman leans down and looks into my eyes. He shakes *Komm Mit!* in front of my nose. "I don't think you're the type of kid who would throw a book at someone. Am I wrong?"

I try to keep my talking to a minimum, afraid the quiver in my voice will betray me. "Well, uh, no . . ."

"*No?* No, you didn't throw this book? Your name is on the inside cover. Did someone take your book?"

"Well, *no*. I mean no. I, uh . . ."

"I've seen you hanging around with Jake Grivas." The compassion leaves his eyes. "He's a bad kid. Are you a bad kid?" He says it like I'm actually a dog.

"No," I say. "No, I'm not." *I'm a good boy.* If I had a tail, I'd be wagging it.

Mr. Hartman is getting frustrated. He's almost out of words. "Well, then," he says, standing up and judging me from his great height. "Why are you lying to me?"

I shrug.

He sighs like a steam engine pulling out of the station as he shoves me toward the stairs.

"C'mon."

He unclips his walkie-talkie and pushes the red button to talk. The speaker crackles, a burst of static so loud it makes me wince. "Hartman, coming down C. I've got Burns with me. Over." Another crackle and a beep as he releases the button. Who the hell is he talking to?

As we walk through the lobby I hear the janitor, Mr. Reali, coming. He has a bristling key ring strapped to his belt, and the million keys jingle like sleigh bells. Everyone calls him Luigi because he's a skinny Italian guy with a mustache and he always wears a green baseball cap. He waves a pair of industrial-size bolt cutters at Mr. Hartman.

"You need these anymore, Frank?"

"No thanks, Mike. Thanks, though."

"You find anything?"

Mr. Hartman frowns and stops walking, hooking a finger in the back of my collar to stop me, too. "Nope," he says sourly.

"Ah. Well, that's good, right?"

"Yeah," he says like he's saying *no.* "Yeah, it is."

"Oh, say," Mr. Reali says, lowering his voice. "That other thing. I'm sorry, but I can't do that thing. I told Mr. Braun and I'm telling you now too. I got a fear of heights."

Mr. Hartman rubs his face, pushing his gold-rimmed aviators up as he pinches the bridge of his nose. "Yeah, yeah, I know. You said."

"And besides," Mr. Reali continues nervously, "that ain't even inside the school, technically, so it ain't even my jury's diction, as they say."

Mr. Hartman nudges me to start walking again. "Yeah, yeah," he says. "I know. It's fine."

As we walk away the janitor calls after us, waving the bolt cutters. "I'm sorry, Frank. It just ain't even my jury's diction!"

Mr. Hartman marches me into the principal's office. The waiting room is small, with a glass wall on the front that looks out onto the lobby and front doors. There's a high counter on the left-hand side for the secretary to sign in visitors, some nice framed photos of covered bridges, and a short row of chairs facing the windows. Tommy's already there, slumped in a chair that's way too small for him, his elbows jutting into the seats on either side of him.

When Mr. Hartman and I walk in, he looks up, and the back of his huge head bumps a framed photo on the wall behind him.

Tommy doesn't look good.

His nose is puffy and lumpy, like a half-mashed potato. His nostrils bulge out, packed with cotton balls. There's a thin line of blood down the front of his jersey that's dried brown. Also, there's a look in his eyes, a fear and pain that seems disproportionate to the amount of trouble we're in.

"Sit," Mr. Hartman says to me, pointing to a chair next to Tommy before passing through the door into Mr. Braun's office. I sit down and think, *Good boy.*

I sit one chair away from Tommy. I'd sit farther away if I could, but I can't. There are only a few seats in the waiting room, all in a row, so this is as far away as I can get.

The secretary, Mrs. Tews, is hidden behind the tall counter on the far side of the room, working on an old computer. After a couple of minutes of clacking loudly on the keyboard with her fake nails, she stands up and goes into a back room. I hear the copier running, but aside from that and the thin whistle of Tommy's breathing, the waiting room is eerily quiet.

I wish I could sit farther away from Tommy. I'm afraid he's going to grab me right here and start punching me. But when I finally work up the courage to glance over at him, he's ignoring me, staring gloomily at the floor, long telephone-pole legs stretched out.

Then he leans forward and puts his head down into his hands and his shoulders start shaking, and I'm shocked to realize that he's crying. He's trying to cry quietly, but I can hear his sobs echoing inside the meat cave his massive hands form around his face.

I'd be less surprised if he jumped onto the coffee table and started tap-dancing. I reach over and pat him on his broad shoulder, as much out of embarrassment as compassion. I know Tommy wants to kill me, but I never thought he'd try to do it by embarrassing us both to death.

"Hey, look, I'm sorry Jake hit you—I mean, I'm sorry your nose . . . got hit," I offer lamely, already trying to rewrite the narrative.

Tommy shrugs me off. He talks into his hands, voice muffled, nose all stuffed up.

"Fuck you. I don't care about my stupid nose or your psycho friend."

He sniffs a couple of times, then takes a shaky breath and collects himself. He lifts his puffy face from his hands, wet with tears, and looks at me.

"I guess you're gonna tell on me for beatin' on you in the stairwell, huh?"

Oh right! That didn't even occur to me! *I can tell on him!* Awesome! But then what about the book? I mean, him hitting me in the stairwell doesn't cancel out the book throwing, but still, it's gotta help.

Tommy mistakes my silence for agreement and nods. "Yup. I thought so." His voice trembles as he whispers, "My dad is going to *kill* me."

Your dad *is going to kill you? You mean, like* you *tried to kill* me *today?* I'm unable to muster much sympathy for Tommy.

"Well, if you don't want to get in trouble at school, maybe you shouldn't be throwing people against walls and shit."

Tommy cocks his head like he must have heard me wrong. Nobody talks to the Richter Scale like that.

His disbelief stokes my anger. "You push people around all the time," I continue. "Maybe you deserve to get pushed back, see how you like it."

Tommy stares at me for so long that I mistake it for confusion, but when he finally responds, his voice is intelligent and clear. "I should see how *I* like it? I don't. I don't like it at all."

He stretches out his left arm and turns it over, palm-side-up, then carefully rolls up the sleeve of his football jersey, revealing an ugly round scar, like a cigarette burn, on the inside of his forearm. The scar looks new, angry pink flesh puckered on his pale skin. He looks at the scar and then back at me angrily, like I'm the one who did it. "Caught me drinking in the woods," he says, pointing at it.

Like a magician performing a grisly trick, he rolls his sleeve up farther, revealing another scar and another . . . and then another. He points to each scar like a tour guide and tells me what he got it for : "Talking back . . . drinking again . . . skipped school . . . can't remember what this one was for . . ." He stops rolling his sleeve up at the elbow, and I count six scars in all. Most of them are old, but a few look newer.

I guess now I know why Tommy wears his long-sleeved football jersey every day.

He yanks the sleeve back down, and I'm relieved when he doesn't glare at me angrily again or say anything else, but instead stretches his legs out, leans back against the wall, and closes his eyes.

I try to summon remorse for yelling at Tommy and am ashamed to discover that I can't. Instead, I feel cheated, robbed of my right to hate him. It's like if someone cuts you off in traffic and you want to honk at them, but then on their rear window you spot one of those pink ribbons that means they're a breast cancer survivor.

I hear snoring and am surprised to see that Tommy is, miraculously, asleep. He snores like a wet kazoo because of his busted nose. *Why does everyone keep falling asleep today?* Are Mr. Hartman and the janitor sneaking opioids into the water fountains?

I can hear muffled arguing behind Mr. Braun's door. I wonder what's going on in the office. Why haven't Tommy and I been called in yet? I squeeze my eyes shut and try to follow Tommy's example. But I can't. The phlegm snoring and muffled argument combine in a very unpleasant way, and I'm about to get up and walk out of the waiting room, maybe keep walking out the front doors and not stop—but then I get an idea. A better solution.

I nudge Tommy and he starts awake with an alarmed snort, his huge head bumping the picture frame behind him again. He looks at me like he's not totally awake yet.

"You don't want to get in trouble with your dad, right?"

Tommy responds slowly, still waking up. "What?"

"You don't want to get in trouble with your dad, *right?*" I repeat.

Tommy takes a second to confirm this, then nods. "Right."

"Okay. And I don't want Jake to get in trouble for hitting you with the book. So I'll make you a deal."

I outline my idea to Tommy, and he listens carefully. At the end of my explanation, he seems to look at me in a new way.

"Wow. I judged you wrong," he says. "I thought you were smart."

CHAPTER 17

A MINUTE LATER, MR. HARTMAN FINALLY WALKS out of Mr. Braun's office with Trey strolling behind him, Trey smiling like Mr. Braun just gave him a student-of-the-year award. Mr. Hartman is fuming. Tommy and I are both concentrating on the scam we're about to pull. Trey's the only person in the room who's happy. When he sees me twisting my hands in the waiting-room chair, he waves. "Hey, Kirb! What are you in for?"

"Uh, well, it's kind of complicated. . . ."

"Bullshit, right?" Trey says before I can finish. "Were you framed just like I was? I bet you were. Did you know they even searched my locker for *drugs*?" He winks at me. "They didn't find anything, though. I'm not *stupid*."

"Hey, hey, hey, no talking." Mr. Hartman grabs Trey by the

arm and shoves him into the chair between Tommy and me. "You. Sit," he growls, then points at Tommy and me. "You two clowns: in there." Clipped to his belt, his walkie-talkie crackles loudly. He swears and flicks a button, turning it off. Then he shoves the principal's door open wider, revealing Mr. Braun dwarfed behind a massive desk.

"Gentlemen," Mr. Braun greets us, beckoning us in with his chubby little hands. "Please come in."

I haven't been in Mr. Braun's office since the first day of school, when he welcomed Mom and me to Upchuck High, but the office is much as I remember it, small and cozy, lined with floor-to-ceiling bookshelves. I had forgotten, however, that the back wall has French doors that open out to the field behind the school. The doors seem out of place, and as Mr. Braun sits at his desk, the light shining through them backlights his tiny form, an elvish god whose eminence is blinding.

Despite the intimidating lighting, Mr. Braun himself is warm and reassuring. He actually looks more like a hobbit than an elf: short and round, old and jolly, wearing a deep green vest over a blue dress shirt. His bald head is so shiny I swear he must polish it twice a day, the dome surrounded by a shock of puffy white hair. He smiles at Tommy and me, and his face folds up along a million well-worn wrinkles.

In the morning, when we all walk in, he stands outside the office like a Walmart greeter and says hello to students whose names he knows.

Just 'cause he's nice doesn't mean he's dumb, though. His clever little eyes shine like wet stones beneath his bristling gray eyebrows. I really hope Tommy and I can pull off my plan. I mean, I'm pretty sure I can hold up my end, but Tommy is dimmer than a box of broken light bulbs.

I can't fail to notice that my German book—the murder weapon, exhibit A—is theatrically placed in the center of his desk. Man, I'm having a lot of trouble with books today.

"Well, Tommy," Mr. Braun says cheerily, "that's quite a bump you've got on your nose! How did that happen?"

Tommy glances at me—which I wish he hadn't done, because giving someone a shifty sideways glance is not something you do right before you tell the truth—then launches into his spiel. He talks mechanically, like a GPS trying to pronounce a difficult street name.

"Well, Mr. Braun, I asked Kirby to give me his German book. And he threw it to me, and it accidentally hit me in the nose."

Mr. Braun's bushy eyebrows draw together, like two caterpillars kissing. "I thought you told Mr. Hartman that Jake Grivas hit you with the book?"

Tommy looks at me again, a threatening glance this time, which I interpret as *You better hold up your end of the bargain.*

"Kirby threw the book at me, yes. But he didn't mean to hit me. It was an accident." Tommy leans forward and a little drop of blood from his nose leaks out around the cotton and splatters onto Mr. Braun's desk.

Mr. Braun quickly moves some papers and looks at me for help. "Kirby, is this true? Did you throw your book at Tommy? Are you sure it wasn't *Jake* who threw the book?"

I'm a little nervous about lying to Mr. Braun, so I ease into it by employing one of Ms. Torres's unanswerable questions.

"Why would Jake throw my book at Tommy?"

"Well, I don't know," Mr. Braun replies immediately. "Why would *you* throw the book at Tommy?"

Dammit. Okay, there's no turning back now. I feel like I'm stepping off a diving board as I jump headfirst into the lie. "You know, it's so crowded in the Thun—I mean, the lobby—and Tommy asked me for my German book, and I couldn't reach him, so I tried to toss it to him, but someone bumped into me and it threw my aim off." I cap off my big stinking lie with what I hope is the smile of an innocent baby.

Mr. Braun leans back a little, either because he's surprised by my brown teeth or because he can actually *smell* the bullshit I'm shoveling. He squints at me for a long time, like he's trying to peer inside my brain. It reminds me of how Mom stares at me when she's trying to figure out if I'm lying.

Finally he asks, "Is Tommy in your German class?"

"Uh . . . no."

"Tommy, do you take German?"

"No," Tommy says. "Spanish."

"Well, then," Mr. Braun asks him, "why would you ask Kirby for his German book?"

Oh. Crap. I can't believe that didn't even occur to us. Now

it's my turn to give Tommy a guilty sideways look. Luckily, we're both saved by the believability of his own ignorance.

"You know what?" Tommy shrugs. "I don't know."

Our exchange is so absurd, it sounds like one of the strange dialogues from my German book.

Mr. Braun: Tommy, do you speak German?
Tommy: No. I speak Spanish.
Mr. Braun: Then why did you ask Kirby for his German book?
Tommy: I do not know.
Kirby: There are many students in the Thunderdome. It is a place of danger.

Mr. Braun runs his hands through his snowy hair and rocks back in his chair, staring at the ceiling like he longs to return to his humble hole in Hobbiton. When he looks at me and Tommy again, all the *gee shucks* friendliness is gone.

Mr. Braun places his hands on his desk with exaggerated calmness and speaks in a deadly quiet voice. "I just want to make sure I have this straight." He points at Tommy. "You're telling me that you asked Kirby for his German book, even though you're not taking German. And then, Kirby, instead of asking him why he'd want your book, or walking over and handing it to him, you threw it at his face *so hard* that it broke his nose."

I utter the first honest sentence I've said since walking into this office. "I'm not very good at throwing."

He looks at Tommy. "Does that sound plausible to you, Tommy?"

Tommy shrugs again.

Mr. Braun knows that we're both lying, but he can't prove it. Also, at this point, it seems like he might not care anymore. I'm glad Trey was in here before us, because I think he wore Mr. Braun down a little bit. He tries to smile at us, but he can only muster a grimace. He pushes *Komm Mit!* at me so hard it almost slides off the edge of the desk.

"See Mrs. Tews at the front desk on your way out; she'll write you both hall passes to return to class."

As Tommy and I walk out of the inner office and close the door behind us, we pass Trey, still in the waiting room. He's sitting backward in one of the chairs, facing the wall and patiently peeling a long strip of wallpaper off.

"Hey," I say. "What are you still doing here?"

He rips the wallpaper strip off and it flutters to the ground. "Oh, they wanna send me home, but they can't because my mom's still at work."

"Sorry to hear that."

"Me too. I wanna get out of this crummy place. Little advice, Kirby: You don't wanna be around when my mom finally gets here. She is gonna be piiiiiiiiiiiissed." His face suddenly lights up. "Hey, did you see me throw the raccoon up onto the roof? Wasn't that awesome?"

Disturbing is what I'd say, but since this is a day for deception, I agree. "Yeah, it was awesome."

"Do you think it's still up there?"

"I guess it must be. It didn't look well enough to climb down on its own."

"Yeah, no duh. But I mean, I thought maybe vultures would have gotten to it by now."

Vultures? Are there vultures around here? I try to picture a flock of them circling the school, black wings flapping behind pink, featherless heads.

"I tried to go up on the roof to check," Trey continues, "but the door behind the drama stage was locked."

I'm struggling to figure out how the hell Trey escaped custody long enough to try to access the roof when Mrs. Tews clears her throat. She's a large woman, rising behind the front desk counter; her dyed red hair and wide, sloping shoulders make her look like an angry volcano.

She flaps two hall passes at Tommy and me. "Boys?" she says threateningly. "Would you like to go back to class, or would you prefer to go back in with Mr. Braun?"

"I think I'd like to go back to class," Trey says, hopping up and reaching for a hall pass.

Mrs. Tews gives him a withering look, and Trey sits back down, smiling. I toss him a jaunty salute as Tommy and I leave.

"Don't forget about me, boys," Trey calls after us. "Tell the girls back home to write!"

Tommy and I leave the principal's office, and I'm turning left to return to English class when Tommy grabs my shoulder. His grip is so strong I'm worried he'll crack my clavicle if he sneezes.

"Hey," he mumbles. "Hey, um . . ."

There's a strange expression on his face, almost a look of pain, like he's constipated.

"You're fucking lucky," he finally blurts. "I don't know how you did it, but you got us out of trouble." He hits me on the back so hard my glasses almost fall off.

"Yeah," I say, pushing them back up my nose. "Well, you know . . ."

"I would've been fucking *dead* if I had gotten in trouble," he continues, trying to sound as tough as possible. "My old man . . ." He whistles. "He would've flipped the fuck *out*."

There's an unfamiliar feeling between us, and it takes me a second to recognize it: *camaraderie*. Tommy's not making fun of me. He's actually trying to be *nice*. For a moment we're just two dudes hanging out.

"Well . . . see you around?" I offer awkwardly.

Tommy groans. "Look, wait . . ." Whatever he wants to say, he can't seem to say it, so instead he says, "You might want to skip lunch today."

"Skip lunch? Why?"

"I don't know. Just maybe you should."

I remember the manic gleam Jake got in his eyes when I

mentioned that Mark would be at lunch, and I remember the wicked blade resting in his palm, and I tell Tommy, "Actually, maybe *you* should skip lunch."

Tommy's expression suddenly goes hard. "What the fuck does that mean? You telling me what to do?" He advances toward me, chest puffed out. "Yo, just 'cause I'm being nice to you for a second doesn't make me a fucking pussy, bro."

I throw my hands up in surrender and backpedal. "What? No, that's not what I meant. I didn't mean it like that—"

Someone knocks on the glass inside the office. It's Mrs. Tews, scowling at us. "Get to class!" she says, her voice muffled by the glass.

Tommy gives me one last dirty look as he stalks away toward Circle A, and I hurry in the opposite direction, toward my locker in the Thunderdome. With the bloody German book in my hand, I feel like a killer who just got away with murder and is about to dispose of the weapon.

CHAPTER 18

ABSURDLY, GIVEN ALL THE ROTTEN STUFF THAT'S happened today, I feel kind of lucky. I guess it's like how you might feel lucky after surviving a car accident, although if you look at it the other way, you're *unlucky* for having gotten in a car accident in the first place.

Whether it's fortune or misfortune, though, today isn't over yet. Tommy's warning that I shouldn't go to lunch means that Mark is probably going to fight me then. Assuming Jake doesn't carve him up like a side of roast beef first.

And then and then and *then*—assuming I live through all that—I get to go home and face the music.

Thinking about it that way, I kind of hope I don't make it past lunch.

I put my German book in my locker and check my phone. There's about twenty minutes left of English class, and after that it's lunch. What the hell am I supposed to do in only twenty minutes?

I slam my locker shut. I wonder if Jake will really stab Mark? I don't have a clue. I feel like I know Jake well, but we've only been hanging out for a couple of months. Maybe I don't know him at all.

Ah, fuck it. Once again I feel guilty for even caring about this little stuff. What a great way to spend Melanie's anniversary, worrying about my petty bullshit.

Why am I going out of my way to protect Jake *or* Mark? I lied to Mr. Braun to get Jake out of trouble—I put my ass on the line—but Jake's just going to get himself back in trouble later today anyhow. And I tried to warn Tommy about Jake, but of course he's too stupid to listen. So fuck 'em both. All those psychopaths can murder each other during lunch if that's what they wanna do. I'd have better luck training the horse dogs to roll over than I would have trying to control these killers.

I feel a little lighter having made that decision. Still, I'm in no rush to return to English—I know it's going to be awkward, and I know Rob is going to embarrass me again—so I take the long way there, strolling slowly around the perimeter of the empty Thunderdome.

I'm walking past the gym when I literally bump into PJ. He stumbles out of the gymnasium doors, struggling to carry the torso of a huge papier-mâché bear. His bow tie hangs untied around his neck like he's a lounge singer. His tuxedo jacket is off and his sleeves are rolled up. I wince as I notice the line of red scars running up his arm where Mark stapled him this morning. Behind PJ, in the gym, a strobe light flickers.

"Hey, PJ. What are you doing?"

"Oh! Hey. I'm just helping with the decorations for the dance. I'm on the party-planning committee."

I shouldn't be surprised. PJ is in every single club in school except for dodgeball, which he was kicked out of because they said he "didn't take it seriously enough." But I mean, who takes dodgeball *seriously*? How boring does your life have to be that you get passionate about dodgeball? Although I take cow painting seriously, so perhaps I can't judge. *People who live in glass houses shouldn't throw dodgeballs* and all that.

PJ gives me a quizzical look. "What are you doing out of class?"

"I just left Mr. Braun's office."

"Oh man, did you get in trouble? What happened?"

"Welllllll, it's a long story. Tommy jumped me in the hallway, and then Jake hit Tommy in the nose with a book, and then Rob embarrassed me in front of the English class, and then I got called into the principal's office, and then Tommy pulled his sleeve up and there were all these crazy burns on it—"

"What? Seriously?!"

"Yeah, *seriously*, and then neither of us got in trouble because I convinced Tommy to lie about it, and then Tommy warned me not to go to lunch—"

PJ interrupts. "Because they're serving tacos today?"

"No, because Mark's going to beat me up then, I guess, and then I warned *Tommy* not to go to lunch—"

"Because they're serving tacos today?"

"No, because Jake has his wicked 'gravity knife,' whatever the fuck that means, and he said he's gonna stab Mark, and I'm pretty sure he means it."

PJ's mouth drops open. "Oh wow. Hold on. Lemme put this down." PJ lowers the bear to the floor and cracks his back, then twists side to side and bounces down to touch his toes. "That bear is heavy!"

He pulls some loose jelly beans out of his pocket. A few nickels and dimes are mixed in with them. "You want some?"

I shake my head, like, *No thanks. I've already had so many jelly beans today.*

PJ pops a few into his mouth and talks around them as he chews. "So, what are you going to do?"

"Nothing," I say proudly. "Not a damn thing. Let those guys fight if they want to. I'm out. I'm done." Saying it makes me feel good, like I'm taking a stand, as opposed to how I should feel, which is cowardly, because I'm doing nothing. But I push that thought down as PJ nods and agrees with me.

"Sensible," he says. "Very sensible."

"Hey, I hate to ruin the mystery, but what are you doing with that bear?"

PJ tosses a jelly bean high into the air and then catches it in his mouth. "I'm helping set up the Fall Fling. Vern is helping too, and I thought it would be a good chance to talk to her, lay a little groundwork before I ask her out at lunch—oh shoot, do you think your fight with Mark is going to mess that up?"

I can't believe PJ is still worried about Vern after I told him our friend might murder someone. "I don't know, man. Maybe?"

"Okay, cool. Well, I guess we'll see. If it doesn't, remember, I need your help with that one part."

I still don't quite understand what PJ's plan consists of, so I try to draw some information out of him by saying, "Oh right, the part with the . . ."

"Boom box. Just push play. Oh, but this bear—we borrowed it from the drama club; it was originally used in *The Winter's Tale*—we had this bear hanging from the ceiling, but then it fell, and Vern was standing right underneath it, so I pushed her out of the way and the bear hit me instead."

He rubs his forehead, and I notice a big bump starting to swell there. "I thought she'd be glad I saved her life, but I think I pushed her a little too hard, because she knocked over a couple of tables full of stuff. The punch bowl and, uh, some cupcakes. Some glasses and plates too . . . the chocolate fountain."

His face flushes red all the way to his ears. He dips down to touch his toes again and arches his back in pain.

"Aaaaaanyway, the teachers said we can't use the bear now because it's too dangerous."

He pulls Mr. Reali's massive key ring out of his pocket, bristling with keys. "So I gotta lug this bear up and lock it behind the drama stage. Bonus: I can get a new shirt, maybe, behind the stage there."

I'm not looking forward to going back to English class after the scene I caused, and I figure I won't be missed if I make another quick detour. Ms. Hunt will just think I'm still at the principal's office.

"I'll give you a hand," I offer.

"Are you sure? Oh, thanks!"

I grab one of the bear's big paws, PJ grabs the head, and we awkwardly shuffle-step the bear across the lobby toward Circle B, where the drama stage/auditorium takes up about a quarter of the second floor.

"Hey, where's your tuxedo jacket?"

PJ grimaces. "I tried gluing my bouquet back together, but I accidentally glued it to my jacket, so I left it soaking in a bucket of water to try to dissolve the glue."

"In a bucket of water? I would think a tuxedo jacket would be dry-clean only."

PJ stops, stricken. "Oh. Crap. Good point." He sighs heavily. "Maybe today isn't the best day to ask Vern out after all. . . ."

I notice that the staple holes on his arm have started bleeding again and nod my head at them. "Dude, you're bleeding."

"Crap! Hold on—" PJ gently puts his end of the bear down. There's a bathroom a couple of feet away, and he runs in.

A minute later PJ shuffles out, pale and serious.

He looks up and down the hall. "Uh, Kirby, c'mere. You might want to see this."

I follow PJ into the men's room, our footsteps echoing on the tiles. Being in the bathroom with PJ reminds me uncomfortably of this morning, when I cowered in a stall while he got beat up. The stillness of the room, the echoes, give the room the feeling of a church, and I badly want to confess to PJ, *I was there. I watched them beat you up.* But before I can say anything, PJ points to a pair of shoes visible under one of the bathroom stalls. Someone is sitting on the toilet.

I recognize the sneakers immediately, black leather with shiny gold trim. Rock-star kicks.

The shoes don't move, not even a little, not even after PJ and I walk over and stand right in front of the stall door.

PJ pauses with his hand on the closed stall door. He looks at me, scared, and pushes the stall open with a creak like the front door of a haunted house.

Jake is slumped on the toilet. Eyes closed, mouth open, a thin line of drool dripping from the corner of his mouth. He doesn't look asleep, like he did this morning in art class. He looks *dead*.

At first I think he really is dead, but then he twitches and I breathe again. PJ clears his throat tentatively, and Jake jerks a little, his eyes opening a crack. He tilts his head back and peers at us between his barely open eyelids.

"Kirb?" he croaks.

PJ and I stand in horrified silence as Jake breaks into a wide smile, like we just threw him a surprise birthday party. "Hey, guys!" he slurs. "Oh man, it's great to see you."

"Jake, what are you doing?"

He looks around groggily, like my question is hard to answer because it's so obvious. "Nothing. What are you guys doing?"

"Are you okay?" PJ asks.

"Yeah," Jake slurs. "Fine." He tries to stand up, and does for a second, then slumps down to the floor on rubbery legs. He sits down on the floor right in front of the toilet, where everybody's pee drips.

This can't be Jake, because the Jake I know would never do that. This is way beyond a little charcoal on the sleeve of his shirt.

"Get the fuck up," I say, disgusted. "Get off the dirty fucking floor."

Normal Jake would launch himself at me like a bobcat for talking to him like that, but this version of Jake just smiles beatifically. "Not that dirty," he says, his eyes closing as he pats the tiles like he's petting a fluffy dog. "Not that dirty. S'fine."

PJ leans over to me. "I think he's on drugs."

"Oh really, PJ?! Is that what you think? Are you sure we shouldn't have the lab boys at CSI run some tests?"

Jake flaps a limp hand at us. "S'fine." He smiles. I've never seen him so happy. "I'm just glad to see you guys."

All the times Jake said he was tired because he was drinking NyQuil, was it actually something else? I guess it was. I know he drinks, and he smokes weed every now and then, but he never told us about anything heavier.

Man, I must be a pretty shitty friend not to have noticed this.

Jake seems to read my mind because the fog in his eyes lifts a little as he looks at me. "Dad must have upped his dosage," he says. "They're usually tens, but I think the doctor must've given him fifteens."

Oh right, his dad's painkillers. I guess that's better than . . . heroin? I'm really reaching for a silver lining here. Jake tries to stand again and manages it this time, but after taking an experimental step toward us, he wobbles to one side and leans against the stall.

"Fifteen . . . maybe twenty."

"You don't look so good," PJ says. "Maybe you should go to the nurse."

Jake laughs, which is encouraging. "Uh, I don't think so."

He straightens up. His slick black hair has flopped down, like it often does, but he doesn't push it back, and I wish he would. He doesn't look like himself that way. "I just need some fresh air."

"Ah yes," I say. "Fresh air. The antidote to drugs."

Jake gives me a dirty look. *Good.*

PJ pulls his phone halfway out of his pocket to check the time. "I hate to say this, but we should probably get going. I still have to drop the bear off and then get these keys back to Mr. Reali." He shakes the massive bundle of keys.

It sure is a lot of keys. Heck, a key ring like that could probably unlock any door in the whole school. I remember Trey asking if I thought the raccoon was still up on the roof, and I'm seized by a strange compulsion.

"If you want some fresh air, I know just the place."

We drop the bear behind the drama stage. PJ looks through the racks of costumes in the wings but can't find a replacement shirt for his battered tuxedo.

Backstage, in the far corner, we find the rickety wooden ladder that leads up to the catwalk that runs through the rafters, high above the stage. I crane my neck back to look up at the catwalk, half hidden in the dark curtains above.

"Are you sure you can do this?" I ask Jake.

"Yeah," he says. "I'm cool."

Jake does seem quite a bit better, although he's still acting weird—he keeps remarking how amazing everything is and saying how much he loves me and PJ—but he's not stumbling or sleepy anymore.

The three of us climb the ladder to the catwalk, the whole thing giving a disturbing shake with every step. It's dark up on the catwalk and it smells like dust. Musty velvet curtains hang around us, muffling the sound of our footsteps on the metal grating. I peer over the railing at the stage far below us, then remind myself not to do that again as I grip the railing with both hands.

At the far end of the catwalk there's another short ladder with a cage around it locked with a silver padlock. PJ hands me the janitor's key ring, and I search through the keys for a silver one. There are three, and the second one works.

We climb up the ladder and push open a trapdoor in the ceiling that opens with a loud creak.

Sunlight pours down, blinding me. I close my eyes and grab the lip of the trapdoor and haul myself up onto the roof. I blink a couple of times, and then I'm looking at blue sky.

We're on the roof.

PJ spreads his arms like wings and runs in a circle, scattering the white gravel that covers the rooftop. "This is awesome!" He crosses to the edge of the roof and leans over so far that I'm afraid he's going to tip over.

"Dude, be careful!"

"It's fine. It's not too high."

I creep toward the edge and peek over to discover that PJ's wrong. It is *way* too high. I look down into the courtyard and see the top of the flagpole below us. A potent rush of vertigo makes my head spin. It's weird that flying with Dad, being one thousand feet up, doesn't bother me, but standing on a roof thirty feet up makes me nervous, but there you have it.

"It's not too high," PJ repeats. "Besides, if I fell, I would just land on that ledge."

He points down to a narrow ledge about five feet below us that circles the outside of the school.

I step back from the edge, and my heart rate dips back to normal. It *is* pretty cool up here. The roof is circular, like the building below us, and covered with little pebbles, like a stony beach.

I look back to check on Jake. He's on the opposite side of the roof, arms crossed, looking out at the woods behind the school.

I try to enjoy the scenery myself. The sky is clear, limitless. It feels like if I could figure out how to *let go*, I could float up, up, and away into the endless blue. It's been so long since I went flying with Dad, I didn't realize how much I missed gaining a little altitude.

Trey would be disappointed to see that there are no vultures circling.

The dead raccoon is a couple of feet away, to our left, and PJ and I walk over to check it out. Getting thrown onto the roof hasn't done anything to improve its condition. Its guts are leaking out in a wide splat, like a dropped cherry pie.

PJ whistles. "Grody."

"Wicked," I agree.

Jake strolls over, elegant as a runway model, smoking a joint.

"GEEZ," I yell. "Don't you ever stop with the fucking drugs?!"

Jake winces. "Not so loud, dude! I'm trying to even out. It's just weed, for fuck's sake."

"It *is* just weed," PJ agrees.

"Thank you," Jake says, pulling another long toke and finally smoothing his hair back, thank God. He takes in the scenery and sighs. "Wow. This is *beautiful*."

He sits down next to the raccoon and dangles his legs over the edge, which makes my heart skip.

PJ sits down next to Jake, pleased to temporarily be in his good graces, although I'm pretty sure it's just the pills making Jake so friendly. PJ dangles his legs over the edge too, kicking them back and forth like a kid on a swing.

I sit down a few feet away from the edge and slowly scoot forward till I reach the lip. I try to stick my legs out over the edge, but I can't. They simply won't do it, so I cross them under me instead.

For a couple of minutes the three of us just chill and stare out over the schoolyard, wrapped in the rich, earthy smell of Jake's joint. It's beautiful up here. I should be enjoying it, but I can't. I'm so annoyed with Jake. First the knife and now this. It doesn't matter if I get him out of trouble; he's just going to get himself back in. He's *wasting* his life. It makes me want to push him off the damn roof.

I pick a smooth little pebble off the roof next to me and examine it. It looks just like all the other pebbles on the roof. It's white, about the size of a large pearl. It's warm in my hand, from sitting in the sun. I turn it over and notice a small vein of gray running up the side. On the side directly opposite the gray line, there's a little pucker in the rock, a kind of fold. The rock is oblong, like an egg. I realize that actually it's different from the other rocks on the roof. It's unique.

I toss it off the roof and watch it fall all the way to the schoolyard below. Then I grab a handful of stones and let them run through my fingers with a clatter. Nobody will ever notice that one rock is missing from all of these.

Clouds float past the sun, creating shifting patterns of light and dark that drift across the parking lot. Beyond the parking lot, cars cruise slowly through the school zone on Main Street.

Jake quietly says, "I think I'm moving to California."

"Uh-huh," I say. "Sure."

Jake says "I'm moving to California" so often, I've gotten used to tuning it out. It's almost his catchphrase. Like one time he asked for avocado on his hot dog at the Shuckburgh Corner Store, and of course they didn't have any, and Jake said, *This is bullshit. I'm moving to California.*

Another time I was at Jake's house and I heard him upstairs getting in a huge fight with his dad. When he came down to the living room where I was watching TV, he was crying. It was the only time I've seen him cry. "My dad's an asshole," he said. "I'm moving to California."

We walked to the drive-in afterward, climbed through a hole in the fence, and watched the end of one of the Fast and the Furious movies. I can't remember which one. The one where they drive their cars fast. Jake spent the whole movie describing how great California is and all the stuff he was gonna do with his sister when he got there.

The whole California thing, it's just a fantasy. One of those daydreams you construct to help you get through the tough parts of the day.

Jake's eyes are half closed as he considers me, smoke drifting out of his nose like a dragon. "I mean it this time, Kirby."

Something in his tone of voice makes me think he's serious. "What?"

"California is nice," PJ offers cheerfully. He points to Jake's joint. "Marijuana is legal there, so that'll be nice for you. And Kirby and I can visit you. We'll come out to the coast, have a few laughs. . . ."

"How are you going to get there?" I ask skeptically.

"There's a bus leaving from the Greyhound station down Main Street today at three thirty. I'll walk over there and buy a ticket."

Wait . . . is he serious? I can never tell when he's kidding. God, I hate him.

"You always say you're gonna move to California." I try to mimic Jake's voice, his deep monotone, as I say, "I'm gonna go to California and learn to surf and go shopping with my sister. Shuckburgh, Sucksburgh, Fuckburgh. School sucks. Everything sucks. Blah, blah, blah." I throw another rock off the roof and then stare Jake right in the eyes to show I'm not scared of him. "Why don't you wake up and smell what you're shoveling?"

Jake looks at the joint between his fingers like it just said something, then tosses it over his shoulder, back onto the roof. He takes a long, shaky breath and looks straight ahead, out over the schoolyard. "I can't stop taking my dad's pills." He says it in a weird voice. He doesn't sound confident like he usually does. It sounds like a sentence he's never said out loud before.

"He doesn't notice," Jake continues. "The bottles are so big and he's zonked out most of the time himself. Or he's not even there. He's on the road so much. . . ." He takes another deep breath and plunges forward. "California is warm. I can go outside and walk on the beach. And it would be nice to see my sister again. It's been years. I bet I'm taller than her now. I don't know if I am or not. Isn't that weird?"

I want to tell Jake that I know how he feels, but I can't.

He turns and sees my expression, which I guess doesn't look great. "I know it annoys you that I talk about my sister so much, but maybe she can help me. . . . I don't know." He moves the pebbles around, raking them into lines with his fingers. "I just gotta do something different."

A little voice in my head suggests, *Maybe you should move to California too, bud.* I could start over. Avoid my parents and all their bullshit and Melanie and all my bullshit—but I can't. As annoyed as I am with my parents, I wouldn't do that to them.

Jake already said when the bus leaves, but I ask again anyhow, to fill the silence. "What time does the bus leave?"

"Three thirty. I'm gonna leave right after school, and by the time my dad gets home from his trip tomorrow and sees I'm not there, I'll be, like, halfway through Texas or whatever. I'm not gonna tell my mom because she'll try to stop me. But once I'm already there"—he throws a handful of pebbles off the roof—"I guess she'll be cool with it."

"You're going to *bus* there?" PJ says. "That's gonna take forever."

Jake shrugs. "I've got more time than money."

"How much money do you have?"

He pulls a crumpled wad of money out of his pocket and smooths the bills out on his leg. I count three tens, a twenty, a couple ones.

I've never taken a bus to California, but I'm pretty sure it costs more than fifty-something bucks. I reach into my pocket and hand Jake another twenty, which is all I have.

Jake protests, pushing it away. "Ah, no, man, c'mon. Don't."

"I honestly don't think you can make it to California with only fifty bucks."

He grudgingly takes the money. "I guess you're right."

PJ hands Jake a two-dollar bill. "Sorry. It's all I've got. I spent the rest on jelly beans."

Jake scrutinizes the bill. "Did you draw sunglasses on George Washington?"

"No. I drew sunglasses on *Thomas Jefferson*. But don't worry. It's still good. They'll take it." PJ nudges Jake. "Treat yourself. Buy some nice marijuana."

"PJ," I say.

"Sorry."

I have a sudden urge to get off this damn roof. "I gotta get back to class."

"Yeah," PJ says, checking the time on his phone, "I have to give these keys back to Mr. Reali, then finish setting up in the gym."

"Okay, cool," Jake says, staring out across the parking lot. "Just give me one more minute. I just want to spend one more minute . . . like this."

- - -

Like I said, Melanie got sick twice. The first time she was five years old and I was only three, so I don't remember it. She got my bone marrow, I got these lovely kitchen-countertop teeth, and she got better.

My parents periodically reminded us of the fact that it was my bone marrow that saved Melanie and that I was *so brave* for donating it, but whenever they brought it up, Melanie and I would give each other unimpressed looks, because, I mean, c'mon, I was only three. It's not like I volunteered.

She got sick the second time when she was seventeen. For a while it seemed like she had a really bad flu, which was strange because it was the end of the summer. Then one day I came home and found Mom and Dad crying together at the kitchen table.

When the school year started, Melanie's teachers gave me homework to bring home to her. I felt weird going into her classes and then lugging all her printouts home. But I felt even worse a few weeks later, when those same teachers *stopped* giving me her homework.

I would've let the doctors take more bone marrow from me—I would've let them saw my fucking legs off and pull every tooth out of my head—but they said a marrow transplant wouldn't help this time.

My parents visited Melanie in the hospital every day, but they only brought me on the weekends, because during the week I had school. But one Wednesday, Mom took me out of school to visit the hospital while Dad was working.

When we got to the hospital, it was weird. Mom and I didn't go into Melanie's room together. Instead, she stopped me in the hallway outside her door. The hallway smelled like bleach, white lights humming overhead like hungry mosquitoes.

Mom kneeled down and looked me in the eyes. "Go talk to your sister."

"Aren't you coming in?"

"Not right now. Just go in and talk to her yourself. It's all right."

But it wasn't all right, and I knew it.

Even though I had been visiting every weekend for the past couple of months and had spent countless hours sitting in the vinyl-covered easy chair next to Melanie's bed, I hadn't talked to her much since she'd gotten sick. It's not that I didn't *want* to talk to her; there just wasn't much to talk about—aside from the obvious subject that we all tried to avoid. Mom and Dad spent most of their time in the room standing over her bed, watching her sleep. She slept a lot near the end.

I wasn't sure why Mom wanted me to go into the room alone and talk to Melanie—but I had a bad feeling that if I thought about it for a second, I could figure it out.

Mom nudged me again. "Go talk to your sister, honey."

I tiptoed in, afraid to break the delicate silence of the hospital room. White machines on poles surrounded Melanie, beeping and breathing quietly like little animals attending her. She was awake, but just barely.

My big sister looked very small in the middle of her huge

hospital bed. The bed had all these complicated controls on the side of it and thick metal bars around it, and it seemed strange to need something so big and sturdy to support her thin body. The head of the bed was elevated, and Melanie was staring vacantly at the top corner of the room. There was a TV bolted to the wall across from her bed, and it was playing *Die Hard* with the sound off, but she wasn't watching. *Who the fuck puts* Die Hard *on in the cancer ward?* I thought, then realized they probably just tuned it to TBS like six hours ago, and no one had been in the room since then.

The room was all white and gray except for the rainbow-colored bracelets that hung loose around Melanie's wrists. They were friendship bracelets that she had woven herself. She would clip a safety pin to the bedsheet and then take a bunch of different colors of thread and attach them to the pin, as an anchor, then weave them around one another for hours and hours until they formed a bracelet. She had made so many during the time she'd been in the hospital that she had gotten really good at it. She'd even made one for me, which I was wearing, already a little dirty and falling apart because I wore it nonstop.

She was bald, and had been for a while, because of the chemotherapy. Remembering it now, picturing her frail body on top of the white bed, barely making a dent in the sheets, I recall her looking very pretty with a shaved head, although I must be remembering that wrong. You don't look pretty when you're dying of cancer, right?

I sat in a chair next to her, and slowly, slowly she turned to look at me. She moved like she was underwater. She gave me a sleepy smile. Her eyes had a faraway look, looking at me but also through me. I wondered if she was seeing things I couldn't see, like the future or the past. Then I realized I was being silly and that she was just on a lot of morphine.

"Hi," I said.

"Hi," she whispered back, and it felt so good to hear her voice, even if it was cracked and barely there.

I knew this was going to be the last conversation we ever had—that's why Mom had brought me today—so I savored every word Melanie said. The only problem was, I couldn't think of any words to say! All the normal conversation openings didn't seem appropriate.

How's it going?

Not great.

What's new?

Not much. Just dying.

The moment was so big, it seemed inane to fill it with small talk. I felt like we should talk about something important—but I didn't want to. I wanted to share one last normal moment with my sister.

But I couldn't hold on to the present. I felt the unstoppable weight of the future barreling toward us.

I closed my eyes and retreated into the past. Melanie and I were sitting together in the station wagon's rear seat, facing backward, watching the road unspool behind our car. It was nighttime, and we were driving away from our home in

Bethlehem, the dark road illuminated by streetlights, our house shrinking smaller and smaller as we drove away.

Something small and warm touched my hand, and I opened my eyes. Melanie was looking at me and holding my hand.

"What's . . . this . . . movie?"

She was looking at me, not the TV, so it took me a second to realize she meant *Die Hard*.

"Uh, it's *Die Hard*," I said.

Her mouth opened in a soundless laugh. "*Too soon*," she croaked.

I wanted to laugh at her joke, but I just couldn't. I wanted to scream. She squeezed my hand, and I calmed down a little bit.

"Please say something," I said.

She was very tired and struggled to focus. "It's hard," she finally said.

She blinked slowly and smiled at me, and that smile broke my heart. I had always thought that a broken heart was just a figure of speech, but I could feel the break, a deep and irreparable break inside me. I embraced the pain, an extension of her, and hoped it would never heal.

"Do you remember when I had a broken leg?"

She nodded.

"Do you remember sitting on my bed and keeping me company?"

She nodded again. We sat in silence for a minute. I looked at the machines around her and wondered what they were supposed to do. They breathed and beeped quietly, dribbling life into her. I looked back at Melanie. She was beautiful.

"I love you," I said, trying very hard not to cry. I didn't want to make her sad.

She nodded again, and she said, "I love you, too." Her voice was smaller than a moth. It flapped in front of my face and then flew away.

Her eyes closed, and that was the end of the conversation.

I stood and turned to look into the hallway, but Mom wasn't there, so I walked into the little bathroom next to Melanie's bed. I closed the door behind me and stood in the dark.

I waited there for a while, and as my eyes adjusted to the dark, the hard geometric planes of the bathroom emerged around me. I put my face close to the wall and looked at the little tiny bumps in the paint. The texture of the wall.

After a long time I finally turned on the bright fluorescent light over the sink. Everything looked different. I realized that the bathroom had been a time machine and I had traveled years into the future—how far I wasn't sure. I prepared myself to step out of the bathroom and find Melanie's room empty. The bed is empty and dressed in fresh, smooth sheets. All the machines are gone and the window curtains are drawn back, letting warm morning light stream in. A janitor pushing a flat mop down the hall sees me standing there and stops. "Are you lost?"

I wondered what future-Kirby looked like, so I turned to inspect myself in the mirror. I was rather alarmed that I didn't recognize the guy staring back at me. Tears were streaming down his face. He stared at me for a long time, until I looked away.

Someone knocked on the door.

It was Mom. "Kirby? Are you in there?"

"Yeah, hold on." I ran cold water and splashed it on my face, then dried off with a couple of scratchy paper towels.

I came out of the bathroom and Mom was waiting for me in the hallway, purse on her shoulder. We were leaving. Melanie was asleep in her bed, a deep sleep, her mouth open.

I hesitated in the doorway. I wanted to go back and talk to Melanie again, see her little smile again, but I was worried that if I walked over to her bed now and nudged her, I'd discover that she wasn't asleep; she was dead. Or—somehow this possibility was even worse—I'd nudge her awake and she'd look at me with drug-fogged eyes, not recognizing me.

Jake and PJ stand up, and PJ notices me still sitting. "Kirb, are you all right?"

"Yeah, I'm fine," I lie. I stand up unsteadily, pins and needles prickling through my legs. I wobble, and Jake grabs my arm before I fall off the roof.

"Whoa, easy, tiger." He grins.

Like an idiot, I give Jake a big hug, almost knocking us *both* off the roof. "I'm going to miss you, man."

Usually he'd push me away or punch me in the balls, but he's either still high or more human than I thought, because instead he actually hugs me back. "Jesus, it's just California," he mutters into my shoulder. "Besides, the day's not over yet. So soak it up while you can, jerk."

He's right; the day isn't over yet.

Still hugging Jake, I reach into his back pocket and feel that the knife is still there.

"Hey, whoa, what are you doing?" Jake asks, kind of laughing. "Don't grab my ass—*wait.*"

He realizes my intentions a second too late and tries to push me away, but I pull the knife out of his back pocket and squirm out of his reach as he tries to grab my arm.

"Motherfucker!" Jake yells, fingers curled like a jungle cat, lunging at me.

I twist and duck under his arms, then take two quick steps toward the edge of the roof and throw the knife over the edge. I lob it lightly, like a dove taking flight from my hand, and for a moment it floats up into the blue before dropping into the courtyard below.

Jake grabs my shoulder and spins me around, eyes burning like green flame. He's about to say something when a sound on the other side of the trapdoor makes us all freeze: the loud crackle of a walkie-talkie.

From the other side of the trapdoor in the middle of the roof comes a muffled voice that's unmistakably Mr. Hartman. "I'm heading up to the roof now," he says. "The cage was open. Tell Mr. Reali to make sure he keeps that thing locked in the future."

We all stare at one another, petrified, then spin around wildly looking for a place to hide. There's no cover. The roof is wide open.

There's only one option.

PJ points to the edge of the roof and says, "The ledge!"

Oh shit. Oh no.

PJ drops down over the edge of the roof, onto the ledge that he pointed out when we first came up here, then frantically waves for Jake and me to follow him. There's no time to think. We get down on our hands and knees and drop over the edge too, onto a ledge that I'm dismayed to discover is only a little wider than our feet, barely enough to stand on. As he steps down, Jake slips on some pebbles on the ledge—probably friends of the little pebble I threw to its doom, hell-bent on revenge—and almost falls two stories to the courtyard below. PJ and I grab the front of his shirt as he windmills his arms desperately. We pull him to the wall, and he hugs it for dear life. We all do.

I reluctantly pry my fingers off the roof's lip above our heads, and a second later we hear the rusty creak of the trapdoor opening. Mr. Hartman huffs and puffs as he hauls himself up onto the roof.

"What's he doing up here?" PJ whispers to me.

"He's probably grabbing the raccoon," I guess.

Standing on the ledge, pressed flat against the wall, we've got maybe six inches of ledge between us and the wide blue yonder. The top of the roof is just above our heads. We have to crouch down to avoid being seen.

I hold my breath as Mr. Hartman's shoes crunch on the pebbles. He's walking away from us, toward the raccoon, like I hoped he would. I hear the flap and ripple of a trash bag opening. Mr. Hartman stops walking, and I expect to hear a heavy *thump* as he scoops the raccoon into the trash bag, but instead there's a long silence.

"What's he doing?" PJ asks.

"I don't know."

I want to peek over the edge to see him, but I'm afraid he'll see me. What if he's looking over here?

"I've got an idea," PJ says. He pulls out his phone and turns on the camera, then slowly raises it above the ledge like a periscope just in time for us to see Mr. Hartman bend down and pick up the joint that's next to the raccoon.

"Well, this is interesting," Jake says.

Mr. Hartman stares at the joint and then looks around the roof. He couldn't be more conspicuous. His bright checked sports coat screams against the blue sky and white pebbles. He glances back in our direction but doesn't see PJ's phone. It's just the tip sticking up over the edge. He scans the roof one more time, considers the joint again, then pulls a lighter out of his pocket.

No.

Way.

I tap record on PJ's phone just as Mr. Hartman lights the joint and takes a deep pull from it. He holds the smoke in for a long time before letting it out with a grateful sigh. He closes his eyes and turns his face toward the sun. He takes a couple more puffs, pinches the joint out, then slides the butt into his jacket's breast pocket. He grabs the raccoon by its tail, flops it into the trash bag, and heads back down the ladder, closing the trapdoor behind him with a loud *clang*.

None of us can believe what we just saw. We climb back up onto the roof and watch it over and over on PJ's phone.

Jake points to the screen, like a referee watching an instant replay. "He's clearly smoking the joint there, right?"

"Absolutely, yeah," I say. "I mean, he lights the damn thing. Why would he do that unless he was smoking it?"

"And look, you can see the smoke there when he exhales," PJ says.

We watch the video maybe a million times, then climb back down the ladder and out of the drama theater. As we hit the hallway, the bell for fifth period rings.

Looks like I missed English class entirely, which is good. Lunch is next, and I should be worried about Mark, but I'm not. I'm not worried about him at all. I threw Jake's knife away, so I don't have to worry about him killing anyone. And if Mark wants to beat me up? Let him. Who gives a shit? It's like getting that little bit of altitude on the roof really did change my perspective. You realize how small each of us is in the grand scheme of things.

We join the crowd of kids heading toward the cafeteria, a general air of fun and happiness in the crowd, everyone excited that for the next forty minutes they won't be learning anything.

"Okay," PJ says seriously, "regarding Vern, at lunch, let's just play it by ear. I'll bring the boom box and the other thing, and if you and Mark don't fight, then we'll still try to ask Vern out. Remember: Hit play when I do the split. Sound good?"

PJ's single-mindedness should bug me, but instead it's a welcome distraction. I give him a thumbs-up. "You got it, pal."

He arranges his shirt and stops walking to pose like a model, leaning nonchalantly against a locker. "How do I look?"

PJ's ruffled tuxedo shirt has gray smudges all over the front from clinging to the ledge. Bloody pinpricks run up the one sleeve and there's a big bump on his forehead where the bear fell on him.

Jake opens his mouth, clearly about to say, *You look like shit*, so I give PJ a manly punch on the arm and say, "Dude, you look great."

"Thanks! Ouch!" He rubs his arm where I hit him. "Careful, I'm still a little bruised."

CHAPTER 19

THE CAFETERIA IS ON THE FAR SIDE OF THE
Thunderdome, next to the gym, so we hit our lockers on the
way there. Jake and I put our books away, and PJ pulls out two
bulging duffel bags. I swear his locker is like the TARDIS; it
must be bigger on the inside than it is on the outside. I guess
one bag has the boom box. I'm not sure all of what's in the
other one, but there's something rattling around inside that
almost sounds like . . . Ping-Pong balls? After all the strange
stuff I've seen pulled out of book bags in the past twenty-four
hours, nothing would surprise me.

As crazy as the Thunderdome is in the morning, it's even
crazier during lunch, when everyone is wide-awake and rammy
from sitting at a desk all day.

PJ, Jake, and I join the herd, down the hallway and into the cafeteria. Loaded up with his big bags, PJ bumps into people every time he turns to talk to Jake or me. "Tacos," he says in an awed hush. "Tacos, tacos, tacos!"

The cafeteria is well designed to handle the crush of students. There are four different doors, each one leading to identical buffet setups with steam tables. Past that, the center of the room has a long island of premade food: chips, drinks, stuff like that. The rest of the wide space is long, tan Formica tables with attached benches.

A few teachers roam the cafeteria aisles to maintain order, although there really aren't enough to cover the whole space; the light teacher presence, along with Mr. Hartman's noticeable absence, makes this an ideal place for Mark to attack.

As soon as we walk into the crowded cafeteria—with the loud *thwack* of plastic trays slapping against tabletops and the redolent smell of cooking hamburger meat—my heart rate spikes. I thought I wasn't worried about Mark anymore. I thought I had bigger problems that made this scuffle seem unimportant, but I guess my brain didn't share that information with my body.

As we join the slow-moving line at the far-left buffet, I try to keep my head down. But Jake stands on his tiptoes, as visible as a lighthouse, swiveling his head and trying to see above the crowd. He's happy, animated.

He slides his hands into the back pockets of his slim black jeans and places one black-and-gold sneaker lightly in front of him, a ballerina relaxing for a moment between pirouettes. "You see anything?" he asks hopefully.

"Ooh! Ooh! I see something!" PJ says. "I! See! *Tacooooooooos!*"

Yes, it's taco day. The smell of hamburger meat is thick in the air, and I can tell that the cooks here have *never* eaten Mexican food before, because it smells like sloppy joes. I grab a mint-green tray with little sections in it for the different foods—the trays are a superheavy plastic that looks like it will still be here a thousand years from now, after the fall of humanity—and start assembling tacos from the steaming buffet before us.

Jake rolls up the sleeves of his white oxford—he has this special roll that makes the sleeves lie flat very neatly—as he grabs a tray and starts loading up his tacos with the different fixin's. "Ooh!" he says with delight. "Guacamole."

I have a tender stomach, so I don't put much on my tacos: tomatoes, lettuce, a little hamburger. PJ gives my barren tacos a pitying glance. "Dude, at least put some cheese on there."

"I can't. Lactose intolerant, remember?" I almost add, *Remember this morning?* But I stop myself just in time.

"Oh right, I forgot your"—PJ flutters his fingers around his stomach—"stomach thing."

"Lactose intolerance," I specify.

"You shouldn't be so intolerant," Jake says. "Open your heart to dairy, Kirbo."

"My heart's not the body part I'll be opening if I eat dairy."

PJ smothers his tacos in jalapeños and hot sauce. He fills a couple of little cups with extra hot sauce, snaps lids on them, and puts them in his pockets too, along with some loose jalapeños.

"What the hell are you doing?"

PJ shrugs. "Never know when they might come in handy."

"Dude, you guys are both crazy," I say.

We leave the line holding our pale green trays of fake Mexican food and wander into the lunchroom proper, a wide space divided by long rows of lunch tables, maybe twenty rows wide, most tables already full of happily talking kids. The tables are tan, the floor an indescribable taupe, the walls a beige that just sucks the life out of you. It's like a desert where colors go to die, our pale green trays the only hue struggling for survival in the tan wasteland.

I scan the lunchroom, but I still don't see Mark, so I try to steer us toward the closest table. "Let's sit over here, in the corner," I suggest.

Jake continues drifting toward the center of the cafeteria. "Nah. C'mon, let's go this way." He smiles.

"Dude, c'mon! Quit messing around!"

And that's when I spot Mark, sitting across the room, at a far-right corner table on the other side of the premade-food island. He's easy to spot because he and Tommy are sitting near each other, and they're the two tallest kids in the room. Also, Mark still has his big black eye, and Tommy's nose is red and swollen. They stick out like two battle-scarred stuntmen at a day care.

Mark sits near the middle of the table, glaring at me with his one good eye as he spits a glob of Skoal juice into a chocolate milk carton. Tommy's on the outside corner of the bench, a dangerous frown under his swollen nose. Myka hangs on his arm, and Cigarettes and Jono sit across from him, on the other side of the table. When Tommy nods in my direction, they both turn around and grin at me like hyenas.

Rob's sitting with them too, and everyone at their table—a couple of other football players and cheerleaders, the cool kids—starts looking our way and chatting excitedly, ready for the big game to begin.

I was hoping Mark might not be mad anymore, but if anything, he looks *angrier* than he did this morning. He doesn't take his cold eyes off me as he idly scratches the scar that runs up the side of his blond crew cut.

Fear stops me in my tracks, and Jake bumps into my back with the edge of his tray. "Yo, dude, what's the holdup?" He follows my gaze to Mark and Tommy's table.

"Hey! Let's go sit with them!" Jake waves at them, and Tommy's eyes bug out as he gives Jake the finger. Mark doesn't react, just keeps staring at me with the focus of a hunter measuring the distance between his bow and a deer.

Jake laughs like Tommy and Mark are old friends he's delighted to see and talks to me over his shoulder as he heads toward them. "Look at Tommy's nose! Holy shit! C'mon, let's say hi."

"No! Dude, c'mon . . ."

"It's fine," Jake says, walking ahead of me and rounding the island. "Those punks ain't gonna do shit. Watch."

"No! Don't! *Jake!*" I grab his arm, but he rolls his shoulder and slides out of my grip gracefully without breaking his stride.

I scan the cafeteria desperately for a teacher and spot Herr

Bronner's safety-orange suspenders way across the room. It looks like he's the closest teacher, but he's still at least a dozen rows away. Not close at all, and looking in the other direction.

Jake strolls lightly between the rows of tables, behind the backs of kids eating, and I follow, pleading with him. "Jake? Please? Stop!"

That familiar charge is building in the air, heat lightning on a summer day, and kids turn—broken taco shells paused halfway to their mouths, the hair on their arms standing straight up—to watch Jake stride past.

Tommy leans down the table to talk to Mark, and I can just hear him ask, "Can I, Mark? Please?"

"Okay," Mark replies, spitting his chewing tobacco onto his plate. "But save Kirby for me."

We're maybe ten steps away, about to cross into the empty aisle between the tables, when Tommy stands up. The kids at his table watch with avid fascination, the cheerleaders stifling mean giggles, everyone delighted to find themselves ringside at an impending fight, even one that's clearly going to last only two seconds. Tommy is a refrigerator, a man cast from iron, his fists two sledgehammers. Jake is half his size, and he looks very slim in his tight black jeans and fitted white oxford. Tommy is going to knock Jake right out of his fancy sneakers with one punch, and we all wince in anticipation of Tommy's fearful blow.

Everyone except Jake, who is so relaxed he's acting like he's still on the school's roof admiring the view, approaching Mark's table with catlike grace, almost dancing. He points at

Tommy's nose and sings in a high, clear voice, "Rudolph the red-nosed reindeeeeeer, had a very shiny nooooooose. . . ."

Tommy lifts his tree-trunk legs over the cafeteria table's bench and steps into the aisle to meet Jake.

I stop at the edge of the aisle, but Jake continues walking into the open space between the rows of tables. Tommy cocks his fist back and shifts his broad shoulders sideways, a freight train of meat bearing down on Jake, but Jake doesn't slow down. He doesn't even put his *tray* down—he's still holding it with both his hands!

Tommy is about to swing forward and knock Jake's head right off his shoulders when Jake tosses his tray at Tommy. He doesn't throw it hard, just lobs it underhand, so for one second, at the top of its arc, the tray hangs suspended in front of Tommy's shocked face, blobs of guacamole and hamburger meat floating weightless in midair.

Tommy jerks back from the mess of flying food, and Jake skips forward the last two steps between them and kicks Tommy in the balls, *hard*, a football player punting a field goal. Tommy bucks forward, grabbing his crotch, and as his face comes down, Jake hits him on the chin with a vicious uppercut.

The tray hits the ground a second before Tommy does. The loud flat *BAM* of the tray, a familiar lunchroom sound, makes everyone within earshot reflexively go, "Ooooooooooh!"

Myka screams. Tommy crumples into a limp pile in the aisle, taco mess dripping all over his football jersey.

I'm still holding my tray, slowly backing away from the aisle. I desperately scan the cafeteria again for a teacher and see with relief that Herr Bronner is at least looking in our direction to see what the commotion is, but he's still halfway across the room, unsure what the disturbance is. Two teachers from other corners of the room are converging as well, one talking urgently into a walkie-talkie.

Jono and Cigarettes jump off the bench, so eager they trip over each other trying to get to Jake first. Jake steps over Tommy's unconscious body and grabs the tray off his chest as he does. Jono is closest to Jake, and as he stumbles over the table's bench, Jake steps forward to meet him, swings in a full circle, and smacks him flat in the face with the tray. There's a dull *crack*, and as Jake pulls the tray back to hit him again, I see for a second that Jono's face is covered in blood. Another flat *crack* and a wet *smooch* as Jake pulls the tray back and drops it with a clatter. Nobody goes "ooooooh" this time. Blood speckles the tan linoleum floor as Jono slides off the bench in a limp pile, and everyone around the carnage shies away in terror. The fun schoolyard scuffle they expected has turned into a horror movie.

Cigarettes tries to get away from Jake, but there's a crowd behind him, and he still has one leg on either side of the bench. Realizing he's cornered, he throws his hands up in surrender, and Jake drives his fist right between the upheld hands, knocking him back onto the table. His body hits a food tray hanging over the edge of the table, and it flips into the air like a catapult, spraying lettuce and salsa everywhere.

Some people are screaming and some are chanting: *"Fight! Fight! Fight!"* One high voice cuts through the noise and cries, *"Somebody, do something!"*

I catch motion on my left, Mark marching toward me from around the other side of the table. He shrugs his jacket off and pushes the sleeves up his muscled forearms, like he's ready to bale some hay.

Jake spots him too and yells, "Not so fast, farm boy!" as he runs toward Mark, but Tommy lurches up off the floor like Jason Voorhees rising from the dead, his face green with guacamole, and tackles Jake in a drunken bear hug in the middle of the aisle. Jake pulls one arm free and punches Tommy over and over in the head, swinging his fist like a hammer, but Tommy holds on, squeezing him in his big meaty arms and ducking his chin so the top of his head absorbs most of the blows.

Mark rounds the corner of the table, coming straight for me, his face twisted with rage. "Fuckin' finally," he snarls, but just as he steps into the aisle in front of me, Herr Bronner runs up and pushes him back, away from Jake and Tommy rolling on the floor. "Stand back, everyone!" he yells, red-faced and out of breath. "Everyone, stand back!"

Tommy rolls on top of Jake and tries to strangle him with his huge hands, but Herr Bronner grabs Tommy by the shoulders. "Let go!" he shouts. "Boys, break it up!"

Tommy lets go of Jake, and the instant he does, Jake punches Tommy in the throat.

Tommy gags and rolls off Jake, onto his side, struggling to breathe.

Herr Bronner is yelling. *Everyone* is yelling. Screams fly around the cafeteria like bats. Separated from me by Herr Bronner and

Tommy and Jake, Mark glares across the aisle like he might leap over the jumble of bodies and attack me anyhow, but then two more teachers run up and push the crowd back farther. The circle of students around the fight is thick now, and I step back, hiding myself in the crowd.

Tommy gasps for breath on the floor, hands around his neck. Herr Bronner gets down on his knees and elevates his head onto his ample lap. "Stay calm," Herr Bronner says in his soothing instructor's voice. *"Breathe."*

Jono and Cigarettes are limp as spaghetti noodles, slumped across the table and covered in tacos. Kids are trying to help them sit up.

"Put pressure on it!" someone yells.

"Get his feet up!" offers another.

One teacher who I don't recognize is yelling into his walkie-talkie. "Where is Hartman? Where is Hartman?!"

Everyone is screaming and horrified except Jake, who rises proud in the middle of the destruction and raises his fists like a champion prizefighter. Doing a slow turn, his arms held aloft, he spots me in the crowd and smiles. He looks way more high than he did when we found him in the bathroom, but it's a different kind of high, not one that turns him into a sleepy, calm Jake I don't recognize. This is the Jake I know, but more so. Like a butterfly breaking free of its chrysalis, spreading its beautiful bloodred wings, this is Jake's final form.

He laughs deliriously. "Yippee ki-yay, motherfucker!"

CHAPTER 20

SOMEONE PUTS THEIR HAND ON MY SHOULDER, AND I have a very small heart attack until I turn and see it's just PJ.

He's looking past me, at the big show. "Wow," he says, shaking his head. "That was . . . wow." He has one hand over his mouth, and every time he tries to lower it, it pops back up like it's on springs.

I don't think Jake could've done more damage if he'd had the knife.

"Jake is in so much trouble," I tell PJ. "He's gonna get expelled for sure."

PJ gives me a funny look.

I'm feeling light-headed, and then I realize it's because my throat is shut tight in a full-blown asthma attack, my breath a thin whistle. I sit down on a bench and try to calm down as I use my inhaler.

Mr. Hartman still hasn't shown up, but a couple of other teachers have, including Mr. Braun and the nurse, who's holding one of Cigarette's eyelids open and shining a penlight into his eye.

While everyone else looks like they were just in a car accident, Jake looks fresh as a daisy, not a scratch on him. A couple teachers have pushed him back into a corner and are surrounding him, like a rabid dog that could break loose at any moment.

After a few minutes the whole group heads to the principal's office, and the two biggest teachers flank Jake like they're transporting Hannibal Lecter.

I watch them walking away and realize I don't want to be left alone in the lunchroom with Mark. Also, I don't know, maybe I can help Jake. Maybe I can tell them that Tommy started it, that he was *about* to hit Jake. Even in my head it sounds lame.

Regardless, I chase after Herr Bronner, who's bringing up the rear of the procession. One of his suspender straps has come unclipped and flaps behind him. *"Entschuldigen Sie, bitte?"* I automatically ask in German.

"Ja, was ist es?" Herr Bronner's curly hair is all disheveled. He shakes his head. *"Ich meine,* uh, yes? What is it, Kirby?"

"Herr Bronner, can I come with you? I saw the fight. I know what happened."

"Uh, *ja.* I mean, *nein.* I mean, uh . . ." The group is pulling away. "Yeah, okay. Fine."

I wave for PJ to follow me as I jog to catch up with Jake.

When we get to the office, Mr. Braun ushers Tommy, Jono, Cigarettes, and Jake straight back into the inner office. I'm worried that someone will kick PJ and me out of the waiting room, but there's so much commotion going on that nobody notices us aside from Trey, who I'm surprised to see is still in the waiting room, still slowly destroying the office furniture—and Mrs. Tews, who asks what we're doing there.

"We saw the fight," I respond. "Mr. Braun wants to talk to us," I lie.

"Okay, okay," she says. She puts her bifocals on and then takes them off again. Her phone rings. "Uh, that's fine. Have a seat."

PJ and I sit in the two chairs next to Trey, who is energized by all the chaos. "What's going on?" he asks me, bouncing in his seat. "What's going on?!"

We tell him about the fight, and he whistles appreciatively. "Oh boy," he says. "Jake is *fucked*."

"I know," I say. "But I'm hoping I can tell Mr. Braun that Tommy started it. He sort of did. He was about to punch Jake. . . ." He was about to punch Jake because Jake and PJ and I painted Mark's farm last night. Are we going to have to get into all of that, too? Shit. This is getting complicated. For once I wish I had listened to Jake and we had spent last night digging up one of his bottles of peach schnapps.

Trey shakes his head sadly. "I don't think you understand. You'll see."

Before I have a chance to ask what he means by that,

Mr. Hartman storms into the office, sports coat unbuttoned and flapping. On his way to Mr. Braun's door, he spots me and points. "You! Burns! Stay right where you are."

He opens Mr. Braun's door, and I almost don't recognize Mr. Braun's voice, it's so angry. "Finally!" he shouts at Mr. Hartman. "Where the hell were you?"

Mr. Hartman slams the door behind him as the two of them argue.

The bell for the end of lunch rings. I watch kids walking to class and chattering in the lobby outside the office, and it feels weird not to be out there with them. The silence in the waiting room is funereal. PJ and I don't talk. He's busy messing with his phone.

A few teachers come and go from Mr. Braun's office, and a couple of minutes later Jono and Cigarettes walk out, escorted by Mr. Hartman. They don't even notice me sitting there; they're still shaken up, soldiers returning from the war.

Mr. Hartman returns a few minutes later with Mr. Reali, who has the big bolt cutters I saw him with earlier, as well as a book bag that it takes me a moment to recognize as Jake's.

Trey stops unscrewing one of the legs from the coffee table long enough to shoot me a significant look. "Game over, dude. Game over."

Shortly thereafter, Mr. Hartman leads Tommy out of the office. Tommy sees me and scowls. Mr. Hartman waves me in, exhausted.

"C'mon, Burns, get in here. Jaramillo, you can go."

"Uh, but PJ saw the fight too," I say.

"*Everyone* saw the fight," Mr. Hartman says, rubbing his bloodshot eyes. "Mrs. Tews, write Pablo a hall pass. Burns, get in here."

As I walk past him, he stops me with a meaty hand on my chest. "I gave you a chance to tell me the truth before and you didn't take it." He lowers his voice and looks me right in the eyes. "This is your last chance."

The sun is higher than the last time I was in Mr. Braun's office, and the godlike glow that surrounded him before has been replaced by slanting shadows that hide his face. Mr. Braun leans forward behind his enormous desk, fingers steepled, his white hair wild like he's been pulling it, and he does not smile or give me a "Welcome! Please come in!" like he did the last time I visited his office. This time I'm not a kitten he's trying to find a home for. I'm a stray cat he's deciding whether or not to drown.

Jake is slumped in a chair, his back to me, and I realize just how screwed he is when I notice his right hand is hand-cuffed to the chair's arm. In the center of Mr. Braun's desk, where my bloody German book sat before, is Jake's book bag. I recognize it immediately because, like all of Jake's clothes, it doesn't look like any of the book bags the other kids carry at school. It's black and strangely square, with the red logo of a horse's head on it.

"Have a seat, Kirby," Mr. Braun says, all business. He is not a happy hobbit. He's Hans Gruber and he wants to know, *Where are my detonators?!*

Mr. Hartman blocks the door behind me, arms crossed, the buttons of his polyester shirt straining against his bulging chest. He breathes loudly through his mouth, and it's kind of gross.

Briefly, I consider offering him my inhaler, but instead I perch on the edge of the chair next to Jake and sneak a glance at him. He doesn't return the look. He just stares at the ground, and it hurts me to see him like this, like a wild horse that's been broken.

Mr. Braun studies my face carefully as he holds both hands up on either side of Jake's book bag, presenting it to me. "What is this?" he asks.

Wait . . . *what?* Why isn't he asking me about the fight?

"Uh . . . that's Jake's book bag, I think."

Mr. Braun's bushy eyebrows draw together as he peers at me like an owl. "Yes. And what's inside it?"

Is this a trick? I don't know what he wants me to say. "Books?" I offer.

Mr. Braun drums his fingers on the desk while he considers me. His shrewd eyes flick over my head to Mr. Hartman. "You checked Kirby's locker too?"

"Yeah," Mr. Hartman growls. "I'm telling you, he's stupid, but he's not that kind of stupid."

Now I'm *really* confused. "Wait, you checked my locker? For what?"

"You honestly don't know?" Mr. Braun studies me again, the

wrinkles around his bright eyes folding up as he squints, then suddenly relaxing. "No, maybe you don't."

He reaches into Jake's book bag and pulls out a big ziplock bag of white pills.

Oh. Right. *That*.

Jake winces and looks away like Mr. Braun pulled a stack of porn out of his backpack. "Those are my *dad's* pills. I guess he put them in my bag by accident."

Mr. Hartman sputters, "Oh yeah! Right! That makes sense!"

Mr. Braun holds up his hand. "Frank, relax. We'll let the police sort it out."

Mr. Hartman snorts. "You're damn right we'll let the police sort it out, and I can tell you what they're going to say: five hundred milligrams of oxycodone? That's a misdemeanor."

A misdemeanor? I finally understand Trey's comment. Jake's not getting *expelled*. He's getting *arrested*.

Mr. Braun sees the alarm on my face and softens a little. "Don't worry, Kirby. You're not in trouble. We're sorry to bring you in, but after the altercation this morning with Tommy and your book—"

"Which we *know* you lied about," Mr. Hartman grumbles.

"Uh, yes, which we *assume* you were lying about"—Mr. Braun scowls at him—"we thought perhaps there might be a connection between you and the drugs we found in Jake's locker."

Jake shifts in his chair, and the handcuffs rattle. "I told you there wasn't."

Mr. Braun gives him a bland look, like, *Sure, we should have taken your word for it.* He opens his desk drawer and drops the big bag of pills inside as Mr. Hartman slaps a heavy hand on my shoulder. "Mrs. Tews will write you a hall pass to go back to class."

I start to panic. They can't send Jake to jail! "Look, you don't understand," I say. "Tommy and those guys have been messing with us all day!"

Mr. Braun dismisses me with a wave of his hand. "Look, we're not even talking about the fight yet, although, yes, that was Mr. Grivas's fault too, and I'm fairly certain the boys' parents will be pressing charges for that as well. Kirby, you seem like a smart kid." He slams his desk drawer shut and locks it with a small key, which he points at Jake. "Do yourself a favor and stay away from this guy. He's poison."

Mr. Hartman's walkie-talkie crackles to life. "Hartman, this is County. Do you copy, over?"

Mr. Hartman picks it up and presses the receiver. "I copy. Over."

"Hit a little snafu, two-eleven on Main Street. We'll be fifteen minutes late. Do you have a secure location to hold the perp?"

"Roger, he's secure here. Over and out."

He clips the walkie-talkie back onto his thick belt and hoists it up under his gut. "Okay, Burns, let's—" Mr. Hartman is interrupted by a yell from the waiting room. Even through Mr. Braun's closed office door we can clearly hear a woman scream, "You made me get outta work and come here for this? A fucking RACCOON?!"

The voice is so piercing, we all jump. Mr. Hartman opens the door a crack and peeks out.

"Mrs. Ch-Ch-Chantry," the secretary stutters. "It is against school rules to—"

The interruption fires Trey's mom up even more. "Oh, there's a rule in your school handbook that says 'No raccoons on campus'? You know how far away I work? You know I get paid by the hour, which means if I'm not at work, I don't get PAID, which means you're costing me MONEY right now? Who's gonna pay me back for this, because I want to talk to them RIGHT. FUCKING. NOW!"

"God, this day just won't end." Mr. Braun swears as he wearily gets out of his chair and rounds the corner of his formidable desk. "Keep them here for a minute," he says to Mr. Hartman, then shuts the door behind him.

Jake looks at me. "Guess I won't be going to California after all," he whispers.

"No talking!" Mr. Hartman barks.

Jake swivels around in his chair, handcuffs rattling, to give Hartman the stink eye. "What are you going to do, arrest me twice? Are the cops gonna throw the book at me for being chatty?"

"Shut. Up!"

Jake smiles up at him sweetly, all sugar and spice. "Hey, why weren't you in the cafeteria? I bet Mr. Braun was wondering where you were when the fight happened, huh?"

Mr. Hartman lets out a long, shaky breath and rubs his face, his big features smooshing like rubber in his hands. As he drops his hands from his face, he takes a step toward Jake, but then he gives me a guilty look and stops. I'm shocked to consider that if I weren't there, he might actually do something to Jake.

"Excuse me, Mr. Hartman," a quiet voice says politely. "Can I show you something?"

Mr. Hartman turns, and all of us are surprised to see PJ standing behind him, in front of the closed door. I didn't hear the door open. How did he get in here?

Mr. Hartman is wondering the same thing. "How'd you get in here?" he asks.

But then I realize how PJ got in here. SECRET NINJA SKILLS.

PJ says nothing, just holds his phone out so Mr. Hartman can see the screen. There, visible in stunning digital clarity, is the video of Mr. Hartman smoking a joint on the school's roof. His back is to us, but he's still completely recognizable, broad shoulders under a tightly stretched checkered sports coat, free hand hooked in the waist of his tan pants. As a plume of smoke rises from his head, he turns and exposes the profile of his large face. He's wearing a blissful expression, and I feel a twinge of pity as I realize it's the first time I've seen him happy.

As he watches the video, Mr. Hartman is the exact opposite of happy, his eyes getting wider and wider until I'm afraid they're going to pop out and fall into my lap.

Jake shakes his head sadly. "Mr. Hartman, I'm surprised. I've always looked up to you as a role model."

Mr. Hartman lunges for the phone, but PJ's a beat ahead of him and hides it behind his back. Mr. Hartman grabs PJ and is about to throw him against the wall and slap a pair of handcuffs on him, too, but PJ blurts out, "I already uploaded it to YouTube. Right now the video is private—but it doesn't have to stay that way. I can make it public."

Mr. Hartman pushes PJ away and takes a step back, bumping into the bookcase behind him. His high forehead glistens with sweat, his eyes darting back and forth between me, PJ, and Jake. "Okay, look," he says shakily. "You boys are in a lot of trouble here. *A lot.* But if you delete the video right now, we can forget about this whole thing."

Jake laughs. "You wish."

"Jake, please," PJ says diplomatically. "I agree with Mr. Hartman. We should forget about this whole thing. Mr. Hartman, I can give you the password to delete the video, and you can watch me delete it from my phone, too, but first I need something from you."

Relief washes over Mr. Hartman. "Yes. Absolutely. I think that's best for everyone. Okay, so, uh . . ." He tries to smile as he says it, but instead his lips curl back in a snarl. "What do you boys want from me?"

"All you have to do is drop the key for Jake's handcuffs on the ground here," PJ says. "Then follow me into the waiting room and don't come back into this room for five minutes.

Then you and I can delete the video, and it'll be like this never happened."

Trey's mom is still yelling behind the door, but none of us is listening.

For a second I'm certain we've pushed Mr. Hartman too far and he's going to throw us all into prison himself, video or no video. A vein beats in his forehead. One of his hands clenches into a fist and the other creeps up to his side, where he probably wore a shoulder holster, back when he was a cop.

"You're suspended!" Mr. Hartman jabs a finger at PJ, spittle flying from his lip. "No. Fuck that. You're expelled! *Forever!*"

PJ doesn't budge. "Expel me and I'll post the video on the school's Facebook page. Unlock the handcuffs and follow me into the waiting room and this all goes away. You have ten seconds to make up your mind."

Jake starts to count down, *fast*. "Ten, nine, eight, seven, six—"

"All right, all right! Wait! Stop!" Mr. Hartman pries a key ring out of his pocket, the keys jangling all over the place because his hand's shaking so bad. It takes him four tries to get the key for the cuffs off the key ring. He holds the little key in the air for a second, daintily, between two thick fingers, then drops it.

The key falls silently onto the plush red carpet. Mr. Hartman looks down his nose at the three of us with the wounded pride of a good cop being forced to go dirty.

Jake picks the key up off the floor and unlocks the cuffs. He rubs his wrist, which is all red.

PJ points at the French doors behind Mr. Braun's desk. "Go out that way," he says to Jake.

"Oh, I was going to walk out through the waiting room, past Mr. Braun," Jake says. "Do you think these doors would be better?"

Mr. Hartman is so angry he can barely speak. "This is blackmail!" he sputters.

"No shit it's blackmail," Jake says to himself, smoothing his thick hair back and straightening his shirt, which is somehow, even after all the mayhem we've been through today, still perfectly ironed and white. He brushes an invisible speck of lint off his sleeve and grabs his book bag off Mr. Braun's desk.

Mr. Hartman points back and forth between me and PJ. "You two little criminals are gonna go along with this story, right?"

"Yes, sir," I say. "Jake stole your key, and then he escaped."

"Good, because if you don't, I'll kill you."

He says it, and a second later we all realize he kind of means it. I think he's shocked to realize it himself, because he doesn't say anything after that.

Jake drops the key back on the floor, in the middle of the carpet, where it's sure to be seen. Mr. Hartman and PJ open the door and walk out, and Trey's mom's voice blows in like a fierce wind.

"I can sue this school for costing me wages and for causing emotional harm. You know that, right?!"

"Now, now," Mr. Braun says, "please, Mrs. Chantry . . . please calm down!"

As Mr. Hartman closes the door behind him, Jake hops up and crosses behind Mr. Braun's desk. He tries to open the center drawer, where Mr. Braun put the bag of pills, but of course it's locked.

"Fuck," he says, looking around the room. "Do you think there's a screwdriver around here?"

"Geez, Jake," I say. "Forget about the pills! You've only got five minutes! Or less, if Mr. Hartman changes his mind."

"Fine," he says. "I just wanted to eliminate the evidence." He opens one of the French doors and pauses on the threshold.

I follow him to the door and feel like I should say something, some cool last words, but all I can think of is, "Have fun in California."

"How could I not? You know how much I love surfing." I enjoy this classic Jake joke for only one second, because suddenly he pivots around on his foot and punches me in the face. My glasses fly off and I fall back, knocking a stack of papers off Mr. Braun's desk.

"What the hell?!"

Jake puts his hands up. "Plausible deniability," he says. "You tried to stop me from escaping, and I clocked you."

Jakes runs out the door and across the lawn, lit blazingly by the sun for a moment, then disappearing into darkness as he enters the woods. I rub the blossom of pain on my cheek and linger in the open doorway. Someone is burning leaves, and the smell is a strong mix of crisp and sweet, dead leaves and smoke.

— — —

When the cops show up a couple of minutes later, they are super-duper pissed that Jake escaped. The magnitude of the situation is conveyed by their use of the word "escaped," a verb reserved for prisoners and magicians. Jake qualifies as both in their opinion.

Mr. Braun literally can't believe it. He keeps asking Mr. Hartman, "What do you mean, 'He's *gone*'?" as PJ and I awkwardly stand in the corner of the office and watch Mr. Braun look under his desk, inside his closet, and even inside the filing cabinet drawers—not because he thinks Jake will be scrunched up inside a manila folder, but because he doesn't know what else to do.

"I told you to watch him!" he screams at Mr. Hartman.

"I'm sorry, sir. I thought you needed help out there."

Mr. Hartman acts angry, but I can tell he's relieved that our scheme seems to be going as planned. We're all in the same boat, and he does everything he can to make sure our story stays afloat.

There are two cops on the scene, an old guy with a mustache and a younger cop whose uniform is one size too large and who is always adjusting his hat. Mr. Braun puts PJ and me back in the waiting room, where we're questioned by the young officer while Officer Mustache, clearly the higher-ranking one, goes over some stuff with Mr. Hartman and Mr. Braun in his office.

I'm not nervous, because even though the lie PJ and I tell the young cop is pretty unbelievable—that Jake pickpocketed the key from Mr. Hartman, then knocked me out—it's more believable than the truth, which is that we blackmailed the school's head of security for smoking marijuana on the roof. Also, the fresh bruise under my right eye is pretty convincing.

Mr. Braun's office door is cracked open, and I'm able to overhear their conversation and learn a few things. Someone has a broken nose. I'm not sure who, but I'm not surprised. I pick out a few other serious-sounding medical terms, including "fracture," "contusion," and something about teeth, which sounds bad. An ambulance has been called, although I'm not sure for who. Most importantly, though, I learn that Tommy, Jono, and Cigarettes (whose real name, surprisingly, turns out to be Xavier) have all been sent home, which is awesome, because it means I don't have to worry about them hassling me—at least not until their bones heal. The Iron Pigs are gonna have a lot of benchwarmers playing in the game tonight.

When the discussion is over in Mr. Braun's office, Mr. Hartman comes out to the waiting room and backs up our story to the young officer. "The kid pickpocketed me, I guess. I don't know how he did it, but I guess he must have." He shakes his head and frowns, perhaps laying it on a bit too thick. "The kid is *good*."

Mr. Braun holds PJ and me in the waiting room a little while longer, for no clear reason except that he knows *something* strange is going on. He knows there must be a connection between me and Tommy and Jake, but if he thought about it for a million years, he'd never guess that the connection is that last night I painted Mark Kruger's cows.

Speaking of which, the longer I'm in the office's waiting room, the longer I'm safe from Mark, so I don't mind if Mr. Braun keeps me here all day. I can't imagine Mark is going to try to fight me today, not after all the insanity that's already happened and the police being here and all, but I don't know. The way he stared daggers at me as Herr Bronner dragged Tommy off Jake . . .

The police "search" the woods behind the school for Jake, but I watch the manhunt through the window, and all the two cops do is stand at the edge of the woods and hit a couple of bushes with their nightsticks. Mr. Hartman is out there with them too, and I bet he's discouraging them from searching too hard. He wants Jake to get away and stay away.

I smile thinking about Jake headed to sunny California. I hope he has better luck out West than he did here. I hope he has fun with his sister. I hope I haven't just helped a future serial killer escape.

Mr. Hartman huffs back into the waiting room from outside just as the bell rings for the end of sixth period. He gives PJ and me a look so dirty it makes me want to wash my hands.

"All right," he growls. "Get outta here. We're done."

PJ and I exchange amazed looks. Holy shit, we're getting off scot-free?

"We're . . . done?" I repeat hopefully.

Mr. Hartman looks around the waiting room. It's empty except for Mrs. Tews leaning down behind the counter, handling some paperwork, not paying attention to us. Mr. Hartman approaches our chairs and kneels down so we're eye to eye. The smell of his cologne is sharp, but it's not strong enough to mask the musky scent of his sweat underneath it. "Yeah," he says quietly, his voice hoarse from years of smoking. "We are absolutely, one hundred percent done. And if you ever tell anybody about what happened today, so are you. Got it?"

"Yes, sir," PJ and I say in unison.

There is a very real possibility that before today is over Mr. Hartman will kill us and stage it to look like an accident.

Well, if he wants to kill me, it's not going to be easy.

He's going to have to wait in line.

CHAPTER 21

PJ AND I MISS ALL OF SIXTH PERIOD, WHICH FOR ME is just a study hall anyhow, and head to biology. I almost can't believe there are only two periods left in this never-ending hellhole of a day. Biology and swim class and then that's it. Only two periods left and I get to go home! Home to my empty room full of boxes. Home to my easy chair and John McClane jumping off Nakatomi Plaza and Mom and Dad placing my notebook on the kitchen table like *Komm Mit!* and warning me, "This is your last chance, Kirby." DEFCON 1. The roof is wired with explosives.

I wonder how long I could live at school. How long would it take Mr. Reali to discover my pup tent on the roof?

Aside from the gym and the pool, the science lab is the

only classroom not in one of the three circles. I heard it's separated for safety reasons because of all the dangerous chemicals in there and the tanks of oxygen and stuff—if the school ever caught on fire, that room would blow up like a paint factory.

It's connected to the main lobby by a long hallway that wraps around the outside of the gymnasium. There are no classrooms along the hallway, just lockers, and halfway down the hall, doors to the girls' and boys' locker rooms. The hallway is great because if it's not too crowded, you can race. The current record was set by Matt Ditty, and I know this because there's a little piece of paper taped to the first locker in the hallway that says:

CURRENT RECORD HOLDER:
MATT "CRAZY LEGS" DITTY
ONE MINUTE TWENTY-THREE
SECONDS

The science lab always reminds me of a morgue because of its gleaming rows of experiment tables, but even more so today because we're going to dissect dead frogs. Inexplicably, everyone is delighted by this prospect.

Probably because they were less expensive, we're getting our frogs alive, which means not only do we have to dissect them, but we've got to *kill them* first. I guess this will teach us the important biology lesson that humans are pack animals, happy to commit unspeakable violence as long as an alpha dog tells us it's all right.

I hope we'll at least kill the frogs in an interesting way—push them down a flight of stairs, perhaps, or take them for a rowboat ride on a secluded lake—but instead Mr. Perry tells us we're just going to use a lethal dose of chloroform. *Booooooooring.*

"All right, everyone," Mr. Perry says, pacing in front of the blackboard in his unnecessary white lab coat, "find a table and break up into dissection teams, groups of two."

PJ and I pair up and grab an experiment table. Each table has a thick glass jar on it with a frog trapped inside, the open end of the jar placed down on the table. Next to the jars gleam metal trays of slender dissection instruments.

PJ slides his two duffel bags under the table and flips through the printed-out pages of anatomy and dissection diagrams next to the tray of scalpels. I watch our frog sit serenely inside the big jar, just chillin', not concerned that it's trapped in an invisible prison surrounded by giants. The soft pale skin on its throat balloons out each time it breathes in that weird way unique to frogs and wealthy older men.

PJ has his full tuxedo on again, although it's looking pretty ragged. After he pulled it out of the bucket of water, he tried to dry it using a hand dryer in one of the bathrooms; it shrank a little, so now it's supertight on him and the sleeves are too short. He's also wearing his shirt backward so the gray smudges on the front won't show, which looks really weird because there are no buttons and the collar goes straight across his throat in a band, like a priest's collar. He looks like a time-traveling prophet from some dystopian future.

"Oh, hey, I've got something for you." PJ looks around the room, then reaches into one of the duffel bags and hands me something under the table.

It's smooth and jiggly. I look down.

"PJ. Is this a . . . water balloon?"

"Yes! Would you like to know what's in it?"

"Water?"

"Oh, no." PJ rubs his hands with glee. "Well . . . yes, water, but not *just* water. Remember the jalapeños and hot sauce I grabbed at lunch? Well, I chopped the jalapeños really fine, and I let them soak in some water, 'infusing'"—he makes air quotes—"the liquid, and then I poured a bunch of hot sauce in there too. Then I funneled all of that into one of the water balloons we didn't use on the cows last night."

He pokes the balloon in my hand, and it jiggles with dangerous potential. "That is a sphere of liquid hellfire. I double ballooned it, to make sure it wouldn't pop accidentally, so make sure you really wing it when you throw it."

He looks at me proudly.

"And you want me to throw this at Mark when he attacks me, I suppose?"

"Precisely," PJ says. "Aim for the face. It will blind him, and if any gets in his mouth or nose, it will also gag him and possibly even make him throw up. Remember the tenets of ninjutsu: deception, evasion—"

"Yeah, yeah, I remember the tenets," I say, carefully placing the balloon into the outer pocket of my book bag, so if it accidentally breaks, it won't get my books wet. I remind myself to throw it away as soon as I find a trash can. "Look, PJ, we just blackmailed a school official. We found out our best friend is addicted to opioids right before he hospitalized three students and fled the law, a crime that we were accomplices to. Also, I didn't get to eat my egg sandwich this morning. This has been, like, the second-worst day of my life." It's the anniversary of the worst day of my life, but I don't tell PJ that. Instead I toss my hands up. "If Mark still wants to come at me—which, I don't know, maybe he's had enough bullshit too—then let him. But either way, I'm not scared. I don't care."

"Okay." PJ shrugs. "I'm staying a little late to help finish decorating the gym, so my mom is going to give me a ride home. I was going to ask if you wanted to ride with me so you don't have to get on the bus with Mark, but—"

"Well, if you insist," I say before PJ can finish his sentence. "Of course I would love a ride." Hey, just 'cause I'm not scared doesn't mean I'm a glutton for punishment. Maybe I can even go to PJ's house after school. I mean, Mom will make me come home eventually, but at least it might buy me an hour or two. And if I can keep buying an hour or two for the next twenty years, then maybe this whole notebook thing will blow over!

Mr. Perry walks around the room and puts a chloroform-soaked cotton ball under each of our jars, lifting the edge of the jar up to slide the cotton in with a pair of forceps. When he puts a poison cotton ball into our jar, at first our frog jumps at the glass, trying to get out, but then the fumes start to take effect and it slows down.

Mr. Perry resumes his spot at the front of the classroom, yanking a cord that pulls down a large diagram of frog anatomy over the blackboard. "Okay, let's give it five minutes, and then we'll begin dissecting."

Our frog stumbles around in circles for a couple of minutes. It's torture.

I close my eyes and try to think of something else, and I remember the machines hooked up to Melanie, beeping and chirping like little animals.

I open my eyes, and the frog is lying down on its side. It's breathing weakly, slower and slower. The paper-thin skin of its frail chest rises up and down, slower and slower, until I can't stand it anymore.

I pick up the jar and carefully scoop the limp frog out from under it. I walk its unconscious body over to the window, cupping it in my hands.

PJ looks up from the dissection instructions. "What are you doing?"

I'm surprised at how emotional my voice sounds and the wave of feeling flowing through me. "I'm giving this frog its freedom," I choke out. I fan my hand in front of its face, trying to give it some air.

PJ squints at our notes. "I don't think that's part of the experiment...."

"Maybe it is, PJ!" I say, louder than I intended, loud enough that a couple of kids stop taking videos of their frogs with their phones and look over. "Maybe this isn't a biology experiment. Maybe it's a *psychology* experiment. Maybe scientists are watching us right now with hidden cameras, to see how many of us are killers. Well, I'll tell you what: *I'm* not. I won't kill this frog." And with that I drop the frog out the window.

PJ grimaces. "Ooh, I hope it's okay."

"What do you mean?"

"Well, we're pretty high up."

I lean out the window and look down. He's right. I forgot that the biology room is on the second floor. There are some bushes under the window. Maybe the frog landed in there. I can't see.

Mr. Perry notices me standing by the window. "Is everything all right over there, Kirby?"

CHAPTER 22

THE BELL MERCIFULLY RINGS AS I FINISH WRITING *I will not disrupt the local ecosystem by releasing lab animals into the wild* for the five hundredth time. I shake my sore hand, shuffle together the stack of papers I filled, and hand them to Mr. Perry as I join the rest of the class filing out the door.

Mr. Perry frowns at me and shoves my pages into his lab coat pocket. "Next time you feel uncomfortable doing something in class, Kirby, please tell me ahead of time."

"Yes, sir."

PJ and I follow the rest of the class out of the classroom, PJ lugging both of his duffel bags like a Sherpa ascending Everest.

"Okay," PJ says when we're out in the hall, "since lunch didn't go as planned, here's my new idea. Vern had gym class this period, which is right down the hall here. She should be finishing up changing as we speak. I figure we wait in the hall outside the locker rooms, and when she comes out, I read her my poem. When I reach the last stanza, you press play on the boom box and do the thing with the other bag, I do the dance, all that, and then we take a bow. I realize it's not perfect, but since Jake messed everything up at lunch, I think this is the best I can do on short notice." He grimaces. "It just drives me crazy. I had this planned out perfectly and then Jake has to mess it all up."

I can't believe PJ is still talking about Vern. I stop walking. "Y'know, saying Jake 'messed everything up' is a little unfair, like you had nothing to do with the trouble we're in."

PJ rolls his eyes.

"This whole fucking disaster started with the cow painting," I say. "And whose idea was it to use the Kool-Aid, PJ?" I scratch my head. "Hmmm. I can't seem to remember. . . . Oh, that's right! It was you. We got in this trouble *together*, and then Jake saved our asses at lunch. Yeah, he went a little overboard—"

"A *little*?" PJ laughs.

"Okay, fine, *a lot*, yeah. But, dude, who dropped their book bag at the farm, huh?" I kick his big dumb duffel bag. "Jake may be crazy, but at least he stood up for us, unlike you. If you hadn't wussed out and told Mark that it was Jake and me with you, Jake wouldn't have fought Tommy at lunch. So, actually, PJ, if you wanna blame all this stuff on one person, that person is"—I get really close and poke him in the chest—"you."

PJ looks at me seriously. "Who said I told on you and Jake?"
Uh-oh.

"I told you that Mark saw us running away," he continues.

I try to act confused. "Oh . . . right. Sorry. I got mixed up. I thought you said—"

"I said that Mark already knew about you and Jake. I know that's what I said, because I remember feeling so bad about lying to you."

Oh man. I am not in the mood for this right now. The day is almost over! I can see the finish line!

"You were in the bathroom, weren't you?" PJ doesn't even ask. He just says it sadly. "It was the cheese, wasn't it?" He sighs. "I *thought* I smelled your farts."

The second bell rings.

"Look, man, I've gotta go. I'm gonna be late for swim class."

I round the corner and jog down the little flight of stairs that leads to the hallway. Right as I push through the double doors that open into the hallway, my Spidey sense tingles, but it's too late. A couple of feet away, blocking the hall, are Rob and Jono, a small crowd of gawking kids behind them. I'm so used to being ambushed by now, I don't turn to run or crouch into a defensive tuck or anything. Instead I point at Jono's battered face and say, "I thought they sent you home."

Jono's right cheekbone is puffy blue, and his lip is split and swollen. He licks his bloody lip. "The nurse wanted to send me home. But I told her nah, I have to play in the game tonight." He cracks his knuckles. "It's a big one."

The hallway is narrow, orange lockers lining the right-hand side. The semicircle of students behind Jono and Rob gawk like spectators at the Colosseum, waiting for the lions to be let loose. A few have their phones out, ready to record if things get interesting. Their sympathy touches me deeply.

I'm surprised not to see Mark here—not that I'm disappointed. I do see Myka, though, standing at the front of the crowd, right behind Jono, scowling at me so meanly that for a second I'm afraid she might try to fight me too. "Fuck you," she says. "Your psycho friend almost killed my Tommy!"

"I'm sorry," I say, and I mean it.

Rob leans against a locker and shakes his head. "You are one *popular* guy today, huh? Jono has a score to settle with your friend Jake, but Jake bounced. So we figured we could settle up with you instead. Is that cool?"

Jono rubs his hands like he's about to eat something delicious.

"Sure." I sigh. "That's fine. Let's just get this over with." I take my glasses off and fold them in my pocket.

I'm done. I almost made it. I was close, but I was stupid to think that I could get out of this. At a certain point you have to accept the inevitable.

Rob nods at Jono, and I close my eyes. The last thing I see is Jono's ugly black-and-blue face pinched into a painful smile as he strides forward, ready to pound the shit out of me.

I clench my stomach muscles and lower my head, not knowing where the first punch will land but hoping to avoid a direct hit on the jaw or a sucker punch in the gut. But instead of a fist in the face, the first notes of "Eye of the Tiger" blast in my ears, very loudly. My eyes fly open, and I see Jono right in front of me, paused in midpunch. Jono, Rob, Myka, and all the other onlookers are confused, staring in shock at something behind and, somehow, above me.

I turn around and see a giant warthog holding a boom box. It's PJ, wearing the head of his Iron Pigs mascot costume—tusks spread wide in a terrifying grin—standing on stilts so tall his bristling head brushes the hallway's drop ceiling. He drops the boom box into my hands as he hoists the two giant duffel bags over his head, unzipped.

"Run!" he screams from inside the warthog head, and then upends the two duffel bags at the same time. Hundreds, maybe thousands, of rainbow-colored Ping-Pong balls tumble out, bouncing all over the hallway. The music is deafening. The balls pop and clatter all around us, and the kids who were expecting a fight break into relieved applause.

"Run!" PJ yells again, pushing me forward. I drop the boom box and stumble past Jono. I bump right into Rob, knocking him over, and I can feel his tiny body crack a little under my feet as I stumble over him and he screams. Jono tries to grab me, but he slips on the Ping-Pong balls covering the ground and goes down onto one knee, his kneecap making a loud *crack!* as it hits the tile.

"Oh geez, I'm sorry!" I say.

"Ow! Shit!" Jono yells, grabbing his knee.

"Run!" PJ yells again, and I do. I run down the hall toward the lobby, away from the pounding bass beat of "Eye of the Tiger" and from PJ screaming like a stuck pig.

I have a pretty good head start, especially since Rob has tiny legs and Jono has a busted knee. I swerve around people as I run down the hall, but a couple of seconds later, much sooner than I expected, I hear Rob's and Jono's sneakers squeaking on tile as they dodge the same people, chasing me.

It takes me a couple of seconds to notice I'm not really breathing.

Oh shit. I'm having an asthma attack again.

I try to suck in air, but it's like breathing through a straw. I won't be able to outrun Rob and Jono like this. If I could make it to the end of the hallway, I could lose them in the chaos of the Thunderdome and there will probably be some teachers there, but I'll never make it to the Thunderdome.

I'm about to stop and let them catch me when I remember the balloon.

A sphere of liquid hellfire.

The front pocket of my bag is already a little unzipped. I pull the balloon out and, incredibly, it's unbroken. It jiggles in my hand, a poisonous spider egg. I drop my book bag as I keep running, and a couple of seconds later Rob curses and a pair of palms slap as they hit the floor.

This is my best chance. I spin and hoist the balloon over my head, cocking my arm back to throw it, hoping that when Rob and Jono round the corner they'll be close together so I can hit them both at the same time—

—but then there's a *pop* and a *whoosh* and suddenly I'm all wet. My head is soaked. Water trickles into my eyes, my nose, my mouth . . .

And the burning begins.

I squeeze my eyes shut, but it's too late. They're already doused in flaming gasoline. Veins pulse red across the backs of my eyelids. Water goes up my nose and down the back of my throat, and the taste is nauseating, spicy but also sickly sweet, and I almost throw up.

Stumbling backward, I try to wipe the water out of my eyes, and a tiny reptile part of my brain shouts, *Run, run, run,* to the beat of approaching footsteps.

Oh right. I'm being chased.

I spin and run blindly down the hall, but the footsteps are getting closer. Then I hear the sound of showers and the rush of steam as a door opens.

The locker rooms.

Water!

I still can't see anything, so I swerve left until I bump into the hallway wall and shuffle forward with my hands out until I feel the metal of the locker room door handle. I jerk the door open and run inside.

Echoes. Humidity. Steam in the air.

Water.

The steamy air helps my chest to loosen up. I greedily gulp air and run toward the sound of the showers, slipping on wet tile. I plunge my flaming face into the stream of water blasting from a showerhead.

Instantly the pain lessens. I hold my face up to the cooling water, and it feels amazing. My clothes are soaking wet, but I don't care.

My relief is shattered by a girl shrieking, her scream echoing off the tile walls.

I turn away from the shower and open my eyes just in time to see a girl wrapped in a pink towel, screaming and stumbling backward, pointing a trembling finger at me like I'm a swamp monster straight out of a B movie. I'd recognize that long blond hair anywhere, even though it's plastered wet around her face.

It's Vern.

I'm in the girls' locker room.

The shower room is big, tile floors and walls shrouded in steam from a dozen showerheads spraying hot water onto the floor, but Vern and I are the only ones in it. Vern is so shocked it seems to be affecting her cognitive skills, because instead of running out of the open doorway into the locker room, she just stands there and screams like a steam whistle.

I'd ask her if she'd like to go to the dance with PJ, but this probably isn't a good time.

Another girl runs in, wearing a damp T-shirt and jogging pants. It's Mary, her short hair spiky wet. She's dragging two other girls with her, and when the three of them see me standing under the spray of the shower like the Creature from the Black Lagoon, their mouths drop open.

Mary screams.

The other two girls scream.

Vern is still screaming.

What the heck? I figure, and I start screaming too.

Peals of terror bounce off the tile walls as I run out of the shower room. The girls shrink back and grab one another like I'm a giant spider scuttling past them. I head for the door back to the hallway, but then I remember that Rob and Jono are probably still out there. I spin around, almost falling over, my wet shoes slipping on the tile, and run back into the locker room. The screams shoot up an octave as the girls see me charging back toward them. I pass them to discover that, blessedly, the rest of the locker room is empty, so I'm able to run through the changing area without traumatizing anyone else.

I slam the door to the gym open and slide to a stop, sopping wet, on the sideline in the middle of the basketball court. Across the court from me are a bank of double doors that lead to the Thunderdome and salvation.

Unfortunately, I can't reach them because the dodgeball club is engaged in an intense barrage in the gym. The opposing teams face each other across the two halves of the basketball court, and they are taking the game *very* seriously, whipping those big red elementary school kickballs at each other with deadly aim. They're so busy throwing and dodging, juking left and right to fake the throwers out, that nobody notices me skid out of the locker room.

Nobody except Jono and Rob, who are walking down the sideline, about to go into the boys' locker room twenty feet to my left. Jono freezes with his hand on the door and unsheathes a smile that splits the cut on his lip, dribbling fresh blood onto his teeth.

I quickly assess my escape routes: There's no way I'm going back through the girls' room, so that's out. A pair of doors on the left leads to the parking lot behind the school, but I'd have to pass Jono and Rob, so that's out too. It's the Thunderdome doors or nothing.

Jono and Rob walk toward me, grinning, and I'm about to run when I notice something at my feet. A power strip with a bunch of thick electrical cords snaking into it.

The dance.

The lights.

I stomp on the red button on the power strip, and the bright lights overhead are replaced by flashing blue strobes and spinning rainbow lasers. *Welcome to the party, pal!*

I race through the middle of the dodgeball game toward the doors. The strobe light turns the gym into a jumble of gyrating limbs, white flashes of motion between blinding stretches of black. I hear the bounce of balls still being thrown around the court, people laughing and hooting. I jump over a fast-moving grounder that bounces between my legs. A ball hits me in the back, another in the leg. One or two balls must hit Jono and Rob because I hear them curse and trip.

"Hey, get off the court!" someone yells.

"Time out! Interference!"

A ball that feels like it was thrown with *intent* smacks me hard in the side of the head, and I stagger sideways, wet socks squishing inside my shoes while I continue to run, carried forward more by momentum than conscious thought until I slam through the double doors and into the bright lights and quiet calm of the Thunderdome.

I run face-first into a terrifying monster—PJ's warthog head, which Ms. Torres is holding up and admiring like a Ming vase. PJ and Ms. Torres are just outside the gym doors, talking together, but they stop abruptly when I careen sopping wet out of the gym.

"Mr. Burns!" Ms. Torres gasps, looking me up and down with alarm. "Are you all right?"

"Uh, yes, great." I'm panting so hard I can barely speak. "I just, uh . . ." I jerk a thumb at the flashing lights on the other side of the slowly closing gym door and stretch against a stitch in my side. "That dodgeball game is *intense*."

Rob and Jono burst through the door a second after it closes, but they screech to a stop when they see Ms. Torres, who gasps in shock again. "Mr. Klein! Mr. Schmoyer!" I notice her tone is a little cooler with them than it was with me as she asks, "What are you two doing?"

"Oh! Uh, sorry," Rob says. A bouncy red ball escapes from the gym, and Rob jogs over to retrieve it. "Sorry about that, Ms. Torres. Dodgeball game getting a little out of hand, I guess." He dribbles the ball and slaps Jono on the arm. "C'mon, Jon boy, let's get back to it."

Jono gives me a baleful glare as he follows Rob back into the gym, where I notice the lights have returned to normal as the door closes behind them.

"Ms. Torres was just admiring the craftsmanship of my mask," PJ tells me.

"Yes. It's magnificent," Ms. Torres agrees. "I had no idea Pablo did this all by himself! So nice to see someone working in papier-mâché. It's a neglected medium."

I smile, thinking that papier-mâché isn't the most unusual medium PJ has worked in. Ms. Torres should see his Kool-Aid and cowhide paintings.

Ms. Torres hands the warthog head back to PJ. "Oh!" PJ says, pulling my backpack out of his duffel. "I grabbed this in the hallway."

"Thanks," I say, taking my bag.

The final bell rings. The few remaining kids in the hall pick up their pace, rushing to class, and Ms. Torres looks at her watch, the band a chunky jumble of beads and baubles. "You boys had better get to class." She looks back and forth between us as she serenely glides away. "Such nice boys," she says to herself.

I realize I should probably tell PJ that I just saw Vern in the shower, and then I remember I have something else to tell him first.

"Hey, PJ . . . I'm sorry."

PJ makes a pained expression and looks away. He doesn't like confrontation. "Uh-huh."

"I'm sorry about being in the bathroom when Mark was beating you up. I was hiding in there, and I was just . . . I was afraid. Okay? It was a shitty thing to do. I'm a shitty friend. I suck, and I was afraid of getting beat up."

PJ looks at me seriously. "Yeah, it was shitty. But I get it. We're all shitty sometimes. I shouldn't have lied about telling on you and Jake. I shouldn't have lied about Mark finding my bag. I'm sorry too."

A young teacher with a Boy Scout haircut and earnest eyes walks past and looks at us curiously, especially me, since a small puddle of water has formed around my feet. "Don't you boys have a class to be in?" He sees the warthog head PJ is holding and adds, "Go hogs."

"Yes, sir! Go hogs!" PJ replies as the teacher walks away. He puts the warthog head into his empty duffel bag. "Well," he says to me without much enthusiasm, "I'm going to geometry now, but I'll head down to the gym afterward to help finish setting up. If you need a ride . . . the offer still stands."

"Thanks, man. You're a lifesaver."

PJ smiles at that as he walks toward Circle A, and I follow him through the lobby as I head toward the pool, which is down a short hall next to the entrance to the circle. As I pass the first locker in the hallway that leads to the science room, I see that someone has modified the piece of paper there. They've scribbled out Matt's name with a black Sharpie and written next to it:

CURRENT RECORD HOLDER:
KIRBY "CHICKEN LEGS" BURNS
ONE MINUTE FIFTEEN SECONDS

CHAPTER 23

I'M SOAKING WET, BUT SINCE MY LAST CLASS IS
swimming, I guess all I did was get a head start. As I hurry down
the empty hallway, I check my poor battered book bag. It still
has my trunks and all my stuff in it, including, saints be praised,
my inhaler. I shake the inhaler, press the button on top, and take
a long, grateful drag.

I rush into the swimming pool locker room. It's empty,
everyone already changed and out in the pool. I throw my bag
in a locker and put on my trunks, and then I drape my wet
clothes over a bench so hopefully they'll dry a little bit before
I have to put them on again. Maybe after swimming I can also
use one of the hand dryers.

I sneak out of the locker room into the swimming area. Our

pool isn't Olympic-size or anything, but it's still big, like the size you'd see at a YMCA or something. Bleachers line one side, and large windows high up near the ceiling let natural light in. There's a diving board down at the deep end and blue-green tile all around the outside of the pool.

The whole class is clustered in the middle of the pool, standing in the water while our swim teacher, Ms. Everett, consults a clipboard and takes roll call from the side of the pool. I slip into the shallow end of the pool without anyone noticing and swim underwater until I see the sunken forest of legs ahead of me. I feel like an alligator as I slip around to the back of the group and surface soundlessly behind them.

A minute later Ms. Everett finishes up the roll call but does a double take when she spots me at the back of the group.

"Burns." She consults her clipboard. "Where were you?"

"Underwater."

She grudgingly checks my name off her list. She's no fool, but she is also not someone who likes to waste time on nonsense. She has a short military crew cut and always wears the exact same outfit: a black bathing suit under blue shorts. Although she's our swim teacher, I've never actually seen her in the pool. She looks more like she teaches kickboxing than swimming.

Myka is in the pool with Mary, who saw me in the girls' locker room only fifteen minutes ago. When Ms. Everett says my name, I expect Mary to level a finger at me and scream, "There he is, Ms. Everett! There's the pervert!" Mr. Hartman will pop out of the water in scuba gear, along with two frogmen, who cry, "We've got you now, Burns!"

But Mary doesn't do that. Instead, she and Myka just turn and glare at me like they want to push my head underwater and hold it there until I stop struggling. They whisper back and forth together, then turn their backs on me.

I feel so shitty, I reflexively dip lower in the water until only my head is visible. I wish I could explain to them, "It was an accident! I'm sorry!" but I don't think they would believe me. Anyhow, I certainly can't do it right now.

One thing I don't understand, though, is, why haven't they told on me? I know I should be happy, but it doesn't make any sense.

Ms. Everett blows her whistle and takes us through a couple of swim drills.

We tread water for three minutes, then do laps.

We do the backstroke, then the sidestroke.

I keep expecting Mr. Hartman to haul me back to the principal's office for running through the girls' locker room, but he doesn't. About halfway through swim class I realize that it's not going to happen.

Ms. Everett gives three sharp blows on her whistle. "Free swim!"

Everyone cheers. We love free swim. Kids dunk one another and play Marco Polo. They do cannonballs off the diving board, trying to get the biggest splash. The cheerleaders stand in the shallow end in a tight circle, talking and running their fingers through their wet hair.

I try to relax. After swim class I'll linger in the locker room until I'm sure all the buses have left. Then I'll go to the gym to meet PJ and get a ride back to his house. I'll stay at his place as late as I can and then worry about my notebook after that. Who knows. Maybe Mom and Dad have calmed down since this morning.

I jump off the diving board into the deep end and hit the water with a satisfying velocity. Underwater, I swim over to one side, then tuck my arms and legs in so I sink to the bottom of the pool. The water is Easter-egg blue. Above me, headless bodies float; legs scissor back and forth as they tread water, and arms wave lazily like sea plants. I close my eyes and sink.

I've always liked swimming because it's relaxing. When our family went to the beach, which was practically every summer except this past one, I would sit down in the surf and let the frothy white water wash over my hot skin. Melanie did the opposite. She would charge full speed into the water and dive headfirst under the crashing waves. She'd paddle out past the breaks, far from shore, then wave for me to join her. But I was always nervous to swim out that far.

When Melanie passed away, Mom said she was in heaven. I asked Mom what heaven was supposed to be like, and she said there were mansions there and lush vineyards and roads made of gold. I don't know if that's true, but I can't imagine Melanie enjoying living in a gaudy-ass place like that. I think she'd enjoy heaven more if it was a big long beach with killer waves.

I hear the low *BOOM* of a cannonball above me, but I'm so

deep that I barely feel its impact in the water. My toes touch the bumpy concrete of the pool bottom.

People describe heaven as whatever their idea of "nice" is, but I bet if being dead is like anything, it's like floating underwater. No sense of time passing. Nothing changing. Not feeling or thinking, just maybe sometimes hearing the *boom* of things above you and remembering dimly that you used to be up there too.

Of course, there's an easy way to find out what heaven is like. If I had the guts to stay down here another minute or two, I could see for myself if Mom is right and heaven looks like Northern California.

Melanie smiles and beckons me to paddle out and join her in the deep water, but as usual, I'm scared to swim out that far.

Distorted by the twelve feet of water above me, Ms. Everett's whistle is a wavering warble, but its piercing note still calls me back to reality.

I realize suddenly that I'm out of air, my lungs *burning*. I push off the bottom of the pool and swim up, panic rising as I realize how far down I still am.

I breach the surface light-headed and gasping for air. Little black dots dance in my vision, and what I expect to be a breath of air turns into a big gulp of water as a wave splashes into my mouth.

I cough and flounder toward the edge of the pool, splashing frantically, and when I finally reach the ledge, I cling to it for a moment to cough up water.

Everyone else has already climbed out of the pool and is heading into the locker rooms, shaking the water off their hair and waddling like penguins on the wet tiles. After a moment I paddle over to a ladder, pull myself out of the water, and join the line.

The boys' locker room is noisy and crowded, guys snapping towels at one another's naked butts, tossing insults around, and hooting like monkeys. I feel like some guys act extra manly in locker rooms just to prove that they're totally comfortable being buck naked and showering with a bunch of strangers. I do not feel this way and make no attempts at such deception. I keep my trunks on as long as possible and always change back into my clothes like lightning, preferably in a corner.

Wooden benches run the length of the long room, with pale green lockers on one side and toilets, sinks, and showers on the other. Unlike the gym locker rooms, thankfully the showers here are all semi-private, separated from one another with little plastic curtains in front of them.

There's a wire rack of dry towels inside the door, and I grab the last one. I hang my suit and towel on a hook outside one of the showers and step inside to wash the chlorine off.

I turn the shower off a minute later and reach outside the curtain for my towel, but it's not there.

Neither is my suit.

I poke my head out from around the flimsy curtain, assuming my clothes must have fallen off the hook, but they're not on the ground, either.

"All right, guys, very funny," I say. "Who took my stuff?"

Guys are pulling shirts over their heads and tying up their

sneakers. None of them will look my way, and a dark foreboding steals over me.

Naked and dripping wet, I tiptoe across the locker room's wet floor, past the other guys who are fully clothed and closing their lockers, to where I had draped my clothes over the bench. But my clothes—as I had feared, as I knew they would be—are gone.

"Hey." I try to sound tough when I say it, but I can't. "Hey, which one of you guys moved my clothes?"

A few guys laugh, but everyone still studiously ignores me.

I open the little locker my book bag was in. I'm not surprised to see that it's gone, but I *am* surprised to see, hanging in its place, a Shuckburgh cheerleading uniform—a miniskirt with an attached low-cut, sleeveless top. There's a note taped to the chest:

WE HOPE THIS IS YOUR SIZE.
YOU PERVERT.
LUV, THE CHEERLEADING SQUAD
XOXOXO

A couple of guys can't resist looking over my shoulder into the locker. Jungle hoots and hyena laughs echo around the locker room as metal lockers clang shut. Liam Spagnaletti walks up behind me and crosses his arms over his chest, regarding me coolly. "You're a real prevert, you know that?"

I cringe in the cold and cover my rapidly shrinking manhood. "Look, man, c'mon, help me out here—"

He shakes his head. "Myka and Mary told us during free swim what you did, ya prevert. You're lucky they're just pulling this prank on you instead of calling the cops."

Steve Decusatis slinks past, carrying a towel. He looks very uncomfortable and keeps an eye on me out of the corner of his eye as he passes. I barely know him, but I lunge at him now like a long-lost brother.

"Steve!" I hold my hands out, literally in naked supplication. "Steve, give me your towel!"

Steve recoils from my touch like I'm a leper as he picks up his pace and hurries out of the locker room.

Spags keeps shaking his head at me. "Nobody is going to give you their towel, dude. Myka said if any of us helps you, Tommy will beat the shit out of us. Although, dude, she didn't have to threaten us. Plenty of dudes happy to stick up for what's right. Ya fucking *prevert*." He spits the last word.

"I wasn't sneaking!" I say. "It was an accident! And also, it's *pervert*, not *prevert*." *Prevert* sounds like what you'd call someone before they did something perverted.

"Whatever, dude," he sneers.

Everyone is dressed and leaving the locker room, and as Spags promised, they're all taking their towels with them. Lockers bang shut and wet sneakers squeak on the tiles. Each time the door to the hall opens and closes, a gust of cold air blows in, and goose bumps break out on my bare legs.

"Guys, wait!" I beg. "C'mon, please, someone leave me a towel!"

Some guys think it's funny, others look angry at me, but most are just confused and uncomfortable, happy to get away from the pleading naked boy as quickly as possible. One or two of the guys seem to consider leaving me their towels, but Spags hustles them out the door. "Uh-uh," he says. "Remember what Myka said. Keep moving. C'mon. Let's go."

"Stop! Please! How am I supposed to get out of here?"

Spags looks at me like I'm something nasty he just stepped in. "Not our problem, ya prevert."

Someone snaps my ass with a wet towel as they hurry past. "Serves ya right, ya prevert!"

"It's *pervert*, not *prevert*," I say. "And it was an accident!"

The last guy out of the locker room besides Spags is Soupbowl. He looks me up and down with his stopped-clock eyes as he walks past, and Spags pats him on the back.

"Okay," Spags says, slapping his hands together in a *that's that* gesture. "Have fun!" Spags walks out, the door swings shut behind him, and I'm alone.

I shiver and rub my hands up and down my arms.

I wonder which I'll die of first, cold or embarrassment.

There's no clock in the locker room, and my phone was in my book bag (wherever the hell that is now, probably at the bottom of the pool), so I have no clue what time it is. How long do I have before PJ leaves? And more important, how am I going to get to the gym, where PJ's waiting? It's a long, long walk from here to there, part of it through the middle of the wide-open Thunderdome.

After a few minutes, I crack the door to the pool room open

and peek inside. The overhead lights are off, but the sun slanting down from the windows up near the ceiling bounces off the surface of the pool and casts rippling reflections on the dark walls.

"Hello?" My voice echoes in the empty room. I don't see Ms. Everett anywhere.

"Helloooooo?"

There's nobody here. I tiptoe back into the locker room. I'm getting pretty damn cold. I shiver and take a hard look at the cheerleading uniform in my locker. It looks warm. Wait, what am I saying?

I am naked and I am alone and I feel like I'm on the worst reality-show spin-off ever.

Clad in a red tuxedo, the show announcer flashes a blinding smile, studio lights shining off his veneers. "Hello. I'm Bing Supernova, and welcome to *Naked and Alone!*"

The audience cheers.

"Tonight's contestant is Kirby Burns, who we join now at Uppityfuck High School, where he is—"

The audience roars in unison, "NAKED! AND! ALONE!"

"Kirby is walking in circles . . . ," Bing narrates. "Now he's checking all the lockers. . . ."

The audience hoots and tears their seats out of the floor and hits one another with them.

"And—wait just a second, folks. Now he's trying to fashion a diaper out of toilet paper!"

The audience runs screaming out of the studio and storms the streets, tipping over cars and setting them on fire.

The announcer is alone in the demolished studio, blood sheeting down his face from a gash on his forehead, but he's still smiling gamely. "Kirby is standing in front of the locker with the cheerleading uniform. He's eyeing up that uniform, folks. . . . OH MY GOD, HE'S PUTTING IT ON!"

Amazingly, the cheerleading skirt fits, although it's pretty snug. The skirt barely goes lower than mid-thigh, but luckily there are little hot pants beneath the skirt. The sleeveless top plunges low enough that you get a nice view of my scrawny chest. For once I'm thankful for my slim, girlish figure. The body of an artist indeed.

Stay calm, Kirby. Keep it together. All I have to do is make it to the gym and PJ will have some clothes for me. It'll probably be a cowboy outfit or a kimono, but it'll still be better than this. Heck, if the buses have left already, I might even make it to the gym without anyone seeing me!

I nudge the hallway door open. There's no one out there. I pause a moment, listening for the sound of footsteps, but I don't hear anything.

The coast is clear.

I creep away from the door, and as soon as I'm far enough away that I can't run back, Myka pops out from around a corner and takes a photo of me, then runs away giggling.

Well, *that's* going online.

Can I even come back to school after this? God, I don't know.

A few feet down the hall I see one of my socks. I pick it up and spot, farther down the hallway, another sock. I sigh and begin the scavenger hunt of humiliation.

If Melanie could see me right now, I bet she'd laugh. But not in a mean way. I bet she'd laugh and then I'd start laughing too and then I'd feel a lot better. This whole thing would seem silly. I'll have to find a new notebook when I get home. It won't be the same as using the real thing, but it'll be better than nothing.

The only blessing among all this misfortune is that it's the end of the day, and as I had hoped, the halls are empty. All the buses have already left. The only students I see are a pair of marching band kids in tall feathered hats, carrying their oboes as I stoop to pick up my belt in the hall to the Thunderdome. Rather than laughing or pointing, they hold their breath and give me a wide berth, as though my bad luck might be contagious.

Fortunately the trail of clothes leads through the lobby and into the gym, where I was headed to meet PJ anyway. I hurry through the Thunderdome without seeing anyone else and pick up my shirt from the floor in front of the bank of double doors that lead to the gym. I gratefully slip the shirt on over the cheerleading outfit, although it doesn't do anything to cover the tiny dress or my thin legs poking out beneath it.

I enter the gym to find PJ teetering on top of a stepladder, hanging a strand of Christmas lights from hooks on the wall. Two kids at the base of the ladder are feeding him the lights, and when the door slams shut behind me, all three turn to look at me and stop in mid-task, frozen like I'm Medusa.

PJ is the first to speak up. "Dude, where are your pants?"

"Somewhere around here, hopefully."

Still up on the ladder, PJ points to the door at the far end of the gym that leads outside. It's propped halfway open with a brick, and one leg of my pants is sticking out, into the gym.

"That them?"

"Finally! Oh, sweet denim, how I've missed you."

The two guys holding the ladder clearly have way more questions than PJ, who resumes messing with the lights. "Mary came in here and tossed them out the door a couple of minutes ago," he says. "What's going on?"

I don't want to explain it all now. I just want to get some pants on before anyone snaps another picture or calls me a *prevert* again. "It's a long story," I say as I speed-walk across the basketball court. "I'll tell you in the car. Hey, have you seen my book bag? Did she have my book bag?"

"I don't think so," PJ says.

I grab the leg of my pants, then push the door all the way open and step out into the school's rarely used back parking lot. It's run-down and gross. Grass pokes up between cracks in the black pavement. The vo-tech building crouches at the far end of the lot. Amid the squalor I hope to see my book bag, and I do. I see it immediately.

Mark Kruger, cold blue eyes shining with merriment, holds my bag up like a record-breaking trout. He's standing on top of a low wall that's lost a couple of bricks, his legs spread wide, dirty blue jeans tucked into his tan work boots. He's trying to look tough, but I guess I must look pretty funny, because he's smiling all the same. It's the way a fox might smile at a chicken with a funny hat on. His bruised eye has turned from black to purple, rimmed with an ugly yellow.

A rusted pickup truck idles behind him, the only car in the

cracked lot. Some scruffy guy I don't recognize is sitting behind the wheel drinking a beer, a dirty Phillies hat pulled low over his stubbly face. He's an honest-to-God adult, and seeing him there, apparently cool with all this, scares me more than anything else. I've always thought that anytime I saw an adult, that meant I was safe. I was *unrichtig*.

Truck guy finishes his beer and cracks open a new can.

The door to the gym is still propped open a crack with the brick. I could run back into the gym and slam the door behind me, locking Mark outside—but I need my bag back. My phone is in there.

And besides, more significantly, I can't keep doing this forever. I can tell Mom I'm sick on Monday, but I'd have to come to school on Tuesday. I can't run forever. I can't throw my egg sandwich away every single day.

I take a step back toward the door and yell into the gym, "Hey, PJ!"

"What?" PJ can barely hear me. I can't see him, but it sounds like he's still up on the ladder.

"Hey, my mom is already here. She's just going to give me a ride home."

"What?!"

"I don't need a ride anymore!" I yell.

There's a pause, then, "All right! If you're sure."

I kick the brick aside and the door swings shut with a metallic *clang* that sounds awfully final.

CHAPTER 24

THE AFTERNOON IS QUIET ENOUGH THAT, FLOATING up from the football field in the distance, I can hear the marching band warming up for tonight's game. The dry machine-gun stutter of snare drums and the moan of trombones sliding up and down the scale.

The grass under my shoeless feet is warm from the sun. The rear parking lot is far from the noise of Main Street, the only sounds back here a few birds and the ragged purr of Mark's idling pickup.

Mark drops my book bag behind him and steps off the low wall. "Don't worry," he says sarcastically. "We'll give you a ride home." He looks over his shoulder at the guy in the truck. "That cool, Will?"

Will leans out the window. "Sure. We can drop him off at the hospital. He can share a room with Tommy."

Mark winces at that, and he's not smiling anymore when he looks back at me. "I never would've thought a little pissant like you could be this much trouble. What the fuck is wrong with you? You vandalize our farm, your boy Jake puts my best friend in the hospital, you attack Vern in the shower—what the fuck is your problem?" His voice climbs higher as he lists my offenses until he's speaking in an incredulous falsetto. "I mean, I was gonna beat you up for punching me, but shit, now I'm doing it as a public fucking service."

Mark steps toward me. I reflexively put my fists up, and Mark's scowl disappears as he bursts into laughter. He looks back at Will again, who starts laughing too. I glance down at my skirt and skinny legs sticking out beneath it. Oh right, I forgot I was dressed like this.

"You see this?" Mark says to Will, who shakes his head, laughing.

Mark laughs so hard that he starts coughing, and the coughing fit gets so serious, he has to spit out the wad of chewing tobacco that was tucked in his lip.

"Oh God!" he cries, wiping tobacco juice off his chin. "Almost swallowed my dip!"

Every time it seems like he's about to stop laughing, he gets going again. "You look so *pretty* in that dress," he says.

I muster a strained smile, showing off my pearly browns.

Mark carefully wipes a tear from the side of his bruised

eye. "Okay, buttercup. Time to get serious," he says, waving his hands back and forth as he composes himself. "I got just one more thing to say, and I want to say it right. My daddy works real hard on our farm. Did you know that?"

"Uh, no, I didn't."

"Yeah, no, you didn't. You don't know shit, do you?" He's mad now, and the rapid shift of his emotions is unnerving. "Daddy doesn't have any help. Just my brother and me." He jerks a thumb back at Will, who hoists his beer can in a wobbly salute. "Got laid off from Bethlehem Steel and had to learn how to farm. Did you know that?"

"No, I did not. And I'm awfully sorry."

"You're sorry?!" Strangely, my apology makes him angrier. "You're *sorry*." He shakes his head in disbelief. "Same thing your jackass friend said. Well, take your sorry and shove it up your dickhole. I know what everyone thinks about our daddy, and yeah," he says defiantly, "some of it's true. But shit, he had to learn how to farm at forty-fucking-five!" He punches his fist into his hand at the end of each sentence. "Yes, he ain't no *farmer*. Yes, it's fucking *hard*." He glares at me, wide-eyed, daring me to disagree.

I speak very carefully. "Look, I don't know anything about your dad or your farm. We just went to your place because it was near my house. We didn't know it was your farm. The fact that we picked your place, it was totally random."

Mark frowns and breathes loudly through his nose as he tries to tell if I'm lying. He spits on the ground and turns back to the truck. "You believe him?" he hollers.

"I don't know," Will hollers back. "Can't hear too well." He spins his finger in a *hurry up* gesture. "C'mon, bro, wrap it up."

"I'm really sorry," I repeat. It's all I can think to say, and I mean it too.

"All right, all right," Mark says, annoyed that I won't escalate the argument. He points back at the truck. "Tell my brother, too."

"I'm very sorry!" I yell.

"Fuck you!" Will yells back, hoisting his beer can out the truck window.

Mark laughs as he shrugs off his Carhartt jacket and rolls up the sleeves of his Under Armour shirt. "Fuckin' Billiam." He starts toward me. "All right. You love saying sorry so much, why don't you see how long you can keep saying it while I beat the shit out of you? I owe you at least one black eye."

Three long strides close the distance between us. Then Mark pivots with frightening speed and drives a brutal right hook into my stomach, stepping into the punch with his legs. All the breath inside me is driven out. My legs fold, and I fall to my knees, a hot ball of lead burrowing into my guts. I'm at the bottom of the pool again. I can't breathe.

Mark barks a harsh laugh. "One punch? No, no, no. We're not done dancing, diddledick. Get up."

I try to get up, but I can't. I still can't even *breathe.* I see a brick on the ground behind Mark, but it's too far away to reach.

"I said get UP!" Mark dances around me and waves his hands in my face. "C'mon, boy, get up!"

"Don't hurt him too bad, Mark," Will chides from a million

miles away, followed by the hollow *ting!* of a beer can hitting the pavement.

Mark leans down into my face so close I can smell the mint Skoal on his breath. "C'mon, sweetheart, get up. Lemme see if you got your sister's underwear on under that dress."

I look him in the eye and pull a single burning breath, enough to ask, "What?"

The last month Melanie was sick, my grandmother came to stay with us, to help take care of me and the house since Mom and Dad were at the hospital pretty much all the time.

It was Thursday evening, the day after Mom took me out of school to talk to Melanie for the last time. Mom and Dad were both at the hospital, and I was at home with Grandma. I was watching TV in the living room when she got a call from Mom. After she hung up, she asked me, "I was thinking about ordering pizza for dinner. What do you think?"

I got excited because, like all sentient beings on this wet blue ball, I *love* pizza, even though it kills me. I don't mind as long as I'm near a toilet, but Mom didn't let me eat it very often because she knew it hurt my stomach. I asked Grandma where we were going to order it from, and she said wherever I wanted, so I called Pizza Hut, which is nothing fancy, but it's the best pie you could get delivered in Bethlehem, Pennsylvania. Grandma even let me order the Meat Lovers Pizza, which Mom would never let me do. She'd at least make me order something with vegetables on it.

A couple of hours later I was lying on the couch watching TV, totally stuffed with pizza. As Grandma was folding the pizza box into the recycling, I heard the garage door open and the car pull in. The garage door slowly ground shut, and then the downstairs door to the garage swung open and closed. I heard my parents walking upstairs and felt that something was wrong, although it took me a moment to realize that what was wrong was that I heard *two* sets of footsteps, not one.

Mom and Dad were both home at the same time.

They trudged up the stairs together, and I was wondering why one of them wasn't staying at the hospital. Then Mom looked at me and said, "I'm sorry, honey." She looked exhausted, like she had walked all the way home from the hospital.

I went to my room, and a little while later I heard Grandma's car pull out of the driveway.

Nobody came into my bedroom to talk to me. I think my parents were too worn out themselves to do anything else. They were wrung out like dishrags.

I lay on my bed and watched it get dark. I couldn't think. All my thoughts felt too big to fit in my brain. I lay on top of the sheets feeling my head stretch, wondering when it would crack.

When my leg was broken, I'd lain in bed without moving or doing anything for hours at a time, so I decided to try that again. I watched the square of sunset from my window creep around the room, the light getting dimmer and dimmer until my room was dark. I didn't turn on the light. I didn't move. I didn't cry. I didn't do *anything*, just waited for that big thought to expand so much it would split the walls and bring the whole house tumbling down around our heads.

I was grateful when it got so dark that my room disappeared.

I've always liked the nighttime because it's so quiet and still and there are no other people around. It feels like the whole world is yours, or like maybe the world doesn't even exist outside of your bedroom. I decided that for all intents and purposes, from this moment on, it didn't. I refused to be a part of the world anymore.

It felt like the only sane thing to do.

I lay on my bed in my clothes and shoes. There was a painful crick in my neck. The pillow was too low, but I didn't shift the pillow to make it feel better because I knew that if I didn't move, the night would last forever. The power of my loss had granted me this one-time magic ability, but I had to prove my devotion by not moving an inch. If I could do that, reality would bend to my will, like light bending around a superdense black hole, and the world wouldn't reappear in the morning.

God, I thought, *that would be great.*

But after a couple of hours I had to take a pee, and I didn't have the commitment to piss the bed.

I got up and opened my bedroom door, and the spell was broken: Sure enough, there was the rest of my house, waiting for me. My big plan hadn't even lasted one night. My stupid life was right where I'd left it. Time hadn't stopped because Melanie died. Melanie stopped, but the world kept going, and no matter how hard I tried, I couldn't stop that. I couldn't even stop *myself.* I just kept moving farther and farther away from where Melanie stopped. That was the worst part about it. I was leaving her behind.

My parents' bedroom door was next to the bathroom door, across from Melanie's empty bedroom. I wanted to go into her room and look at her things—her little purple boom box, her hair scrunchies that she hadn't been able to use for months but that she'd still sometimes wear around her wrists, her My Little Ponies, which she was too old for but whose hair she liked to comb—look at her stuff and maybe even lie down on the carpet, sleep on the floor there. But I didn't. It seemed too weird.

Instead I looked at my parents' door and pictured them lying together on their bed. Were they holding each other? Were they crying? I had no desire to open that door and find out.

I was already dreading the next morning when I'd have to see them at breakfast, black bags under their sad eyes as we sat across the kitchen table from one another, going through the charade of living, shoveling calories into our food holes because our bodies demanded it.

After breakfast we'd want to smash the plates or throw them out the window, but instead we'd wash them, because that's what you do if you don't want bugs and mice all over your house. Mom would even wipe the counter, because that's what you do after you put the dishes away.

I would try very, very hard not to say a word, but eventually I'd have to ask Mom something dumb like, "Are we all out of orange juice?"

"Yes," she'd say. "I'll pick more up this afternoon."

When, come on, fuck the orange juice. Burn the orange groves. Detonate a series of controlled explosions along the northern border of Florida and let the whole shattered state float out to sea. How could I care about orange juice at a time like this?

Easy: I'm thirsty, and orange juice is refreshing. My tongue doesn't care that Melanie is dead. My body wants food, the Earth wants to spin, time moves forward and wants to keep moving. *We must always walk along the path of the clock, so it is written in the tablets of Nardorock.*

Standing in the hallway outside the bathroom and knowing I'd do all those things again made me hate myself. If Melanie's death meant anything to me, I would refuse to circle the sun. I'd defy the Earth's rotation and float into space.

Instead I went to the bathroom, because I drank so much soda with the pizza that I had to pee really bad. My mouth tasted like garlic, so I brushed my teeth, too. I even placed the toothbrush back in the Garfield jelly glass next to the sink. I briefly considered smashing the Garfield glass—I even raised it above my head and was about to throw it down onto the floor—but I was worried Mom or Dad might cut their foot on a piece of glass later in the night.

I shuffled back across the hall and crawled into bed.

The next morning I woke up to the sweet smell of waffles cooking out in the kitchen. I crept out, and Mom had already set the table with sunny yellow place mats under the plates and silverware, napkins folded into neat triangles under the forks. The kitchen table looked nice, but there were only three place settings instead of four, and Mom's eyes were dead and gray like a turned-off TV screen. "How are you feeling?" she asked me in a monotone voice.

"Fine," I lied.

I sat down at one of the settings, and Mom put a warm waffle on my plate. It smelled heavenly, but when I took a bite, the batter tasted like cardboard in my mouth.

"Hey, Mom . . . can I have some syrup?"

I draw another burning breath and ask "What?" again.

Mark is still leaning down with his hands on his knees, a shit-eating grin on his weathered face. He can tell he's hit a nerve.

"I saaaaiiiid," he drawls flirtatiously, "do you got your sister's underwear on under that dress?"

I scream in his face and punch him in the balls so hard my fist hits his tailbone. He folds up, clutching his crotch. I lunge forward and try to bite his nose, but he jerks back and my teeth clack empty air. Fire flows up through me and I scream again, random curse words, ancient tongues, the language of the Old Ones. My fists are hot-forged iron as I stand and swing a looping uppercut at Mark's jaw and miss completely, but then throw a left and hit him right in the face. A shower of red sparks spills through the air. The rooftop of Nakatomi Plaza explodes. I am God's hammer.

"Mark?" his brother yells from the truck. *"Mark!"*

Mark stumbles back and swings at my face, so dizzy he misses by a mile. I storm forward and wrap my fingers around his neck, soft in my iron grip. All my hate flows into my hands, and I squeeze hard, the veins in Mark's neck pulsing in my palms.

A world away, the truck door slams shut. "Hey! Hey! Get your hands off my brother!"

Mark grabs my wrists, but he's helpless. Every muscle in my body is flexed as tight as if I were grabbing an electric fence—I couldn't let go if I wanted to. Mark's eyes bulge and his mouth gapes like a fish trying to breathe in the bottom of a boat.

Mark's brother runs toward us. "Let go! Get your hands off him, you psycho!"

He grabs me around the waist but can't pull me off Mark. Little red veins race zigzag patterns through the whites of Mark's eyes, and then something hits me in the side of the head and the world comes unglued.

The blue sky slides past like a fast train.

The ground rushes up to kiss me.

I go through a tunnel.

I come out the other side and stand up spinning. Mark is curled on the ground and Will is standing over his body defensively, brandishing a brick smeared with blood. He looks scared. He's scared of me.

He should be.

I dip down and grab a brick of my own and wing it at Mark's brother's head. He ducks and the brick knocks his Phillies hat

off, then flies over his head and smashes the windshield of the
pickup truck behind him.

"Whoa!" Will yells, popping back up. "Whoa, whoa, whoa!"
He cocks his brick back like he means to throw it if I get any
closer, but I lunge at him anyhow. Instead of throwing the brick,
he drops it and punches me neatly on the chin, a quick clip that
stops me in my tracks. It must knock loose a couple cables in
my brain, because I totter backward and fall down again.

I try to get up, but before I can get a knee under me, Mark's
brother sits on my chest. I claw at him and he grabs my wrists
in his hard, calloused hands.

I try to bite his arms, but I can't quite reach. He stares at me
in shock, and I know I'm acting like an animal but I can't stop
myself.

"Dude! Chill! Dude!"

Mark limps over, massaging his throat, and kicks me in the
side of the face. "Motherfucker!" he croaks.

"Whoa! Whoa! Whoa!" Will releases one of my hands to
hold Mark back, and when he does, I wriggle out from under
him and scuttle toward Mark again like Gollum scrambling for
the ring. Something deep inside me struggles to emerge. I can
hear it growling as it claws its way up my throat.

Mark yelps and stumbles back just as strong arms grab me
around my waist and hoist me up. The sky spins and tumbles
past me as Mark's brother throws me over his shoulder. My
glasses go flying off as the ground rushes up once again and fills
my mouth with grass.

Another tunnel, this one longer than the first. Then I roll over onto my back and, with an effort, up onto my hands and knees.

I stand up unsteadily and am about to rush Mark again, but Will is ready for me. He slams me backward, pinning me against the truck, the engine warm through the grille, but still I struggle to reach Mark.

"Dude!" Mark's brother marvels. "What the fuck is wrong with you?!"

I can't speak, and for a moment I panic. I feel like an animal who used to be a man but has lost the power of speech. But finally I remember how to speak, and there's a hitch in my voice as I point at Mark and yell, "He made fun of my sister!"

Will stares at me in disbelief. "So the fuck what?"

"Yeah!" Mark yells from a safe distance. "So the fuck what?!"

"My sister is dead, you fucking asshole!" And as I admit it, a valve opens inside me and a great pressure is released. I can hear the air escaping in an agonized wail. I'm crying so hard that the sounds coming out of my throat feel like solid things that I'm throwing up. Stones that have been sitting in the bottom of my stomach for a year. Old batteries and rocks and bile tumble out of me.

Will lets go of me. My eyes are wide open, but I have trouble seeing as the world wavers underwater, Mark and Will shimmering quadruplets backing away from me.

I shake. Am I having a seizure? I'm falling apart, but it feels obscenely good.

I stagger away from the warmth of the truck, carried uncontrollably by the force of my crying. The parking lot teeters back and forth, the pitching deck of a ship in a terrible storm.

I'm screaming. I'm crying. I yell as loud as I can, the wail leaving me like a monstrous bat flying out of a cave, and I realize it was the last thing inside me.

I'm empty.

I'm gone.

CHAPTER 25

I SHARE THIS WISDOM AS SOMEONE WHO HAS learned from experience: No matter how long or how hard you cry, eventually you have to stop and put your pants back on.

After stumbling around the woods for I don't know how long, I circle back to the vo-tech parking lot and find my pants where I dropped them outside the back door to the gym. I also find my glasses—after a lot of nearsighted peering and crawling around on my hands and knees—miraculously unbroken, in the grass a few feet away.

I peel the cheerleading dress off, not giving a good gosh golly who sees my pale ass. I can't believe I beat Mark up while I was wearing this.

I catch movement in my peripheral vision, near the gym

door, and I'm ready to explain myself to Mr. Reali, but when I turn, I see that it's not the janitor; it's a frog. It hops up to the gym's back exit and sits there, looking at me with bulging, inquisitive eyes.

"Oh my God. Are you . . . ? Are you the frog from biology class?"

The frog doesn't answer me—no surprise there. But he doesn't hop away, either. He just keeps staring at me.

"You don't want to go back in there," I say, pointing at the school. "It's a jungle. Believe me, you're safer in the woods."

I know he can't understand me. I know he's just a frog. But still, he starts hopping away from the school.

I salute him as he disappears into the high, unmowed grass at the edge of the parking lot. "Good luck, little guy."

With the utmost trepidation, I call Mom. It's 4:10, right about the time she would expect me to be walking through the front door.

The phone rings a long time before she picks up, and when she does, I hear water running in the background.

"Hello? Kirby?"

"Hey, Mom. Hey, uh, can you come pick me up?"

"Pick you up?" She's confused. "From the corner? Are those darn dogs out again?"

"No, no. Uh . . ."

"Are you all right?" Her mom radar is very keen. "Your voice sounds funny. Do you have a cold?"

My throat is scraped raw from screaming. I must sound like a frog myself. "No, I don't have a cold. I'm at school."

"At school?!" She shifts into full mom mode. "Why are you at school?"

"Well, I missed the bus and ah . . ."

Mom puts the phone down to turn off the water. "I'm right in the middle of making dinner," she says. "The roast is in the oven. I'll have to turn it off. . . ." She sighs dramatically. "Okay, mister. I'll be there in twenty minutes."

I wait in front of the school. Cars and minivans are starting to drive into the main parking lot for the game when Mom pulls up in front of me and absolutely flips out, before her car has even stopped rolling, when she sees I'm all banged up. As I limp around to the passenger's side and catch my reflection in the car's window, I almost flip out myself. There's a huge, bleeding lump on the left side of my forehead where Will hit me with the brick, and half my face is covered in dirt and grass stains from one of the many times I hit the ground. My eyes are red and puffy from crying. I look *awful*.

Strangely though, I *feel* good.

I slide into the passenger seat and wince, discovering new bruises on my hip, my back—everywhere, pretty much. Mom gapes at me in horror, hands over her mouth.

"My Lord, Kirby . . . what happened?!"

"I got into a fight."

"A fight? Who? Why?!"

"It's kind of a long story, but a guy made fun of Melanie, and I sort of flipped out on him."

"Melanie?!" Mom is so shocked that she doesn't know what to say. I'm pretty sure it's the first time she's heard me say Melanie's name since she died. She's probably also shocked because she just found out that some stranger made fun of her dead daughter.

"Why would someone make fun of her?"

"Well, he didn't mean to, specifically. He just said 'your sister,' and I just, ah . . . I kind of lost it, and uh . . ." I can't help it; hot tears spring to my eyes. I'm surprised I have any left in me. Usually I wouldn't cry in front of Mom like this—as a matter of fact, I think crying is another thing she hasn't seen me do in the past year—but I force myself to look at Mom and let her see me.

Mom gives me that look of concern that always makes me so angry. I'm about to get annoyed with her. I'm about to regret ever having brought up Melanie. But then I see something else in her expression: understanding. Her face softens, and she puts her hand on top of mine on the armrest between the seats, and for the first time in a long time, I don't pull away.

She doesn't say anything, which is good, because it would probably ruin the moment. Instead she pats my hand and then starts the car. I can see she's crying a little bit too, but just a little bit.

We both cry, just a little bit, as we drive home together.

— — —

After ten minutes or so of quiet communal grieving, Mom breaks the respectful silence and gets down to the brass tacks of who the sorry sack of a shit was who beat up her son. I tell her that I don't want to say who it was, that it was sort of my fault too, and that I also beat him up. I tell her that no, I don't want to call the police, and no, I don't think we should call the young man's parents.

She asks ten times if anything is broken, and I say I don't think so, although "I think I have dirt up my nose." I don't tell her that I got hit with a brick. I say the bump is from my head hitting the ground. Even so, she says that we'll have to go to the doctor tomorrow to make sure I don't have a concussion, and she warns me ominously that "Your father will have something to say when he gets home." This reminds me about my notebook, but surprisingly, thinking about the notebook doesn't make me panic anymore. The fear is gone.

Mom looks at me sideways and clucks her tongue. "I bet that friend of yours, Jake, was involved, wasn't he?"

I remain conspicuously silent, which I suppose is a pretty clear yes.

When we get home I take a long, hot shower. I feel wrung out, but also strangely cleansed, like I just finished one of those thirty-day lemon juice and cayenne pepper diets where, at the end, you shit out all the toxic gunk that had built up in the bottom of your intestines over the years. A kid told me he knew a girl who did that once, and at the very end, the last thing she pooped out was a tiny green rock, glowing with toxic radiation. I *love* that story. It's such a beautiful lie.

I step out of the bathroom into my bedroom and look at the cardboard boxes stacked all over the room. How have I been living like this for so long? I tear the duct tape off the nearest box and start unpacking it.

An hour or so later I hear the garage door rumble up, a sound that makes my stomach flip.

Dad's home.

I know he's going to be upset about the fight. He will *definitely* want to call Mark's parents and the school and probably the president of the United States too. I hear him and Mom talking in the kitchen for a long time—Dad raises his voice a few times—but Mom must do a pretty good job calming him down, because when he knocks on my door, he seems relatively chill.

He's still wearing his navy suit from work, but his green striped tie is loosened. He knocks on my door with one knuckle as he enters and asks, "Can I come in?"

I place a stack of books on the shelf. "I think you're already in."

Dad looks around like he must be in the wrong room. I don't know what he's more surprised by, my beat-up face or the fact that I'm standing in the midst of a couple of unpacked boxes, putting things away.

He stands, shocked, for a moment before saying, "Oh my God . . . did you accidentally unpack a box of whoop ass?"

We both laugh, but laughing makes my face hurt, and I have

to stop and hold my hand up against my jaw. "Ow! Ow, ow, ow."

Dad suddenly gets serious. "Hey, I'm sorry." He walks over and puts his hand on my shoulder, then examines my face. "Oof. Are you all right, bud?"

I tell him the truth. "I wasn't doing so good. But I'm doing better now."

"Good. That's good."

Dad sits down on the edge of my bed. He doesn't say anything, but it doesn't feel awkward. I love that about him, that he doesn't feel the need to say something just to fill the silence. Sometimes he just sits there and enjoys being in the same room together. His dress pants are hiked up above his high blue socks and shiny brown loafers.

"Hey," he says, like the thought just occurred to him. "Hey, uh . . . about your . . ."

"Notebook," I say.

He shakes his head with finality, a friend saying, *No way. I can't let you pay for dinner.* "Look, you've had a bad day. I know we said we'd talk about it today, but we don't have to."

"Yes, we do."

Dad is surprised. "What?"

"Yes, we do. We have to talk about it today. We have to talk about it right now, because . . ." Geez, this is hard. It's getting harder every second, which is why I have to keep going. "We have to talk about the notebook now, because if we don't, I'll change my mind."

— — —

Mom makes herself a cup of herbal tea, Dad changes out of his suit into a blue chamois shirt and jeans, and the three of us sit around the kitchen table in the breakfast nook. Beside the breakfast nook, outside the sliding-glass door, our never-ending backyard is dark. The house is quiet.

Mom places my notebook in the middle of the table, spotlighted dramatically by the stained-glass light hanging overhead. We all look at it like it's the Ark of the Covenant, although of course it's just a red spiral-bound notebook with a rubber band around it, the date 11/7/18 written on the weathered cover in black Sharpie.

Even though this is exactly what Mom and Dad wanted, they seem more scared than I am. Mom's face is set, hard and grave. Dad seems a little embarrassed. For my part, I am energized by a grim determination.

I slide the journal toward Mom. "Go ahead and read it."

Mom takes her hands off the table and puts them into her lap, like I just pushed a mousetrap toward her. She can't have heard me right. This must be a trick. "Just . . . read it?"

I don't mean to be a jerk, but I can't help feeling impatient. I roll my eyes as I pick up the journal. "Here, I'll do it." I open the notebook, flip to a random page, and start reading. I start at the top of the page, but it's in the middle of a sentence.

"'So then I rode my bike down to the park, but nobody was there. I guess because it's too cold out. I parked my bike anyhow and sat on a swing for a little bit, but I felt silly. Swings are for kids, and also it really was cold, so I just biked back home. . . .' Huh," I say, riffling through the pages. "I don't remember writing that." I've never gone back and reread any of the things I've written in here, so, like my parents, I'm almost hearing this for the first time.

I flip forward in the notebook and choose another section at random. "'I like the part where John first meets Takagi at the party, when they're making awkward small talk. Takagi makes a joke about Pearl Harbor, and nobody laughs, of course; it's just so perfectly awkward and exactly the type of thing you see in real life but rarely in movies—'" I laugh humorlessly. "Ah, yes, the *Die Hard* notes; they begin. I started to get pretty obsessed around the time we moved. I think because I had run out of things to say. Also, I don't know why, but it sometimes made writing easier, when I focused on that. Frankly, I think I ran out of things to say a while ago."

Mom and Dad share a look with each other, baffled and a little concerned.

I take a deep breath as I flip back closer to the beginning of the notebook. I don't have the guts to go back to the first page, but I stop somewhere in the first quarter. I steel myself like I'm preparing to take a punch, and as I read my familiar handwriting in black ballpoint on the blue ruled pages, it does feel like someone hits me, right in the heart.

It takes me a minute to find my voice, and when I do, I can't speak above a whisper. "'Hopefully you'll be better in time for us to go to the beach again this summer. This time I promise to swim all the way out with you. I know it's dumb, but I'm afraid of sharks. I know there are no sharks at the Jersey Shore, but it's not being able to see what's under my feet that makes me nervous. Remember the old station wagon we used to have? Remember how much you liked it? I said it made me carsick, but really it made me afraid, not being able to see what was coming. But I promise that when you're better this summer, when we go to the beach, I'll swim out as far as you want to.'"

I'm embarrassed, but I also feel strangely light. Like I'm naked, but only because I took off a heavy suit of armor that's been weighing me down.

I'm relieved to see that Mom and Dad look nothing like how I dreaded they would when I imagined this happening. Mom doesn't give me a sad look of pity. Dad doesn't give me a long, boring lecture. Mom looks straight at me, her wary look gone. She looks at me like I'm an adult. Dad stares at the table, but not because he's embarrassed. He's just thinking.

A tear falls on the page, and I blot it off with my sleeve, smearing the ballpoint ink a little. I take a shaky breath, close the journal, and toss it back into the middle of the table. I realize—and the thought both shocks and delights me—that I'm never going to write in that notebook again.

"I was telling you the truth when I said it wasn't a diary," I tell Mom, pointing at the notebook. "Or at least, that's not how I thought of it. I always thought of it like a—and this is going to sound crazy—but like a time machine. A way to go back to Melanie's hospital room that Wednesday, the last time I visited her, and relive our conversation. At first I thought I was trying to do a better job, make our final conversation count, but since we moved, I think I was using it more as a way to . . . I don't know. Spend more time in the past? Keep her alive, sort of."

I expected Mom and Dad to look happy or victorious at this moment, but they don't. They look a lot more like they did the night they came home together and told me Melanie was gone. They look tired. And I realize that all this time I was ignoring them, putting my thoughts into this goddamn journal and living in the past, they were here in the present, walking the same hard path that I was.

"You thought we wouldn't understand this?" Mom asks.

I shrug, embarrassed.

"Honey, we're in this together."

"Yeah, I know."

"And Melanie is gone," Dad says.

That hurts. But I have to admit it. "Yeah," I say. "I know."

"But we're not," Mom says. "We're still here."

She's right. It's true.

We're here together.

The next morning is Saturday, and it's such a nice day that Dad and I decide to fly to the Kutztown Airport and get some pie at the diner there.

I step out the garage's side door and zip up my sweatshirt. The morning is crisp and chilly. Clear skies overhead, which means no turbulence. I look left, at the Blue Mountain, not so blue anymore, the leaves on the trees confetti orange, yellow, and red, nature's last hurrah before that party pooper winter covers the landscape in a blanket of white.

Dad has already opened up the front of the hangar and pulled the ultralight out. He's standing on a stepladder, pouring gasoline into the wing tanks as I walk up.

"Morning, bud," Dad says.

I give him a lazy salute, like I'm a veteran pilot who's flown many missions and has a cavalier disregard for regulations.

Dad squints up at the light-blue sky. "Good day for flying, huh?"

"Yessir," I agree.

Dad and I zip up our warm leather flight jackets, put on our helmets, and climb into the ultralight. We taxi to the end of the property, to the fence that runs along the edge of the horse farm behind us. Then Dad turns the plane around, pointing us back toward the house, and guns the two-stroke engine.

The prop becomes a blur.

We bounce along over the bumpy field, engine roaring, and then all of a sudden we're weightless; we're a leaf. We float up and over the house as the world drops away.

As we fly low above the big gray barn across the street, the horse dogs chase our shadow over the field. They gallop gracefully, loping across the brown hill, keeping pace with the silhouette of our wings as they ripple across the parallel lines of plowed rows, their beautiful geometry tracing the shape of the land.

We swoop around and circle the house, then bank right and follow the Blue Mountain range east, the whole world spread out beneath us like a lovingly detailed miniature. The sun is fat and orange and bathes everything in a warm glow.

Dad pushes the stick right, then left, making the plane do lazy wingovers, sliding down sideways one way and then climbing back up the other, before we climb to a stable altitude and level out.

Flying toward the sun, we throttle back and cruise. I look out the plexiglass cockpit on my left and count the trees below us, fiery autumn confetti. Tiny cars drive along the winding roads that snake between the bright trees and the green fields. I look forward, at the back of Dad's helmet in the seat in front of me, and am overcome by a surge of gratitude. Dad was right; it's a good day for flying. And I bet tomorrow will be too.

ACKNOWLEDGMENTS

Thanks to Jason Rekulak, Dan Lazar, Jim Thomas, Liesa Abrams, Valerie Shea, Elizabeth Mims, Sarah Creech, Adams Carvalho, Rebecca Vitkus, Matt Ditty, OJ, Nick, and Jen. Also, and especially, thanks to my mom and dad for being such wonderful parents. You're the best.

ABOUT THE AUTHOR

Doogie Horner is the author of *Some Very Interesting Cats Perhaps You Weren't Aware Of*, *A Die Hard Christmas*, *Everything Explained Through Flowcharts*, and other books. His comedy album *A Delicate Man* was an AV Club staff pick. You can follow him online @doogiehorner or learn more at doogiehorner.com.